BLACK BEAR
ALIBI

BLACK BEAR
ALIBI

A ROCKFISH ISLAND MYSTERY BOOK I

BY J.C. FULLER

CHAPTER 1

Philip Russell pointed the Parks & Rec's pickup towards the public entrance, the yellow steel gate moved to the side of the road, and began his morning circulation of Rockfish Island's National Park.

With the heady smell of exhaust floating upon the crisp air, he inched down the road, plumes of white vapor pouring from the truck's tailpipe, and briefly let go of the steering wheel as he vigorously rubbed his hands together, the sting of bitter cold felt in his fingertips from the heavy frost lining the gate.

"Brrrr."

He reached over, keeping one eye on the road, and cranked the heater up to its highest setting before lifting a coffee-filled thermos lid from the dash and taking a tentative sip of the steaming hot liquid.

The island didn't have a Starbucks.

Coming to a gradual stop, Philip squinted through the passenger's window at the outdoor bulletin board, seeing nothing different from the day before, nor any notes to bring anything to his attention. Even the park brochures and small payment envelopes were still fully stocked.

Noting this was a good start to his day and satisfied all was in order, he continued to meander down the park's graveled dirt road at a safe fifteen miles per hour.

As a park ranger, Philip knew a deer or elk could unexpectedly dart across the road, and having received a new patrol truck, he was wanting to keep it as shiny and unblemished as long as possible. It was also the safe and lazy pace of a man, having only slept a few hours the night before, to get an extra cup of coffee down his gullet before hitting the office.

Doing his best to suppress a yawn, Philip slowed the truck even more. He was approaching the third curve, a favorite spot for deer due to the long grass lining the side, when a small black furball suddenly rambled out in front.

He slammed his foot down and let out a curse as hot coffee splashed down his thigh.

Another ball of fur scurried into the middle of the road, and a third one quickly followed.

"Well, I'll be damned."

Philip smiled to himself, knowing as well as anyone what black bear cubs looked like, and placed his empty mug on the dash before slowly reaching over and grabbing the shotgun resting in the rack by his seat.

He flicked the safety off.

Three cubs were sure to be followed by a mama bear, and there was never any messing with one of those.

The last two cubs, who had tumbled together in a play fight, stopped to take a curious look at the truck. When one of them bravely began to approach the vehicle, Philip gave the horn a light honk and sent both bundles of fur flying backwards.

A deep warning growl suddenly came from the left side of the road, and Philip got a good look at the black bear sow. She had materialized out of nowhere, her black fur bristled, muscles moving smoothly beneath.

Resting on all fours, her heavy dark paws found the road and lifted her out of the forest trench, her shoulders as high as the hood of his truck. She let out a loud huff of air and quickly paced herself over to her cubs. Encouraging them with her huge body mass to keep moving.

Philip noticed two things about her immediately.

First, she was tagged.

A bright orange-colored marker was attached to each of her round ears, which meant she was one of the three females on the island and, apparently, she'd had three cubs over the winter. A rarity for bears. He would need to let the Department of Wildlife know so they could come out and tag the little critters.

Second, her tan muzzle was colored reddish-brown with blood.

This didn't alarm Philip. It was just a curious thing to note. He assumed she'd taken a small fawn or a baby elk and had been enjoying her breakfast when her offspring decided to run off.

When all four had safely reached the other side of the road, the sow gave Philip a long stare before disappearing into the woods. Even with his eyes trained on her backside, she and her cubs were out of sight, or at least, out of eye perception within seconds.

Philip exhaled in relief and returned his shotgun to the secured rack in the middle console. He also poured himself another cup of coffee and sat with the engine purring, sipping from the thermos cup, keeping his eyes peeled for the possibly returning sow.

When his cup was finally empty, he climbed out of the truck, gun in hand again, and considered the coast somewhat clear, heading in the opposite direction of the bears, starting his trek into the woods.

His purpose was to haul out whatever carcass the black bear had left behind, in hopes of preventing her from returning and most importantly, deterring the cubs from coming too close to the range road and possible human contact.

He'd marched a good half-mile in, carefully watching his steps, the morning mist and shifting early light making it hard to see the forest floor. The last thing he wanted to do was twist an ankle. Not only would it be painful, but it would make it awfully hard to run if ever the need for it came.

He kept his ears open as well. Bears for their massive size were surprisingly quiet. So quiet, you could walk up on one without even knowing.

As his old Granddad used to tell him...

"They blend awfully good, boy, and they won't let you know they're there unless they WANT you to know." The memory of his grandfather's warning made the hairs on the back of Philip's neck prickle.

Starting to wonder if he'd already passed the kill, Philip suddenly came upon it.

It wasn't a deer or a small elk.

He stood stunned for a half-second, his mind trying to comprehend what he was seeing. With dawning realization, he quickly brought the shotgun to his shoulder, sweat beading his brow despite the cold, and steadily turned in a full circle. His full attention focused on the tree line, seeing nothing but a dark, dense forest.

Only a few feet away was a thin and bloodied hand poking out from behind a large stump, it resting upon the ground at an odd angle. Though it was mostly encrusted with pine needles and dried blood, the skin had a bluish hue, a sure sign the owner was dead.

Philip's gut reaction was the black bear had killed a human and he proceeded forward, his gun still poised at the ready, his steps slow and deliberate. A kill of that kind would attract other bears. He would need to be careful.

Gripping his gun tighter, he ventured closer and spied, scarcely a foot away, a scalp of long hair, an apparent play toy for the cubs as several small paw prints were scattered about it.

The sight stopped him dead, along with the smell of death, the cloying scent overwhelming, his morning coffee threatening the back of his throat. He clutched at his tie and swiftly brought the cloth to his face and covered his mouth and nose, the stench of rot filling his nostrils.

"Jesus." It wasn't a curse as much as a plea.

He'd never seen anything like it.

The bloodied hand was indeed attached to a female body, the center eaten out, ribs exposed. The leftover limbs left slumped in a pile next to the fallen tree trunk, the whiteness of bone bright against the muddy red of eaten flesh, bits of gore, and pieces of organs strewn around it.

He closed his eyes and tried to settle his stomach, counting to ten.

When he opened them again, Philip began to take inventory.

There wasn't a knapsack or tent, no indication the woman had been attempting to camp, and he hadn't seen any deserted vehicles on the road. Though someone might have easily come from the opposite direction and hiked in.

He looked at the corpse's feet and saw she was wearing plain canvas tennis shoes... So, she wasn't a hiker.

She looked young... What was she doing out here?

He peered at the bloodied hand again, this time noticing a ring on the index finger, a possible indicator of identity, and fumbled his cell phone from his pocket.

He needed the authorities, but there was no reception this far out, and he dared not approach the body, his federal training having taught him that much.

Instead, he started taking pictures from where he stood, his tie still pressed against his mouth and nose, his breaths shallow.

Finished, Philip tucked the phone into his shirt pocket and turned his back on the carcass, a collection of gruesome photos now stored on his cell.

"Jesus," he whispered to heaven and started back to his truck.

CHAPTER 2

"Kody, this is Phil on route 201 park path." Philip released the button on his two-way radio and leaned up against the truck, waiting for a reply.

"Kody, here. Morning, Phil!"

"Kody, I need you to radio the mainland sheriff's department. We have a dead body in the park. Possible bear attack."

"No way! Really?" Kody's voice came over the radio in a surprised hush. "Where is your exact location?"

"It's east of the third curve on the north side just past mile marker six. Have Jerry meet me out here. He'll see my truck no problem."

"Not the game warden?"

"Derrick? He's up in Seattle at a conference. I need someone closer."

"Sure, Phil. I gotcha. I'll call Jerry. Um, is it anybody we know?" Kody was the only other park ranger for the island, usually working the summer months while in college, though this year, still enrolled in school, he had decided to skip the spring quarter.

"Kody, ...I honestly can't tell. Over and out." Philip hung the handset back up on the dash and played with the coiled cord as he thought.

It was a good question.

Did he know who the woman was? It was hard to discern any facial features, and the mangled scalp was dirty from dust and saliva, so even the hair color was hard to recall.

He thought back on the clothes.

Her grimy tank top might have been yellow originally, and the cutoff shorts were most likely homemade from a pair of old jeans.

Philip frowned and thought about the ring on her index finger.

Silver. Looked like a whale with its tail spiraled around the knuckle to keep it in place. An orca, he guessed by the bits of black and white visible through the blood smears. It might be something a woman would wear if she were in her mid-twenties or younger? Most likely younger.

Maybe someone who had come up their way to whale watch?

Philip pulled out his cell phone and brought the pictures up on the screen. He zoomed in on the ring, telling himself to focus on the silver circle and ignore the fact it was attached to a lifeless hand.

He recognized the ring, now that he thought about it. A bunch were in a box at the cash register of Hattie's General store, next to the pepperoni sticks, each ring sitting in its own Styrofoam socket. Nothing special about them from what he could recall. Just a typical cheap souvenir ring.

Of course, this information helped and, it didn't. Might be a local woman who was out there, or it might be a tourist. But at least they could figure she'd been in Hattie's at some point.

"Phil, you there?" Kody's voice came over the radio again.

"Yup."

"Jerry said he's about three minutes out. He was already in town when I got a hold of him. He's hauling ass to you now."

"Roger. Sheriff's department?"

"They're sending someone by the ferry. Should be there within the half-hour."

"Did they say who?" Philip hoped it wasn't Geres. The old coot should have retired eons ago and wouldn't even make it five feet off the trail to the body.

"No, just that someone was en route. Oh, and for you not to disturb anything."

"Roger that. Go ahead and call the game warden's office. Ask Derrick to head our way when he can. Check in again if something changes. Over and out." Philip hung up the radio, the rumbling sound of an engine catching his ear.

Jerry Holmes, who had indeed been hauling ass, had arrived.

He stopped his quad cab pickup with a loud screech of the tires and put the truck into park before grabbing the gun case out of the passenger seat and hopping out.

"Hey, Phil! Let me get the tranquilizers out of the back." Jerry opened the second-cab door and pulled out what looked like a small briefcase. "So, you think it's a bear attack?"

Jerry was the island's veterinarian and occasional animal trapper. He stood a few inches short of Philip's six foot four, with dark hair and a mustache, which he styled curled up at the ends.

"Mornin', Jerry. Honestly, I can't tell. Saw one of the sows with three small cubs this morning. She had blood on her muzzle. Black bears though... they're not known for."

"I know. They're not known for attacking humans. They'd rather run. But a mama and her cubs just out of hibernation?" Jerry slipped a red tasseled shot into the gun. "Three cubs, you say? That's good news. We'll have to have wildlife come out and tag 'em."

"Got a call out to Derrick already."

"Did you get her number?" Jerry walked over to

Philip and extended his hand out in welcome.

"Might have been eighty-one. Was more focused on the cubs, to be honest." Philip took Jerry's out-stretched hand and gave it a hardy shake.

"Jeez, Phil. You're shaking like a leaf!" Jerry put the rifle down, letting it lean against his leg, and grabbed Philip's shoulder, giving it a firm squeeze.

"I'm fine. It's just the adrenaline rush. Didn't ex-pect to find what I did, ya know? Was more expect-ing a deer," Philip's voice trailed off as Jerry nodded in understanding.

"I bet, I bet. Well... um. Do you want me to start looking for the sow? I can—"

"No. Let's wait till the sheriff's department gets here. We'll just keep an eye out for her, in case she decides on coming back this way." Philip pulled his thermos out, his hands still trembling slightly. "Coffee?"

"Sure." Jerry smiled and looked around him. "Did you recognize who it was?"

"No. It was... it was too hard to tell. Female, though. Young, maybe early twenties?"

"Tourist? Local? Runaway?" Jerry speculated, running down a list of possibilities.

Philip shrugged his shoulders and frowned at the idea of a runaway.

They didn't get many of those on the island. Well, not those who ran TO the island. Had plenty of young people jump on the ferry and never look back.

"Maybe you should take a closer look at the missing posters when you get back into the office?" Jerry snatched the rifle by its strap and slung it over his shoulder.

"I suppose so." Philip mulled the idea over, knowing what he saw in the clearing wouldn't resemble any photos posted on the WSP Missing Persons website.

He shook the thought out of his head as he offered Jerry the lid of his thermos and poured the remaining morning coffee.

"Thanks." Jerry looked around them and surveyed the trees, his voice casual, "You'd tell me if you knew who it was, wouldn't you, Phil?" He looked back at his friend and gave him a nervous smile.

"It's not Amy, Jerry."

"No?" Jerry gave Philip a hard look, searching his face for any well-meant deception.

Philip shook his head and added, "I'm sure of it."

Amy was Jerry's twenty-something daughter, who had decided she wanted to enjoy life off the island. She had left last summer to go live with her mom, Jerry's ex-wife... but didn't like the rules over there any better than the rules Jerry enforced. Stubbornly, she then decided to try to strike it out on her own. Philip knew Jerry got calls every now and then when she was running low on money or needed a favor.

He had shared that much over a beer or two.

Philip didn't think the young girl was homeless per se but decidedly crashed a lot of couches. They both knew it wouldn't have been far-fetched for the girl to suddenly come back home. Maybe she had decided it was easier to sleep in a tent in the park than crash on a reluctant friend's couch? He didn't blame his friend for wondering.

Jerry nodded his acknowledgment of Philip's comment and finished off the coffee, handing him back the thermos cap.

"So, not a local?"

Philip shook his head and shrugged his shoulders at the same time.

"Might have been a hiker. Except..." Philip screwed the lid back onto his thermos. "She wasn't wearing hiking boots. Of course, the body might have been dragged quite a ways from a day campsite."

"Could've," Jerry mused with him, pondering the situation as well, growing silent.

Both he and Philip looked down at their boots as the conversation stalled. Like most islanders, the two men knew how to dress for the Pacific Northwest's inclement climate, choosing boots that were sturdy, warm, and laced high above the ankle, well-made for the terrain and cold spring weather.

There was a sudden loud whoop of a siren, and both men jumped, startled out of their reveries. A few seconds later, a sheriff's truck appeared around the bend, coming to a complete stop in front of their vehicles.

"That was fast!" Philip glanced at his watch, surprised at the turnaround time since Kody had radioed in.

"Probably was already coming off the ferry when the call came through," Jerry guessed.

Philip bobbled his head to see who was in the driver's seat, the morning sunlight glaring off the windshield. He assumed by the size of the small frame it was Geres and started brainstorming on how they were going to get the old man out to the clearing.

"Hello. Is one of you gentlemen, Philip Russell?" A petite blonde in a tan and green sheriff's uniform stepped out of the patrol truck and addressed the two men.

Jerry and Philip stared.

This wasn't who they'd been expecting.

She waited a polite thirty seconds... "Gentlemen? I'm looking for Philip Russell?" she repeated, consciously placing her hand on her sidearm.

"Um. Yes, ma'am. That's me. I mean, I am." Philip took a small step forward and nodded his head in acknowledgment. "Park Ranger Philip Russell. This here is our local vet, Jerry Holmes."

"Ma'am." Jerry gave a light wave, accompanied by an overly friendly smile.

The sheriff closed the squad truck door and approached the men, taking out what looked like a black leather notepad.

"Park Ranger Russell, you reported a dead body?" She waited patiently as both men stood slack-jawed staring.

At five foot three, a hundred and twenty pounds, (Fifteen pounds being her duty belt and sidearm) Lieutenant Sheriff Lane made quite the cutting figure. Jerry couldn't help but notice the nice athletic form of her arms and the generous swell of her chest. While Philip was distracted by her tight bun hairdo and piercing blue-eyed glare...which wasn't as friendly as he'd like.

"Yes, ma'a... err, Sheriff. I was doing my morning patrol of the grounds. We check to make sure the roads are clear of debris and that the gates are still closed to the off-road paths... that sort of thing. I observed three cubs and a black bear sow crossing the road, and the sow had blood on her muzzle. I assumed it was a game kill. Decided to find the carcass and remove it to keep her from coming back so close to the road, and that's when I found the body."

"I see. Bear attack, then." She scribbled the words down on her pad.

For the third time that morning, Philip said he was unsure.

She looked up, puzzled.

"Unsure? What does that mean?"

"Well, it means the body is too mangled to know for sure."

"Mangled because a bear had them for breakfast," she muttered to herself and flipped the notepad closed with a snap.

"Would you like to see the body?" Philip asked, then looked at Jerry, including him in the invitation.

"Yes, Ranger Russell." Sheriff Lane tucked her notepad away and headed to her vehicle. "Let me grab my parka," she called back, a few drops of rain pattering down onto the hood.

Waiting, Jerry hefted the tranquilizer gun onto his shoulder as Philip grabbed the shotgun from his rig.

The sheriff returned, wearing a bright yellow parka, four sizes too big.

"Mr. Holmes, I'm sure you know how to handle that weapon?" She looked sternly at Jerry and then twisted her hand, palm out in a "lead the way" gesture.

Jerry mumbled, "Yes, Sheriff." and they stepped off the range road.

CHAPTER 3

Philip hadn't known exactly what to expect of his companions when they saw the body. Jerry had lost his morning breakfast within minutes, retching heavily in the bushes. This had perplexed Philip, who gave the veterinarian a questioning look. After all, the man's job sometimes dealt with blood and dead carcasses, but all Jerry could do was shake his head and empty his stomach again. Philip concluded it was the stench of the eviscerated and decomposing body, the putrid smell causing his stomach to roll as well.

Sheriff Lane had been equally surprising. She had taken one look at the weirdly angled hand sticking out from behind the stump and pivoted on her heels, heading back up the self-made path towards the gravel road.

"Ma'a... Sheriff? Where are you going?" Philip called after her.

"Camera. I... I need... I'll be right back!" she yelled over her shoulder, not stopping. She returned, a good fifteen minutes later... with no camera. However, she didn't look as green as she had before.

"It must be back at the office," she said evasively, as she marched past them and made her way to the body.

Philip followed a few paces behind, careful to give her space, and stopped short of the log, peering down at the disturbing scene. Though his heart still raced, his hands had steadied, the initial shock of the find having faded.

He bent down, resting back on his haunches, and let his eyes roam across the bloody remains.

"Sheriff Lane... I think I see something over here."

"What is it?" She nimbly stepped closer, mindful of the prints on the ground.

"Looks like a knife. A bowie knife... a big one at that." Philip looked over at the sheriff and then back to where Jerry was standing behind them.

"Is there any other kind?" Jerry jeered back.

The island's veterinarian had taken point, facing away from the clearing and them, his eyes glued to the forest trees.

Philip ignored him and stretched his neck to see the weapon better. It was bloody, much like everything else at the scene, covered in muck and dried pine needles. The knife's stag horn handle barely visible, it decorated with two black stripes right below the bolster.

Even from a distance, the knife looked dangerously sharp.

"Think she used it to try to fight the bear off?" Sheriff Lane had joined Philip, squatting down as well. She held her forearm up to her nose in an effort to block the penetrating foul smell.

"Possibly." Philip took out his cell phone.

"You can get service out here?" she asked, skeptically.

"No. But since you came back without your camera, I thought we could take a few pictures so we can get in there and take a closer look at that knife."

"No!" Sheriff Lane hopped up. "I should probably call this in. Get someone from the forensics team to come out."

"Excuse me, Sheriff," Jerry called over, twisting at the waist to face them. "But all that body is going to do is attract more wildlife. In fact, we're not safe here now. Phil is right. Best to take as many pictures as you can before something else comes along and does more damage. There's no way you're going to be able to preserve this site till they get here. It might already be compromised by all sorts of roaming wildlife." Jerry turned back and continued to survey the woods behind them.

The sheriff frowned pensively at his back and then turned to Philip.

"I still think—"

"I've had my federal training as a park ranger, and Jerry here is a volunteer sheriff. So, we both know the protocol." Philip straightened up as well, towering over the little yellow-clad sheriff.

She bit her lip and frowned deeper, indecisively. "Alright," she said, after a minute. "But I'll need you to send me copies of the photos." She met his eyes. "I hope I can count on your discretion with them as well, Ranger." She gave Philip a stern, icy glare, which made him more than a little uncomfortable.

Doing his best to meet her scowl with all serious- ness, Philip gave a clipped, "Yes, ma'am," in response.

The small sheriff eyed him a moment longer. She was trying to decide if he was earnest or being a smart ass and came to the conclusion it was proba- bly both. With another frown, she indicated for him to start.

Minutes later, the three stood directly next to the body, and each looked squeamish. Being this close, it was clear it was not a bear attack that had killed the young woman but a slit throat, from ear to ear, and Philip had a good notion the bowie knife was what had done it.

CHAPTER 4

Hey, Phil!" Kody practically sprinted from the park's small office. "You're back!"

"Hey, kid," Philip said tiredly, unloading his gear from the truck cab.

"So... so what happened?" Kody eagerly grabbed Philip's lunch box and thermos, pacing alongside him. "What did the sheriff's office have to say? Did Jerry shoot the bears? Do we need to barricade—?"

"Slow up, Kody. Slow up," Philip cut him off as he swung the office door open. "I'll tell you all about it. Just... just let me get a cup of coffee first."

"Sure." Kody practically threw Philip's lunch into the station's small fridge and rushed to the coffee pot. "Here. I'll get it for you."

"Thanks, kid."

Securing his shotgun, Philip watched as Kody

filled his coffee mug with what he guessed was yesterday's coffee. This was a valid concern since all Kody ever drank was energy drinks, and Philip hadn't yet been to the office.

Peering over his shoulder, Kody noticed Philip watching and started eagerly, "It's just usually, nothing exciting like this happens around here. Don't get me wrong. When that little boy went missing for a few hours last summer, that got the blood pumping. But a dead body! Man, that's just..."

"Not as glamorous as you'd think, Kody. Believe me." Philip grimaced at the coffee mug. It was most definitely yesterday's coffee. "I've already got it barricaded and taped off. We'll just need to keep an eye out for news crews if the story gets out."

"Oh, I'm sure it will. There hasn't been a bear attack, in what? Thirty plus years?" Kody plopped down behind his tiny desk, which was pushed tightly into a corner, and put his feet on top, garnering a disapproving glower from Philip.

"There still isn't." Philip put the coffee mug down and got up to make a new pot.

"What? Was it a cougar?" Kody slowly slipped his feet from the desk and placed them on the floor.

"No... human. It was a murder." Philip looked at his young ranger with a warning. "And it's hush, hush. Sheriff's office doesn't want anyone talking till they decide to make a statement. Understand me?"

Kody nodded his head and ran his fingers through his curly blonde hair.

"Wow. Murder. Wait, how does a bear...?"

"Mother and cubs stumbled across the body and made a mess of it. But it was murder. Slit throat, young female."

"And it's nobody you know?" Kody watched Philip closely, anxious curiosity in his eyes.

"Honest to God, Kody, I couldn't tell. There was so much blood, and not everything was where it was supposed to be." Philip motioned over his own tall figure, moving his hands to the general stomach and groin area.

"Ohhhh... that's disturbing."

"Now you're understanding." Philip dumped the cold coffee out of his mug and refilled it from the peculating fresh pot. "And it was. Very."

"So... What did Jerry think?"

Philip shrugged his shoulders. "He guesses it might be someone from out of town. Maybe a tourist from last Sunday?"

"And you don't?"

Philip shook his head.

"My gut tells me it's someone from here. The body was wearing regular canvas shoes and there wasn't any camping gear, no hiking boots. Nothing to indicate they'd been staying out there on purpose."

"Maybe it was a canoe? I mean, someone who kayaks?" Kody sat up. "Canvas shoes? Maybe a boater?"

"Yeah... maybe." Philip's eyebrows raised in consideration.

Their small island, garnering its name from a local fish located in the beautiful Pacific Northwest, had initially been a trading post in the early 1800s. It had furnished pelts and trappings for many a fur trader until a large forest fire decimated the island in 1825. It sat semi-vacant with a few people calling it home till, in the early 1900s, a small fishing village took root. Eventually, the island became popular for logging. When rumored a large logging company had plans to buy out the entire island, the Federal Government swooped in and declared the haven a National Park in the 1960s, and thus today, it was a modern-day outdoor enthusiast's paradise.

In the springtime, wildlife photographers came to enjoy the newly bloomed flowers and the freshly rested hibernated animals arriving on the forest floor. Summer brought the onslaught of whale watchers, kayaks, canoes, hikers, campers, and novice rock climbers. The last was a newer trend for the island, which was home to a very large and rocky hill, not a towering mountain by any stretch of the imagination. Locally known as The Mole Hill, the steep mound lent an aerial view of the whole island at its crest. Within the last couple of years, this attraction had become appealing to amateur mountain climbers who viewed the island's pinnacle as a beginner's course.

Then come fall, there was always the last of the seasonal boaters and more photographers trying to catch autumn's last hurrah. In addition, were the few hunters allowed to thin the herds of deer and elk that resided in the forest. And lastly, winter, a season that typically sent everyone home.

Last year the park boasted over eight thousand visitors to its shores.

Philip shook the last dusty bits of powdered creamer into his black coffee. "We're out of creamer." He sat down with a loud sigh.

"I can head over to Hattie's and get you some!" Kody jumped up, the youthfulness of needing to have action and the desire to see if the news had hit the small town plain on his face.

Philip had half a mind to let him go, but his thoughts returned to the orca ring.

"No, I need to pick up a few things anyway. You stay here. Make sure no reporters show up. With the sheriff's car heading over on the ferry this morning, that might have drawn some attention." Philip tossed the coffee into the sink and grabbed his jacket.

"Yes, sir," Kody, deflated, slowly sat back down.

"And if a Sheriff Lane comes by, you know NOTHING. Got it?"

"Hey, I'm a park ranger too. Why can't I know?"

Kody whined, kicking his feet back up on the desk with a loud clunk.

"NOTHING, Kody. Hear me? All you know is there was a body found in the park, possible bear attack. Let her fill you in if she so decides and then report to me when I get back."

"Her? Is she cute?" Kody gave Philip his most debonair smile and made as if he was trying to straighten his tie.

Philip chuckled and shook his head.

"Sure, kid. Oh, let me give you a little pointer. Be polite. Call her ma'am as much as you can. She'll like you for that. Shows respect."

CHAPTER 5

Philip hopped into his truck and decided he'd head to the docks first before heading downtown. He wanted to check the Park and Ride lot to see if any vehicles had been left overnight or maybe longer. Their mystery girl was either a towner or an out-of-towner, and if Philip had his preference... she'd be an out-of-towner.

He'd traveled the ten miles to the coast at a fairly quick clip and pulled into the Park and Ride lot just in time to see the two o'clock ferry pull out. He climbed out of the truck and surveyed the five cars left in the lot. He recognized three as island residents.

One was Jeff Johnson's. The owner of the town's only sit-down restaurant and bar, The Royal Fork. Jeff drove a green Ford Explorer and had parked next to the town's semi-retired lawyer, Mike Allister's new Mercedes Benz. Parked next to the Mercedes was a beat-up pickup truck, encrusted with dark bloodstains smeared all over the truck bed and tailgate... This, of course, belonged to the town's butcher, Henry Allan, who was seventy-two. Not the most physical suspect one could hope for. The other two vehicles Philip didn't recognize and he decided he'd swing by later when the ferry was done running for the night.

On a whim, the ranger grabbed his phone and took a quick picture of each vehicle and its license plate.

He was lucky to still have his cell phone as the less than trusting Sheriff Lane had wanted to confiscate the mobile device. However, after some minor but quick negotiations, he'd convinced her to let him transfer the photos to her laptop directly, upon which she then insisted he let her erase the crime scene photos herself from his phone. When the terms of the negotiation had been completed, only then did she allow him to have his cell back. Philip had quickly snatched it from her hand and made a swift retreat to the park office before she could change her mind.

Done snapping photos, Philip surveyed the rest of the area.

There was the parking lot he was in, which sat next to the large pull-up dock for the ferry to load and unload. Bordering on its left, a half-mile down, stood two docks filled with boats belonging to the island residents, and on the left, two more. These designated, as a general rule, for day fishermen, tourists, and curious seals, who sometimes ventured from the rock crops to beg a piece of fish.

Philip turned away from the docks and looked towards Rockfish Island's first mini-mart gas station. It was built last year and stayed open twenty-four-seven... which most of the townsfolk thought was a waste of power and money. It was brightly lit and bragged of four gas pumps. Considering the single gas pump which sat across the street from Hattie's General had furnished the whole island for years, it hadn't really impressed the locals.

Thus, the new mini-mart wasn't very busy most of the time. But Philip figured, between the increase of tourism to the island, and as soon as the town warmed up to the idea... it would get there.

Across the road was Bert's Outdoor Supply and Kayak Rentals. It was the only place on the island anyone could rent kayaks or buy camping and hiking gear. Bert's was the hot spot of the docks.

Philip had decided he'd drive over and see if maybe Bert had seen or heard of anything, when it so happened, Bert came to the front door of the shop with a cup of coffee in hand. Philip smiled and turned the key to the engine over.

"Phil, it's Kody. You there? Over," Kody's voice

crackled over the two-way.

Philip frowned and peered over at Bert, who was still standing in the doorway looking at him.

"Yeah, I'm here."

"Thought I'd let you know the game warden's office called back about the cubs. Derrick can be here by Thursday at the earliest. Also, Sheriff Lane left about fifteen minutes ago and I think is heading your way. She asked where you went, and I told her you'd gone over to Hattie's. Over."

"Okay. Thanks, Kody. Heading there now."

"Oh and, Phil? Piece of advice. Do NOT call her ma'am. She didn't like it very much." Kody sounded vexed and embarrassed.

"Roger and out." Philip chuckled and put the CB into its cradle then looked back at Bert, giving a friendly wave goodbye.

Bert, in return, smiled, lifting the coffee mug in salute, and walked back into the store.

Philip smiled at the sight and shook his head fondly before heading in the direction of what the locals called "Downtown."

Downtown consisted of a two-way single road lined with diagonal parking spots and storefronts. It ran a total of a mile before it turned back into forest and the occasional driveway to a cabin or home. Once off the main road, it was three miles before the local charter primary/middle school came into view and an additional two miles from there, before spotting the newly built high school. The new addition had a large football field, which doubled as a baseball diamond during the offseason. There had been talk of clearing a second field for a soccer complex... but the town board wasn't exactly thrilled at the idea.

In a few short minutes, he found himself in the heart of downtown and pulled in front of Hattie's General Store.

Hattie's General, or just plain Hattie's, as the place was mostly referred to, was the town's only one-stop-shop, each aisle dedicated to something different. There was a gardening aisle, an automotive aisle, electronics, lumber, chips and dips, chainsaws, beverages... You name it, Hattie's had it. And if Hattie's didn't have it, then you were making a trip to the mainland for it.

Hattie's was owned by Ms. Hattie Vickers, who boasted of being a hundred-two and a half. Her grandson, Harry Vickers ran the general store for her now. That's not to say Hattie's General was just in name only. Locals could find Hattie at the general store every day, sitting in a comfortable rocking chair, visiting with customers, and occasionally taking a nap in the back office when the whim hit her.

The golden bell on the storefront door chimed as Philip walked in.

Harry Vickers looked up from the register as he counted out the daily cash and gave a friendly shout.

"Howdy, Phil! You're off early again today." Harry wrote down the number of one-dollar bills and picked up a small stack of fives, the general store empty, the morning rush having already gone by.

"Still on the clock. Just ran out of creamer at the office." Philip strolled up to the counter and picked up the Styrofoam case that the orca rings sat in. "Sell a lot of these?"

Harry glanced over in mid-count and shrugged his shoulders.

"Guess so. Got three left out of thirty." He wrote the number of fives and picked up the stack of tens. "Popular with the tourists."

"I can see that," Philip said, conversationally. "How long have you had these in stock?"

Harry suddenly glanced up at his customer with curiosity and watched as Philip took one of the rings from its Styrofoam slot.

"I don't know... Why? You want to buy a bunch for Christmas or something?"

"Maybe," Philip said, with non-committal distraction. "Hey Har, do you think you'd be able to pull a receipt of when those rings were sold? Or possibly who they were sold to?" Philip slipped the tiny ring onto his pinkie finger and gave it a closer inspection.

"I suppose I could if you had a warrant." Harry

wrote down the number of tens and returned the stack to the register, closing the door with a bit of a slam. "Or you could just tell me why you're playing detective all of a sudden." Harry beamed a knowing smile at his best friend and leaned onto the counter, eager to hear all about it.

Philip winced and looked up at his buddy. "So, you've already heard?" Philip opened the pepperoni stick jar, helping himself.

"I heard a couple of law enforcement vehicles came over the ferry, and that the hearse headed up to the park. But nothing more than that," Harry admitted. "Some climber hurt themselves or did we have another drowning?"

"No... there wasn't an accident. Mind if I have a seat?" Philip asked through a mouthful of pepperoni.

"Feel free, buddy. Table is all yours." Harry nodded towards a wooden picnic bench parked in front of the large glass store window.

The picnic table, which had been sitting in the store for years, was actually for sale. However, everyone used it as the town's communication hub and coffee circle. Beside it, a few feet away, sat Hattie's rocking chair with a sign hung on the front, "Hattie's chair," then in smaller print below, "Not for sale."

Once seated, Philip glanced at his watch and then casually over his shoulder towards the front door.

"Harry, in a few minutes, a mainland sheriff is

gonna walk through those doors, looking for me. So, I'm gonna share something with you, but you've got to use that famous poker face of yours and play it like you don't know anything."

Harry sprung up from the counter and opened the till again, pulling out the twenties to count. He looked up and gave Philip his best straight face.

"Hit me."

"I found a dead body in the park this morning. A young female. Thought it was a bear attack at first. Come to find out the girl was murdered."

Harry's poker face didn't waver.

"You're pulling my leg."

Philip shook his head. "Wish I was." He stood up and walked over to Harry with his ringed pinkie sticking up. "The victim was wearing one of these cheap rings."

The gold bell above the front door suddenly chimed and both men gave a startled jerk at the sound.

"Ranger Russell, may I have a moment of your time?" Sheriff Lane's small figure filled the door, mostly because of the billowing yellow parka she was still wearing.

Philip gave Harry a meaningful look and then turned to the new sheriff.

"Yes, ma'am. Have a seat." He pointed to the picnic table with a smile.

Sheriff Lane looked from him to the picnic table, her brow furrowed.

"Here? Isn't this... isn't this for sale?" She grasped the large sales ticket dangling from the side of the table.

"Sure is, ma'am!" Harry slammed the register door closed with a smile, forgetting to write the number of twenties down. "But feel free to try it out!" His smile widened in welcome as he propped himself up by his elbows and leaned upon the register counter, enjoying the yellow-enhanced view.

She gave him a brief nod and then muttered under her breath, "Everyone's got manners here."

Philip gave Harry a quick nod, motioning for him to stand up.

"Sheriff Lane, this is Harry Vickers. He manages the general store. Hattie the owner, I would imagine, is in the office?" Philip looked to his buddy for confirmation.

"Yup. Taking her late afternoon nap," Harry confirmed.

Sheriff Lane, in mid-sitting motion, looked up. "Napping?"

"Hattie is a hundred and two."

"And a half!" Harry chimed in.

"She's worked almost every day of her life, but that doesn't stop her from taking her afternoon naps," Philip explained and glanced back at Harry. "Mind if I grab us a couple of sodas?"

"Don't mind at all." Harry straightened his tie and shop smock, all the while smiling at the very pretty sheriff.

Philip half-turned to Lane, mid-step, and tossed over his shoulder, "What do you want to drink? Diet something, I suppose?"

He made his way to the refrigerated wall as sheriff Lane settled herself comfortably on the picnic bench.

"Regular Coke... please," she answered, emphasizing the "regular."

"So, you're new to town?" Harry gave his best smile, having made his way around the counter. He was decidedly heading towards the picnic table, intent on joining their conversation.

"Yes, Mr. Vickers, I am. I've been assigned to your lovely island. Just waiting for the completion of the sheriff's office at the end of the street. Thank you for asking," she continued on before Harry could interrupt further. "Would you mind terribly, Mr. Vickers, if I spoke with Park Ranger Russell in private? Just for a few minutes?" The new town sheriff gave her most polite but expectant smile.

"Oh... sure. Of course! Nooo, problem!" Harry started to walk backwards, away from the table, as if he was planning on going in the opposite direction all along. "I've got some stuff to do back there. Gotta move some kitty litter around. You know, do some heavy lifting." Harry flexed his arms in an attempt to show some muscle.

Sheriff Lane, barely paying him any attention, didn't seem to notice if it made much of a difference.

"But!" He pointed playfully at her. "If you need anything, I'll be down aisle four." Harry gave his most engaging smile before turning around to find the correct aisle.

Sheriff Lane mumbled dismissively, "Thank you, Mr. Vickers, for your co-operation."

Philip returned half a minute later, with two cold Coke cans in hand, to find the sheriff busily trying to pull her notepad out of her back pocket and adjust the large parka at the same time.

"So, what can I help you with, Sheriff?" Philip took a seat and pushed a can in her direction. "I've already given my statement, and you still can't have my cell phone."

The sheriff ignored his comment and focused on his question.

"Well, for starters. I was wondering why you weren't at your post? Your partner... um, Kody." She referred to her notepad for his name. "Stated that you felt the dire need to get to the store for more coffee creamer. I would have thought you'd have more pressing matters to attend to." She put the open pad down on the table and looked Philip in the eye. "Don't you have reports to fill out like the rest of us?"

"I do. However, I find I concentrate better with coffee, and I can't drink mine black." Philip smiled and took a slurping sip of soda. "Can I ask you a question, Sheriff?"

"Sure." The new sheriff unconsciously straightened her back and closed her notepad, placing her pen on top.

"What are you doing in town looking for me? Shouldn't you be out there looking for a killer?" Philip asked smugly as he cocked a questioning eyebrow.

Lane decided to ignore the last question and answered the first one.

"I actually came in search of you for what I hope will be considered a good reason." She took a drink from her can as well and continued, "You handled yourself very well at the discovery site, and when I drove down to the docks, I noticed your truck there. You seemed to be surveying the area. Can I ask what you were doing, Ranger Russell?"

Philip paused, debating if he should make an excuse or be truthful. With a heavy sigh, he decided on the latter.

"I was seeing if there were any abandoned cars in the Park and Ride lot."

"I see." She picked up her pen and notepad. "So was I."

"It was the logical thing to do. She might be an out-of-towner and left her car behind. Was hoping to find a lead to who she is...was."

"Which you would have shared with the sheriff's department, I'm sure?"

"Of course."

"And what brought you here?" The notepad was flipped back open.

"Coffee creamer." Philip gave a crooked smile and took another sip.

"No, not just creamer. Though I noticed the empty container in the garbage can. What else?"

Philip hesitated again and looked down at his pinky ringed hand.

He knew what was coming, though he'd hoped he could have held it at bay for longer than a couple of measly hours. He was about to be told to stand down and to not interfere with official sheriff business. For him to stop playing detective, as Harry had guessed earlier, and let the professionals handle the snooping around. No need to make a pest of himself, his help was not needed or wanted.

Sheriff Lane continued, "Unless I miss my guess it has to do with the ring on your pinkie finger? The orca ring? Same as the one on the victim's index finger."

"You noticed." Philip took the ring off and handed it over, placing it onto the sheriff's outstretched palm.

"Yes... it's like those dolphin rings. Except for its black and white. It caught my eye right away when I tagged it into evidence." She turned the ring over a few times and then put it on her own index finger. It slid all the way past the second knuckle. "So, you came here to find out who bought it?"

Philip nodded his head, admitting the fact. "I was hoping Harry could tell me at least when they were sold and possibly who bought them. There's just a few left."

"Can I ask why you're compelled to involve yourself in this investigation? Hopefully, not just for morbid or idle curiosity?" She slipped the ring off and placed it between them on the picnic table.

"No, not for morbid or idle curiosity!" Philip answered hotly.

Sheriff Lane raised an eyebrow and continued calmly, "Why then?"

Philip took a deep breath and said more coolly, "She might be someone I know, someone who grew up in our community. But then again, she might be a stranger. Either way, she was in my park, and I found her. I feel..." Philip shook his head to clear it of the images that were rising. "Responsible to her."

"As do I." Sheriff Lane nodded her head and then tilted it to the side, giving Philip an analyzing once over. "This is going to be my first official investigation on the island, and as soon as the sheriff's office is finished being built, I'll be permanently stationed here. So, I would like to propose a... partnership."

Philip leaned back from the table in surprise.

Her suggestion was not at all what he expected.

He slit his eyes in suspicion.

"Meaning?"

"Meaning... we do this together. I'm new to the area, and you, I take it, have grown up here? People trust you?"

Philip nodded.

"We also seem to be on the same wavelength. We both thought to check the docks and the possible source of the ring. If I were to guess, your next stop would have been the Outdoor Supply store, yes?"

"That shop sees the most coming and going on the island as far as tourists. Then I wanted to hit the mini-mart."

"I, as well. So, I would like to propose we do it together. I am assuming if I asked you to step away from this, you'd most likely refuse. I'd rather not have to race you to these destinations and ask questions that I might not get the answers to as an outsider, but you'll get as a hometown boy."

"Okay... but there has to be an understanding between us," he said, wanting to set some ground rules. In the short hours they'd known each other, the two had already bumped heads more than once.

"Agreed. Number one. I am the lead on this. No one on the force can know you are taking part. In fact, I feel obligated at this time to let you know I consider you a suspect having found the body. You'll need to give me your whereabouts for last night and early this morning."

"You've got to be kidding me! Suspect? That's the dumbest—" Philip bit his tongue and stopped the smart retort that was about to follow.

Lane watched with a smirk on her face. She was getting under his skin, and she knew it.

He took another deep breath and rolled his eyes in understanding.

"Yeah, okay. I see what you're thinking. I'd be the perfect person to lure someone into the park and then randomly find the body."

Lane nodded, acknowledging the thought.

"But I'm telling you, I saw the bear." He leaned in. "And that body was definitely mauled by a bear."

"Still doesn't mean you weren't the one to kill her." Lane eyed him closely.

Philip leaned back, annoyed.

"Innocent till proven guilty. Did they cover that in sheriff school?" Philip asked sarcastically. "Because if they didn't... they really should have."

"I simply said it was a possibility. I'm not accusing you," Lane clarified.

"Well, that's a relief," Philip huffed.

"Glad you understand," Lane closed the subject. "Number two. Anything you find out, and I mean ANYTHING, you will share it with me. No holding anything close to the chest. I need to be in the know so that I—"

"WE," Philip interrupted.

She sighed, annoyed at the interruption.

"So, WE can make educated deductions."

"Number three," Philip took over. "If I agree to this, we should be on more... agreeable terms with each other. I can't go around referring to you as Sheriff Lane." Sheriff Lane's eyebrows perked up in surprise. "At least, not when it's just us. What's your first name?"

"Lane will do just fine then," she said, impassively.

"Oh, come on," Philip insisted.

"Do you want in on this or not?" she threatened, starting to put away her notepad.

"All right, all right. Lane will do, I guess."

"Good," she said with a satisfied smile, and once again, unconsciously straightened her parka.

"And LANE," Philip emphasized her name. "You can call me by my first name. Instead of Ranger Russell, I'm Philip. Phil, to my friends." Philip stuck his hand out to be shaken. It was... stiffly.

"Number four," he continued on, "You share all the evidence. Every print, photo, DNA sample report... everything."

"Agreed," Lane said tartly and rushed on, "Speaking on that, I'll need to get a print of the bottom of your boots for exclusion reasons. Rule out the footprints we made by the body."

"You'll need Jerry's as well." Philip looked down at his own hiking boots as she nodded in agreement. "And I suppose our fingerprints?"

"Actually, I already have those. I collected Mr. Holmes's from his file with the sheriff's office and yours from your Federal Government record." Lane gave Philip a smart look and changed the subject, "I should tell you. I think I may have found where the killer came in. There was a side trail a few feet over from where we entered further south. You can clearly see boot impressions. I requested a cast to be made. The footprints seem to indicate it was the way in and the way out, however... it's only boot impressions. There were no footprints that matched the victim's canvas shoes."

"About that." Philip leaned in eagerly. "I don't think anyone with two brain cells about this island would've tried to go hiking in canvas shoes or dress in the manner she was. I mean, it's early spring... but the park is still super cold. She might get away with it for a half-hour, but anything longer? Forget it."

"So, you think she was brought in and not staying somewhere else in the park?"

"Maybe swiped from the docks? Early season kayaker? It's hard to say."

Lane nodded once again her agreement and added, earnestly, "Here is another thought. Could it be suicide?"

"HA!" Philip leaned back. "Suicide? No." He shook his head humored by the idea. "Not a chance."

"Just wait!" It was Lane's turn to lean in. "She's out there for whatever reason... She's gotten lost. To meet friends. Inexperienced hiker. Whatever, okay? She stumbles across the bear and her cubs. She's petrified but not defenseless. She has a weapon. The bowie knife, as big as it is, would look pretty small compared to the size of a black bear. She envisions her limbs being torn from her body and can't face it. So, instead of being mauled to death, she cuts her own throat." Lane leaned back, lifting her arms from the table in an expressive manner. "It's a theory."

"It's a ridiculous one. First of all, we're not dealing with a mad man-eating grizzly bear. I agree. No bear is anything to mess with, especially shortly out of hibernation and with cubs. BUT, having said that, black bears are the most docile of all the bears in the Northwest. Besides, it's typically lone males that attack humans when they're hungry, and there is plenty of food in the park. Plus, black bears are easy to scare off. As a general rule, they would rather run than fight. If that girl made any kind of scream or commotion, those cubs and mama likely would've headed in the opposite direction and in a hurry."

Lane agreed with a frustrated but thoughtful frown. "It sounded plausible. Back to the canvas shoes for a second." She peered over her shoulder as

Harry exited aisle four with a big goofy smile and pointed at aisle five.

"I'll just be over here now. Lifting more heavy stuff," Harry called over.

"Thanks, Har. Won't be much longer," Philip called back, not really paying him any attention.
Lane simply ignored him.

"We couldn't find any canvas prints. Keep in mind the bears had tromped all over the place. Though, I did find this interesting. When looking at her shoes, if you ignored all the blood and smeared dirt, there wasn't any mud stuck at the bottom edges. I mean, the ground is still pretty damp out there, and you're gonna sink down just a bit, you know? Keeps that ring of mud grouped around the edges of the sole of the shoe."

Philip couldn't help but look down at his own boots, noticing the dried clumps of dirt on the rims.

"So, she might have been carried in? Maybe it's just where the body was dumped? Not the actual murder scene. That reminds me. When will you get the coroner's report?"

"I'm actually meeting with him first thing tomorrow. He's coming over on the ferry. The body is in the morgue of the funeral home here on the island."

"I want to be there tomorrow."

"NO!" Lane said, her tone firm.

"What do you mean, no? I told you," Philip started defensively.

"I mean NO, as in... How do I explain your presence there?"

"To identify the body! I mean, I found her. I might know who she is."

"The coroner might think differently. You are a suspect, remember?"

"He doesn't know that." Philip watched Lane advert her eyes. "Does he? Don't tell me you've started telling people that I'm—"

"Of course, not." She cut him off and then added begrudgingly, "We're meeting at ten."

"That's better." Philip snatched up the orca ring from the table. "Okay, let's move on. Where are you staying?" He took the final swallow of his Coke and crushed the can, getting up from the picnic table.

"I beg your pardon?" Lane followed his lead and swung her right leg over the bench.

"You're not going back over on the ferry tonight, are you?"

"I was planning on it."

"You haven't found somewhere to stay?" he asked, surprised.

"Um, I've been looking for a place to rent... but, I wasn't planning on moving over here for another week or so, till the office was completed. I have to go home."

"Well, pack a few things tonight to bring with

you tomorrow. Harry has a room to rent over the store here. You can stay there."

Before Lane could object, Philip called Harry over.

"What can I do for you?" Harry quickly came around the corner, holding a couple of bags of Cheetos puffs.

"The room upstairs. Is it still for rent?"

"Yeah, a bit dusty, but I can fix it up." He turned to the sheriff. "I rent it out to hunters during the season."

She nodded in understanding and began to swing her other leg over the bench. "Thank you, Mr. Vickers, but I don't think I'll...,"

Philip grabbed her elbow, helping her untangle her leg from the bench and the big yellow parka. She mumbled a quick, "Thank you." And then tried to pull her elbow back with a slight jerk. Philip ignored her and held on.

"You married? Got a live-in boyfriend?" he asked, bluntly.

"No. Not that it is any of your busi—," Lane started to say.

"Got pets? A dog, a few hundred cats?" Philip ignored her.

"Nooo," she said, sternly.

"Any house plants?" Philip's mouth quirked at the corners.

"No," Lane huffed, finally realizing where he was going with his inquiries.

"Good." Philip smiled. "Listen, Sheriff, people will open up to you more if you stay on the island. Shows you're invested. You keep hopping back over to the mainland each night and they will never think of you as a local."

Slightly wide-eyed, she gently disentangled her arm from Philip's grip.

"Thank you for your explanation, Ranger Russell. I see your point." The sheriff addressed Harry again. "I'll take the room as long as it is priced reasonably."

"Oh! Yes, ma'am. I only charge two hundred and fifty for the room during the offseason. It's got a small kitchen, an even smaller bathroom, and a twin-size bed. But there's a window that lets in plenty of sunshine and a small balcony. It's got its own private access on the backside of the building. Keep in mind, though, the butcher will be right below you. We share the freezer. Hattie rents out the back part of the building to Mr. Allan. Oh, and you'll have to park out on the street. There's no parking in the alley," Harry explained as he busied himself behind the counter again. He pulled out a rabbit foot keychain linked to a single key. "Here you go if you want to take a look."

Lane took the key and grimaced at the white-furred rabbit foot attached.

"No need, Mr. Vickers. I'll take it and move in the day after tomorrow." She pocketed the rabbit foot and flipped open her notepad. "Now, can you recall to who you've sold these orca rings?" She nodded towards the little Styrofoam stand next to the pepperoni sticks.

"Well... not really. We started with thirty of them, and I'm not here all the time. Sometimes Hattie rings people up, and then we've got our two part-time gals... Stacy and Melissa. You might have to ask them?"

"Stacy. Let's start with her. What is Stacy's last name, Mr. Vickers?"

"Stacy Jensen. She typically works the late shift during the week. Comes in for the 6 p.m. to 10 p.m. shift, Monday through Friday. She's the high school cheerleading coach and the Baptist Church youth group leader."

"Busy lady. When could I speak with her?"

"Well... if you want to talk to her HERE? I'd say come back at six. If you want to find her now. I'd suggest heading over to the high school gym."

"Thank you, I might do that." Lane gave another polite smile.

Philip, standing behind her, rolled his eyes impatiently. She was a little too "by the book" for his taste.

"And Melissa? Her information, please."

"Well, Missy. That's what we call her. Missy Dean, she works all day Saturday and Sundays for us from ten to ten. She comes over from the mainland. None of the high school kids seem interested in working at a general store. They'd rather help down at the docks or over at the antique shop or the ice cream deli. She won't be back over till this Saturday."

Philip was ready to get a move on.

"Hey, Har. Any way you can pull a report or anything for us on those rings?"

"Well, we're kind of old fashion here. In fact, we barely got a camera system last year and—"

"Wait, you have a camera system? How far does it record back?" Lane interrupted.

"Oh, it records over each day," Harry practically whispered as a group of schoolboys came through the door and headed towards the snack aisle. "Hi, fellas!" Harry called out to the kids, who waved in return.

"Har, back to the report?" Philip nodded, bringing Harry's attention back around.

"Yeah. Um, well... let me think. Cash transactions? I could only give you the date the rings were sold, and even then, I'd have to look it up by the SKU number. But if you wanted credit card purchases, I'd have to correlate them with the daily receipts to see if the totals matched up and make a list of names from the matched totals. Of course, if I did that... I'd be here all night," Harry chuckled at the thought.

Sheriff Lane icily stared at Harry for a full minute then abruptly turned on Philip.

"Park Ranger, this gentleman knows, doesn't he?"

"Well, no. Not exactly," Harry piped up, quickly glancing over at Philip, looking somewhat startled. Philip groaned at Harry's nervous interjection which was basically a confession.

"Have you been eavesdropping, Mr. Vickers?" Lane turned back on Harry, taking a step closer and flourishing her notepad.

"No, ma'am!" Harry squeaked, a guilty flood of red rushing over his face.

"So much for your poker face." Philip glared at Harry, handing him the ring back. He then tapped Lane's shoulder, and she turned back to face him. "All he knows is there has been a murder in the park and the victim was wearing the ring. I shared nothing beyond that."

"I see. That would explain his lack of curiosity as to why I'm asking all these questions. I shouldn't have to explain to you, Mr. Vickers, that this is a sheriff's investigation, and you are under no circumstances to tell anyone what you've learned today." The pretty blonde sheriff's blue eyes looked extremely steely to Harry Vickers.

"Yes, ma'am."

"Wonderful, Mr. Vickers. The sheriff's department appreciates any assistance you can give as far as hearsay or gossip you may pick up from the picnic table. Also, I'll check in with you come morning to find out your results with the purchase report for those rings." Lane gave Harry a brief nod, another expectant smile, and started to make for the front door.

"Hold on, now! Just a second. I have plans tonight!" Harry called after her, shooting a pleading look at Philip.

Philip shrugged his shoulders as if to say, "Nothing I can do about it," and tossed him five bucks for the Cokes and yelled, as a farewell, "Thanks a bunch, Harry!" as he followed sheriff Lane out the door.

The golden bell chimed the departure, and Harry stared after them, now in a disgruntled mood as he watched as the two climbed into their respective vehicles and drove off in the direction of the docks.

"Well... crud."

CHAPTER 6

Philip cleared his throat and arrested Lane's progress to the front door of Bert's Outdoor Supply and Kayak Rental Shop.

"I... uh. I think I should make you aware of something." He met her eyes but lowered his voice as a small group of ferry riders passed by on their way into the shop.

She looked at him, questioning, and gave a nod of encouragement.

"Go ahead."

"I wanted to let you know I was with Bert last night. Bert is my alibi. Not that I should need one." Philip cleared his throat again and then causally glanced behind his shoulder to see if anyone was standing too close.

Lane gave him an "And?" look while shaking her

head for him to continue.

"We uh, we spent the night together." Philip lowered his voice and added, "I didn't leave till about four in the morning."

"You're ga...?" Sheriff Lane started and stopped. "I... I didn't realize that you were..." she stopped again and shook her head. "I mean to say... I usually have a radar about...," she haltingly finished the sentence, "these things." Philip frowned, and her eyes got wide. "I. am. so. sorry! I never should have said that! That was completely unprofessional of me. It's just, you don't look the type. Not that—"

Philip interrupted her, "Radar?"

Sheriff Lane turned her back on him and started towards the shop's door. "I know... So unprofessional. Let's go."

"But that's not all of it."

"For gracious sakes...," she muttered under her breath.

"And it's... well, it's sort of delicate," Philip admitted, lowering his voice to a practical whisper.

"You know, Ranger, I don't really need to know all the intimate details of your night." She looked around them, making sure no one was near enough to eavesdrop. "Uh, let's just get in there, see if we can find out anything about our Jane Doe, and you can tell me later when I question you officially." Sheriff Lane's face was flushed with embarrassment.

"You sure, you don't want to know now?" Philip, his tone amused, pushed.

"I'm sure," she said, curtly, her face reddening even more.

"All right then..." Philip shrugged his shoulders in resignation. He then subconsciously patted down his hair as he sucked in his slight gut, and opened the door of the Outdoor Supply Shop.

The door gave an electronic beep, unlike the jingling golden bell at Hattie's, to announce their arrival.

Lane immediately noticed the shop had a modern "outdoorsy" feel, enhanced by the large wilderness and outdoor sporting photos placed above each department. The back wall of the store was covered with a large climbing wall which had a minor waterfall feature trickling through it, the flowing water leading to a fountain placed in the middle of the sales floor. On the side walls, facing away from the entrance, were displays of kayaks for purchase or rent, along with paddles and expensive fishing poles. However, the main attraction was a stuffed black bear climbing a tree in front of the store window, the store's guests, casually milling around the display of nature as they browsed through the many clothing and boot racks spread across the shop floor.

At the very front was stationed a large counter and cash register, the latter being manipulated by a young girl roughly the age of sixteen. She wore dangling earrings and a bright pink baseball cap with her hair in a ponytail.

Philip bent down close to Sheriff Lane's ear and whispered while nodding towards the register girl.

"That's Bert's daughter."

She looked at him and then back at the cashier.

"Bert has a daughter? Adopted?"

"No." Philip grinned slyly. "She's all Bert's."

Sheriff Lane looked behind and up at Philip perplexed.

A door at the back of the store opened, and an attractive woman, without a stitch of make-up, exited, holding a few shoe boxes in hand. She appeared to be in excellent athletic condition with long dark hair and pretty brown eyes, aged around forty.

The woman spotted the two and gave Philip a bright and friendly smile as she wove her way through customers, one grabbing her before she could reach them.

"And that... is Bert!" Philip said, with a genuinely cheesy grin on his face.

"THAT'S Bert? I thought Bert was a..."

"I know you did," Philip chuckled. "Bert is short for Roberta."

"So, why so hush-hush about her then?"

Philip's smile faltered.

"She's still married. Legally separated, though.

We've been keeping it on the down-low till her divorce goes through. Small island, big tales... that sort of thing."

Bert pointed her customer in the direction of the register and then broke away.

"Well, hello!" Bert's voice was light and friendly.

"Hey, Bert! I would like you to meet our new sheriff for the island. This is Sheriff Lane. She was hoping we could talk to you for a minute. Could we step in back?"

"Well, sure. I'm... I'm not in trouble, am I?" she laughed and pointed them towards the door she'd come from before turning to the register. "Shelby, if you need me. I'll be in the back, honey." Her daughter nodded, along with her dangly earrings, and then greeted the next customer in line.

The backroom was small, with a lone desk crammed against the far wall and a long corridor to the side, lined with metal shelving and stocked full of inventory. There were three picture frames on the wall hanging above the desk, the store's first dollar bill, a current business license, and a photo of an attractive young couple holding a baby, the young couple pictured standing next to an older man in front of the outdoor supply shop.

Bert noticed Sheriff Lane looking at the last.

"That was taken before dad got ill. He was the original owner of Bert's Supply and my namesake.

My Shelby girl was just a baby."

Lane smiled. "Looks like you've got a very successful shop here."

"Thank you. Here, let me get you a seat." Bert grabbed two folded chairs from up against the wall and handed one to Philip. "Help me out here, Phil."

Philip obliged and unfolded a chair for the sheriff.

"Thanks, Bert. This won't take too long. I was telling Sheriff Lane how your shop is the hub of the docks and about the number of tourists that come through," Philip started the conversation.

"Yes. Dad was pretty smart to put the shop here instead of downtown. Though, I know there are still some hard feelings about that."

"To start, how many employees do you have?" Lane gave what she hoped was a friendly smile.

"Oh, just myself mostly. Ernie Reames comes in a few days a week to close and my daughter Shelby, you saw her upfront, she helps out after school and on weekends." Bert brushed aside a lock of hair that had fallen into her eyes, and Lane took notice of her hands. They were roughly callused and strong, the nails short and rough. Not what you would call feminine at all. Lane surmised Bert enjoyed rock climbing as a hobby.

"We don't stay open late, pretty much eight to six. In the summer, I hire extra help. Usually, a couple of high school kids and extend the hours to eight in the evening."

"I see, and roughly, how many tourists do you see in a day?" Lane flipped to a new page on her notepad.

"Well... in the summer and early fall, it's anywhere from a hundred people and up. Winter, just a hand full."

"Early spring? Like, today, for instance?"

"On a weekday like this? Fifteen? On a weekend it might jump up to thirty, thirty-five."

"And the renting of the kayaks? Any recent issues with those? None missing?" Philip asked casually, but a tad too eagerly.

"No." A slight crease came across Bert's forehead. "No, they've all been returned and were undamaged." She caught Lane's eye. "I make sure to take a deposit upfront. Keeps people honest."

Lane gave a polite smile and made a notation as Philip suddenly looked about the room, craning his neck.

"You've got a camera system, don't you, Bert?" He spotted a small lens facing the back door.

"Oh, yes. No sound, though." She peered at the two of them, her eyes slitting into a cautious expression. "This isn't a friendly trying to get to know the area talk, is this?"

"Just trying to get a feel for the place. I'm curious, though, if you ever see anything odd in a town this size and with so many visitors from the mainland?"

Sheriff Lane looked up from her pad expectantly, trying to bypass Bert's own curiosity.

"Odd? Like what?" Bert half-chuckled at the question.

"Like couples fighting? Or someone lurking around? Anything suspicious?"

Bert looked to Philip and then back at the new sheriff.

"Can I ask... why you're asking?"

"Like I said, just curious," Lane said with a pleasant smile.

Bert frowned at the answer and then turned to Philip in concern. "Phil, what's going on?"

She hadn't been fooled.

Philip cleared his throat and looked for the nod of permission from Lane, stating, "Bert, on my rounds this morning I stumbled across a dead body."

"Oh, Phil! That's... that's terrible! Are you all right?" Bert quickly grabbed Philip's hand and clutched it to her chest.

"It was a shock, but I'm okay." He smiled softly at her.

Sheriff Lane, put off by the sudden show of affection, busied herself with writing something else in her notepad.

"Who was it?" Bert turned to Sheriff Lane. "Can I know that? Can he tell me? Is it someone I know?" Bert abruptly dropped Philip's hand and looked panicked. "Oh, tell me it isn't..."

"No. It isn't Tim," Philip reassured her as Bert took a deep breath of relief.

Philip faced Lane.

"Tim is her husband. He's, um... well... he left a few months ago without a trace."

"I wouldn't say without a trace! He packed his clothes and emptied out our bank account before he left." Bert's temporary worry for Tim's well-being was cut short with scorn. "Left me with a teenage daughter to raise, a second mortgage on the house, and a business to run with no money."

"So, back to seeing anything suspicious?" Lane glanced over at Philip and changed the subject, not interested in Bert's marital woes.

The shop owner shook her head in the negative.

"Not that stands out. You always have the snot-ty ferry folks and the occasional grouchy old fisher-men. Typical crowd around the docks."

"And the camera system. How long does it record?"

"It's an older system. We change the tape out every day and we typically keep it for at least a month before we record over it again. I plan on upgrading the system here soon. There can be a lot of sticky fingers when it comes to some of the ferry visitors."

"That's good to know. We may need to ask to look at those later if the need arises." Lane smiled. "Would that be alright with you?"

Lane waited for an answer, and as she did, she realized the park ranger and shop owner complemented each other.

Bert was very natural-looking, not dolled up or what some people might consider 'put together', her style matching Philip's own dark looks and heavy muscular build. (If you ignored the slight beer belly he was always trying to hide.)

Lane thought that Philip's dark brown eyes and handsome square jaw lent to the idea that he would be more comfortable in lumberjack plaids than in his park ranger uniform.

She concluded that the two looked well together.

"Oh sure, anything I can do to help." Bert had regained her friendly and upbeat manner. "But I'd still like to know who it was you found, Phil?"

"We haven't identified the body yet. It was a young female. My guess is around early to mid-twenties. Possibly blonde."

"Possibly? What do you mean, possibly?" Bert looked between the two.

"The body had been mauled by a black bear. Everything was covered in dirt and... gore." Philip scooted his chair in his discomfort, making a large screeching sound against the floor.

"Bear attack!" Bert looked even more surprised than before.

"That's what we thought at first, but it wasn't.

Easy to do with all the blo... err... It was not a bear attack." Philip cleared his throat, unwanted mental images popping into his head. "But the body had been mauled by one," Philip clarified lamely, hoping to end the confusion and close the subject.

"So, what killed her then?" Bert's face was scrunched up in a puzzled frown.

"I'm sorry, Mrs., uh... sorry. What is your last name?" Sheriff Lane readied her pen over her pad again.

"Esten. Roberta Esten. I'll be switching back to my maiden name here as soon as my divorce goes through. It'll be Kerns then." Bert gave Philip a shy smile, which he returned.

"Well as I started to say, Mrs. Esten, we can't share any more details as this is an ongoing investigation. I want to ask that you not share this information with any of your family and neighbors. If you hear anything which might be of assistance to the sheriff's department while people are in your shop or within the community, I ask you to report it to me right away. We're hoping to be able to make an official release of information sometime tomorrow afternoon." The sheriff stood up. "Oh, one last question. On a personal note, does your store carry bowie knives?"

"No. We don't even carry guns. I leave that up to the bigger stores on the mainland." Bert looked over at Philip and shrugged her shoulders, bemused by the question.

"I see," Lane noted and extended her hand. "It was nice to meet you, Mrs. Esten."

CHAPTER 7

Leaving Bert's Supply, Lane and Philip drove across the street to speak with the owner of the new mini-mart, Mr. Chang.

Sadly, Mr. Chang had the same answer to all of Sheriff Lane's questions. He didn't see anybody, didn't talk to anybody, and didn't know anybody. Philip had a funny feeling even if Mr. Chang had, he wasn't going to tell them. Business was poor as is, and if word got out that someone might have been abducted from his gas station, the new business owner might as well pack it all in.

Lane argued it was a strong motive for murder if the victim had been someone trying to blackmail or cause harm to the budding business. Philip doubted it. Mr. Chang didn't strike him as the murdering type, but rather, the keep my mouth shut, and it's none of my business type.

Undeterred by his silence, they had asked nicely for access to the store's video and were even more politely turned down, which meant more work for Lane if she was serious about viewing the surveillance tapes. In an attempt to lean on Mr. Chang, the sheriff warned the mini-mart owner she would have to request a warrant, and it would be much easier if he complied. Not blinking at the semi-threat, Mr. Chang said he'd wait for the legal writ, and thus thwarted, Lane vowed she would duly be back.

Mr. Chang, full of polite apologies, offered them free end-of-the-day corn dogs.

Sheriff Lane declined.

"I've got to get back..." Philip swallowed a bite of corn dog. "Got to help Kody close up the park."

"Close? What's there to close?" Lane's lip wrinkled in mild disgust as Philip pulled the last bite of corn dog off the stick with his teeth.

"Well, there's no overnight camping allowed this early in the season. Gotta close the main gate and then finish up the rest of it."

"Which is doing what?"

"It's more of a patrol. Make sure all the off-road Jeep trails are still secured and gated. Double check there are no abandoned cars. That type of thing. Then lock up the office till the next day." He flicked the corn dog stick into a nearby garbage bin.

"I see. Walk me to my truck?" Lane's voice made it sound like a request, but Philip knew it wasn't.

"Sure."

"So, delicateness aside, tell me your whereabouts last night and before you found the body this morning."

"Alright. Um... Monday. Arrived at work at five in the morning. Had Kody in tow most of the day. I got off work at three. Went home, and took a bit of a nap. Around four-thirtyish, I headed over to Hattie's and did some grocery shopping."

"What did you buy exactly?" Lane pulled out her notepad.

Philip shrugged.

"Groceries. You know."

"I think you know, I don't know, Ranger Russell. That's why I asked." She didn't bother to look up from her notepad, her pen waiting.

Philip clenched his fists in annoyance.

"Well, I can tell you it wasn't rope, duct tape, and a big bowie knife!"

Lane looked up and gave a steady cool glare.

"What did you buy then?"

"I bought some wine, flowers, a box of Cheerios, and a box of condoms."

Sheriff Lane nodded, writing down the list, a slight smirk on her face.

"We're both adults here, Ranger Russell. Go on,

where did you go from there?"

"I then headed home. Had a bowl of Cheerios and then got ready for my date. Left the house a little before six and made my way over to Bert's."

"I'm sorry." Lane looked up, annoyed. "Can we stop calling her Bert? Her name is Roberta."

"But everyone calls her Bert. We've ALWAYS called her Bert," Philip explained, as if it was blatantly obvious, she shouldn't be called anything else.

"So, you arrived at Roberta's house and then...?"

"And then we had dinner and watched a movie on the couch."

"Oh, what movie?" Lane looked up, her eyes genuinely interested.

"I don't know. Some movie on TV. There wasn't..." Philip looked down at his boots. "Wasn't much watching going on."

"Uh-huh. Go on."

"Then we retired for the night."

"I'm sure you got your full eight hours of sleep," Lane said, a slight lilt to her voice.

"Adults here," Philip chided.

Sheriff Lane's smile widened and she quickly nodded as if to say, "All right."

Philip continued, "Then I got up way before dawn, around four in the morning. Headed home. Took a shower, made a pot of coffee, and was on the road to the park by five. You know the rest from my statement earlier today."

"Thank you, Ranger Russell." Lane snapped her notepad closed and opened the truck door. "I'm heading home now. I don't think I have to tell you I'd like you to stay on the island."

"No, ma'am. You don't." Philip gave her a playful salute.

"Good. See you tomorrow at the funeral home. Have a pleasant night." Lane climbed into her vehicle, and Philip lightly closed the door for her.

Giving a parting wave, he watched the sheriff drive onto the ferry and then turned to face the Park and Ride lot, making a mental note it was now sitting empty, which meant no unclaimed vehicles.

Slightly disappointed, Philip then returned to his truck and waited until the ferry pulled out before cranking the engine over and heading back to the office.

CHAPTER 8

"Sorry I've been gone so long, Kody. Go on and head home. I can finish up here." Philip started for the coffee pot and stopped short, realizing he'd forgotten to buy creamer while at Hattie's. "Crud."

"What's the matter?" Kody had jumped up and was already gathering his coat and hat from the hook on the back of the door.

"Ah, nothing." Philip tiredly sat down at his desk and brought up the login screen for his computer. "It's late. Head on home, kid."

"You sure?" Kody hesitated by the door, jacket already on, and lunch box in hand.

"Yeah. I've got these reports to finish up, and I'm gonna be here a while." Philip rubbed his eyes and squinted at the screen.

"You want one of my energy drinks?" Kody began to dig into his lunch box.

"Ugh, heavens no. You trying to give me a heart attack, kid?" Philip waved him off.

"So uh, I did a drive through the park before you came in, and it was all clear. I'll just lock the main gate on my way out. You can let yourself through when you decide to leave."

"Will do." Philip pulled his readers from his shirt pocket and put them on. He glanced up to see if Kody was leaving.

"The park was practically buzzing today with all of those patrol cars." Kody lingered.

"How many showed up?" Philip pulled his readers down to the tip of his nose to look at his young partner.

"Two."

"Oh, yeah. Buzzing." Philip pushed the glasses up and looked down at his computer screen.

"And then there was the funeral hearse."

"Hmm, hmm." Philip was only half-listening as he struggled with the mouse pointer, it not going where he wanted, the thing probably needing new batteries.

"And the tow truck."

"Tow truck?" He looked up, interested. "Whose vehicle was towed?"

"Oh, there wasn't one. The tow guy said he saw all the commotion and figured there was a car wreck somewhere."

"Ambulance chaser."

"Ambulance, what?"

"Nothin'."

"Phil, ...there wasn't an ambulance," Kody said, his tone serious, not understanding the reference.

"Yeah. I know, kid. It's a saying. Just forget it." Philip chuckled and then added under his breath, "Damn generation gap."

"Okkkaayy." Kody shook his head and continued, "Anyway, he said to call him if we have any more breakdowns in the park."

Philip nodded and returned his focus to the screen.

"So, did Sheriff Lane track you down?" Kody now had his hand on the doorknob, but pure curiosity kept him from turning it.

"Did she ever. Which reminds me. I have a meeting downtown tomorrow morning at ten. Don't know how long it's going to take. In fact, I might take some much-needed vacation time here this week. You feel comfortable running the ship without me?" Philip had started to henpeck his way across the keyboard.

"Sure, man! You probably need some time off after finding—" Kody stopped awkwardly and gave a wiggled shiver. "Just seeing the hearse drive by freaked me out. I can't imagine how you're feeling."

Philip looked up from the keyboard, confused, and then decided it was best to go with Kody's assumption.

"It was a shock all right. Just need to... you know,

get past it."

"No worries, Phil. I can hold the fort down, no problem. Take all the time you need."

"Thanks, Kody. We'll see you in the morning."

"Sounds good. Night, Phil." Kody opened the door and bounded over to his truck. Philip tried to remember the last time he had the energy Kody possessed and decided it hurt too much to think back that far.

CHAPTER 9

A sprinkling of morning rain cascaded down upon Philip, who stood on the ferry dock holding his thermos and a large plastic bag. The ranger was patiently waiting for the sheriff's patrol truck to disembark from the ferry.

It was easy enough to spot her with the bright yellow parka.

"What are you doing down here?" Lane called through the truck window, having slowly pulled alongside, surprised to see Philip in jeans and a flannel plaid shirt.

"Trying to catch a ride." He reached out and took a hold of the truck door handle. He found it locked.

"I thought we were going to meet up at the funeral home?" Lane tilted her head and peered up at the rearview mirror, noticing another car coming off the platform.

Philip yanked on the door handle. It was still locked.

"We were. But I'm here now." He yanked again.

"Yeah, but that wasn't the plan," she called back.

"Plans change." He tried again.

Still locked.

Frowning in annoyance, Lane glanced at her mirror again and hit the unlock button begrudgingly. Philip hopped in and shut the door with a triumphant smile.

"But we said we'd meet at the funeral home... and why do you need a ride? Where's YOUR truck?"

"At the park with Kody. I don't have a car." Philip unscrewed the lid of his thermos. "I'm on vacation."

"Vacation? I already told you. You can't leave the island," Lane said, crossly.

"And I heard you. I'm not going anywhere. Don't worry." Philip gave her an easy smile as he poured coffee into the thermos cap. "Work trucks are only for work. Thus, Kody dropped me off so I could get a ride with you." He placed the thermos between his legs and screwed the lid back on. "Besides, I brought you something in trade." Philip hefted the large plastic bag with his left hand into the air.

"What's in there?" Lane's eyes darted to the mysterious garbage bag.

"My boots. And Jerry's too. I swung by and picked

them up last night." He abruptly dropped the bag onto the truck floor and it flopped open.

"How thoughtful. I can actually smell them from here."

"Well, we're working men and sometimes we sweat—."

"And why aren't you in uniform?" Lane gave him a fleeting once over before returning her attention to the road.

"Gee, lady. What don't you understand about vacation?" Philip pointed the thermos cap across his body towards a side road. "Hey, take this left. We can park in the back." Lane obliged and he continued, "I can't be of much help to you if I'm working all the time, can I? And I've got a crap ton of vacation built up, so I took some. You have me for a week."

"You do realize if a murder case is not solved within forty-eight hours, it might never be. I most likely won't need you for the full week." Lane pulled into the back parking lot of the funeral home and parked next to the coroner's car.

"Ah, but you'll have me all the same. You sure you don't want any coffee?" He smiled and held up the thermos, waving it back and forth in a tempting fashion.

"I don't like creamer in my coffee." She pulled the keys from the ignition. "By the way, how did you sleep last night?"

She was honestly curious as she hadn't gotten a wink. The images of the mangled body, seared into the back of her eyelids, had forced her to stare at the ceiling, causing a long and sleepless night.

"Sleep?" Philip answered, between quick gulps. "Never heard of it."

Lane nodded in mutual understanding, spotting a barrel-chested man with a long white beard. He had come out the back door of the funeral home and was lighting up a cigarette.

"Who is that?" Lane tilted her head in the man's direction.

"That's George Barnes." Philip screwed the cap back on the thermos. "I was hoping it would just be the coroner here today."

"George Barnes?" She dutifully pulled out her notepad.

"He owns the funeral home." The funeral director, dressed in black, gave a wave from the porch as he spotted the patrol truck, beckoning them over. "He's married to the town's biggest gossip. Good luck keeping this under wraps."

The two exited the vehicle and crossed the parking lot to George, who was quickly finishing the last puffs of his cigarette.

"Mornin', George!" Philip greeted warmly, extending his hand.

"Well, Good Morning!" George pumped his arm

generously. "Ma'am."

"George, this is Sheriff Lane with the sheriff's department. She's here to—"

"To meet with the coroner. You uh, you're also going to be our local constable too, aren't ya? No more having to wait for the mainland to get themselves over here." George dropped his cigarette and smashed it with his huge booted foot. "I suppose you're here to identify the body, Phil?"

"He's here—," Sheriff Lane began.

"Well, you're too late. She's already been I-dent-TI-FIED!" George said, with gusto.

"By whom? No one should have had access—," Lane started.

"By whom? By me! After the coroner looked over the body, I decided to do some cleaning up. Start the proper and dignified procedure of taking care of the dead." George puffed out his chest as he spoke of his profession. "I cleaned up some of the muck and blood off her face. Put her hair back on top of her head, and I knew exactly who it was!" George smiled, clearly enjoying their avid attention.

"And...?" Philip lightly nudged George's arm, encouraging him to go on.

"It's Stacy. You know, the churchy cheerleader gal." George beamed knowing he'd just answered the million-dollar question.

"Stacy... cheerleader..." Sheriff Lane flipped towards the front of her notepad. "Stacy Jensen?"

"It's her, for sure." George opened the back door to the funeral home. "Come on, I'll take you down to see her. You tell me it's not her, Phil."

Philip and Lane followed him into the tiny funeral home decorated with Roman columns, cheap plastic flower arrangements, and overused velvet furniture.

Soft music played in the background as the director took them past the viewing rooms and through the chapel into the salesroom, leading them downstairs to the basement and morgue section of the funeral home.

The music slowly faded, and their footsteps began to echo, accompanied by the panting breath of George, who was no small man. They continued down a single bulb lit hallway and entered a large cold room, the morgue, freezing, causing Lane to shiver inside her parka and unconsciously step closer to Philip for warmth.

Inside sat a man on a folded chair next to a card table, drinking coffee, busily checking items from a list on a clipboard. He was skinny, fragile-looking, roughly around seventy, way past retirement age, and dressed in a business suit. He wore an oversized feather-down jacket, the coat practically swallowing his frame, and a stocking cap down over his ears.

"They don't believe me that it's Stacy, Ralph. Can you believe that?" George's voice, which bellowed naturally, boomed through the small room. Coroner Ralph Ames looked up from his paperwork and gave a small smile.

"You must be Sheriff Lane? Hello, Ranger Russell." The coroner stood up and shook hands. "I've met Philip a few times between boating accidents and accidental drownings," he explained in greeting and then handed Philip a small jar. "It's for below your nose," he advised kindly. "Helps with the smell."

"Tell 'em it's her," George insisted as he pulled a white-sheeted body from a refrigerated cavern in the wall and threw back the cover with a flourish, revealing a pale and rigid female body, it looking cleaner than it had the day before.

The small group moved to the gurney and peered down upon the remains, a large portion missing.

The young woman was Stacy Jensen.

"George, would you mind getting me another cup of your wife's amazing coffee? These rooms just chill me to the bone." Coroner Ames turned and smiled warmly at the funeral owner. "And maybe another one of her yummy cookies? Two, if she's feeling generous?"

"Sure, Ralph. Sure thing." George knew it was an excuse to be rid of him and have the room to themselves. He hit Philip's arm on the way out. "Told you it was her."

Philip nodded his head, unable to look away

from the pale face staring back, George slipping out the door, his boots echoing down the hallway.

"Well, let's make use of the short amount of time we have," Coroner Ames slipped on a pair of exam gloves, his clipboard held under his arm.

Sheriff Lane, green and queasy, uneasily edged closer, ready with her notepad.

"Time of death. Roughly around three or four p.m. Monday. Cause of death. Slashed throat. NOT... bear attack. No signs of a severe struggle, no signs of any kind of bindings, no signs of rape, or sexual mutilation. However, a few strange things of note. Victim was scalped... AND." He put the clipboard down on the side of the gurney and gingerly lifted the right leg, holding it by the ankle.

"A sticky substance, most likely honey, has been poured over the body. I'll have to run a test or two to confirm." He touched the skin and a short string of goo clung to his gloved hand. "I'm sure that's what encouraged your bear to partake." The corner pinched his fingers together and opened them, the gloves making a squelching sound with each separation.

"Wait. Somebody literally poured honey all over her?" Lane asked, shocked.

"Yes." He pulled the gloves off, tossing them lightly into a large garbage bin, and then grabbed a fresh pair. "Victim has been identified as Stacy Jensen, twenty-two years old and a lifelong resident of the island. From the parts that I could examine, she seemed to be a healthy female. No signs of disease, cancer, or anything like that. Though most of her major organs are missing so that information might be incorrect." Ralph looked over at the sheriff and Philip. "I'm declaring it a homicide. Murder by person or persons unknown."

"So, not suicide?" Lane looked sheepishly at Philip before returning her questioning gaze to the coroner.

"No. I found broken nails. Might have been from grabbing at someone or it might be from the bear dragging her around. I've taken clippings of her fingernails for DNA samples. There is also some bruising under her chin where someone could have grabbed her roughly from behind, forcing her neck up, slicing it with the knife."

"So, she didn't smother herself in honey and then cut her own throat, is what you're saying?" Philip pointedly looked at Lane.

"That's what I am saying." Coroner Ames returned to the card table and pulled out the folded chair, taking the seat.

"Okay, okay. So... she's lured out to the park, then? You said, NO signs of a struggle or being bound?" Lane leaned over the body and took a closer look, the sheriff turning greener by the second.

"Not even any residue of duct tape on the lips. She wasn't gagged either." The coroner busied himself signing papers.

"How can you tell?" Philip leaned over and peered closely at the blue lips.

"No bruising around the corners of the mouth. Most victims work their gags between their lips and teeth, so they can try to talk or scream. This causes strain on the sides of the mouth."

"And the scalping of the hair?" Philip was now able to recognize Stacy, viewing the body with the hair piece positioned at the top of the head and the dirt and gore removed, which went to show how badly bloodied and tumbled her body had been from the bear mauling.

"Well, at first, I thought maybe the bear had somehow ripped it off. But bears don't typically go for limbs or the head. They focus on the guts, your stomach, and fatty areas. So, I took a closer look, and the cuts on the scalp match the serration of the bowie knife found at the scene."

"Trophy?" Lane suggested.

"Possible," the coroner conjectured.

"That would lean towards a serial killer, or someone who has killed for the first time?" She looked over at Philip, panic suddenly filling her usually steady blue eyes.

"But you take a trophy with you. What if it had a meaning of some sort? A sign. A message?" Philip speculated, nodding at the coroner for direction, who shrugged in return.

"I'll let the sheriff here figure that out. I'm due back on the mainland in an hour. I've got another two lined up today." The thin man paused as the door swung open, and George, cookies and coffee in hand, passed the goodies to the coroner, who graciously accepted. "Thanks, George." He smiled his thanks and then added, "Sheriff, I'll be making a statement at 5 p.m. tonight."

CHAPTER 10

"We should head to the high school next. That's where Stacy's boyfriend, Rick, works. He's the baseball coach." Philip busied himself with clipping on his seat belt.

"Don't you think it's wiser to notify the first of kin? Parents, siblings?" Lane lowered the truck's window and tried to ease the smell of work boots from the cab.

"Parents are Snow Birds, and they're still in Arizona. Plus, she's an only child."

Lane nodded.

"That simplifies things. I'll radio the station and ask them to make the appropriate call down to Arizona."

"And then, if Rick checks out, we'll want to hit the Baptist Church. Maybe even try the—"

"Actually, we're going straight to Hattie's. I want

to have another chat with Harry." Lane decidedly pointed the truck in the direction of the general store.

"Why Harry?" Philip was surprised. "Rick is the one dating her."

"Because Harry didn't report her missing. Yesterday, he told us Stacy works from six to ten every Monday through Friday. If she was killed Monday afternoon, that means Stacy didn't show up to her scheduled shift that Monday night, and when we talked to him about a dead body in the park on Tuesday, he didn't bother to mention his cashier not showing up for their Monday shift. That seems a bit suspicious to me."

"Pfffttt... Harry wouldn't hurt a fly." Philip twisted in his seat to face her, the sheriff in return, giving him a look that said, "Are you sure?"

"He wouldn't," he insisted.

"Still doesn't explain why he didn't say anything," Lane persisted.

"Fine. We'll head over there, but I'm telling you, he had nothing to do with it." Philip crossed his arms stubbornly and looked out the truck window at the passing scenery, irritated that they weren't heading to the high school as he had suggested. He remained quiet for the short drive from the funeral home to the general store while Lane, ignoring his childish silence, radioed the station requesting a next of kin call to the girl's parents. The second they were parked, Philip hopped out and made for the store.

Lane jumped out as well and quickened her steps, Philip politely but impatiently holding the door.

"We're wasting time," he hissed in a low whisper as she squeezed past.

"So, you say." She stopped short and flipped the "Open" sign to "Closed," the door shutting behind them.

At first glance, Hattie's General appeared deserted, except for a handful of half-empty coffee cups sitting on the picnic table, an indictor the two had just missed the community gossip hour, and for the little, ruby-cheeked old lady asleep in the rocking chair stationed by the picnic bench, snoring lightly.

At the sound of the golden bell, she was startled awake.

"Hello, Miss Hattie. How are you this morning?" Philip approached the rocking chair and lightly put a hand on her shoulder.

Hattie blinked her runny blue eyes and looked up at the towering man, giving him a big denture smile.

"Oh, Phil! I'm dandy, just dandy. How are you?"

"I'm dandy as well, Miss Hattie. Is Harry here?"

"Suppose so. If he's not sitting at the register, he's in the office. Go on back there. I'll keep an eye out up here." She reached up and patted Philip's hand resting on her shoulder.

"Thanks, Miss Hattie." He nodded to his right,

signaling for Lane to come along.

Catching his meaning, Lane gave a polite nod to Hattie as she passed and followed Philip's lead.

Together, they walked down the length of aisle one, finding a pair of swing doors. Philip gave them a firm rap as he pushed through.

"Hey Har, it's Phil and company. You in here?" he called out.

"Yeah, come on through!" Harry's voice carried from somewhere to the right.

They walked through the doors and found themselves in a dimly lit stock room.

Metal shelves sprung towards the ceiling, filled with various groceries, and stacks of unbroken-down cardboard boxes lined the floor. To the left of the shelving stood three empty grocery freezers, two plugged in, one dark, and to the right, emanated a pale light, indicating the office.

Lane continued to follow behind Philip and stepped through the office door, spying a large window facing the store's interior, the tinted glass placed slightly higher than the register counter. She quickly realized it was a two-way mirror, a way to keep an eye on the floor when no one was upfront.

In the far corner of the cramped room was an oversized, comfortable-looking La-Z-Boy chair, most likely belonging to Hattie, a quilt draped over the arm. Placed alongside it was a dinner tray with the remains of a half-eaten breakfast and a small TV on a stand against the far wall. Positioned directly below the two-way mirror, was a long desk, displaying a litany of disheveled papers, a dozen half-filled coffee mugs, and one very tired-looking Harry.

"Been here all night figuring out that receipt and credit card list for you, Sheriff," Harry said, his words quickly followed by a yawn.

Lane politely smiled and paused before speaking, giving Harry a closer inspection, neglecting the day before to notice any particular details about the grocery manager.

Plump and shy of middle age, Harry was on the short side, around five foot eight, with light sandy brown hair, the top of his head balding. She noted, with Philip standing beside him, that Harry was the polar opposite, lacking his friend's strapping stature, board shoulders, and rugged good looks, though the five o'clock shadow lining his jaw from the night before didn't hurt the illusion. Harry did, however, have a much rounder belly than his beer buddy.

Harry, stifling another yawn, noticed the sheriff's scrutinizing gaze and quickly broke out into an encouraging grin.

"Can I get you some coffee, Sheriff?" he offered, randomly grabbing a mug from his desk and starting to stand.

"No. No, thank you, Mr. Vickers. I'll pass on the

coffee, but thank you for the offer." Lane smiled politely and asked, "You were here all night, you were saying?"

"Sure was! Doing my civic duty." Harry, this time, gave a wink to go with the smile.

Philip decided to cut in before his friend made a fool of himself.

"Thanks for doing that, Har. But we've got something to tell you. The body has been identified." Philip looked to his new partner, who had her notepad in hand and pen ready. She nodded with the go-ahead. "The girl in the park?" he reminded.

"Oh, that was fast. She ended up being one of ours?" Harry gave his eyes a good rub. "That's a shame."

"Afraid so. It's Stacy Jensen."

Philip thought Harry looked stunned while Lane thought he looked tired AND stunned.

"Stacy? Stacy, who works here?" Harry asked, flabbergasted.

Lane nodded and stepped forward.

"The coroner says she was dead by 4 p.m. on Monday afternoon. Which means she wasn't at her shift Monday night, Mr. Vickers." She tilted her head as if to say, "You want to explain that?"

"No... she wouldn't have been." Harry put his head in his hands, running his fingers through his thin hair.

Philip and Lane locked eyes over Harry's head.

"I mean to say, Stacy asked Missy to cover for her Monday night and Missy stayed with her aunt here on the island instead of returning to the mainland like she usually does on Monday mornings. She covered the shift for Stacy."

"But, what about last night? When Stacy didn't show up? Didn't you start to wonder, if maybe?" Philip sat down on the arm of the La-Z-Boy, moving the quilt to the side.

"Well, NO! I just thought maybe Missy misunderstood, and Stacy asked her to cover Tuesday night too. I just can't believe it. Wow... Stacy." Harry sat up, shaking his head. "It's shocking!"

"I know." Philip frowned at his friend. "Were you really here all night, Har?"

"Yeah. When neither Stacy nor Missy showed up at six for the shift change, I had to stay. I asked the neighbor to drive Hattie home and then back into town this morning. Decided it was better to crash here since I'd have to be back in the morning anyway and just worked on the receipt list all night. Which reminds me..." Harry reached over and pulled several sheets off the printer. "This is the best I could do... I—" he stopped himself. "I guess you're not needing this anymore, huh?"

"Sorry, Harry." Philip lightly patted his friend's shoulder.

"Mr. Vickers, do you know why someone would want to kill Stacy?"

Harry looked up at Lane, his eyes widening.

"No! I can't even... I mean, she was a good-looking girl. Everyone seemed to like her. Customers never complained."

"Anybody pay her any special attention?" Philip asked.

"Oh, only every high school boy who came through the door. Everybody flirted with her, but all the towners knew she was dating Rick. Out-of-towners were always hitting on her."

"Did she confide in you at all? Tell you if she was nervous about anybody or if she and Rick were having any issues?"

Harry slowly shook his head.

Lane gently took the list from his hand, the grocery manager still holding it out numbly.

"Can you tell me your comings and goings of Monday?"

Harry let out a long puff of air.

"Um. Let's see. Usual day. I woke up, got ready, and was at the store by six. Stayed here all day, till about two-thirty." He gave a slight shrug. "Right after I saw you, Phil, I ran Hattie home real quick. She wasn't feeling so good. Then I came straight back here and left at 6 p.m. when Missy arrived."

"And after that?" she encouraged.

"I went home, cooked dinner, and crashed out around eleven. I always stay up until after the store closes. Just in case one of the girls has any trouble or questions."

"Do you know why Stacy needed Missy to cover her shift Monday night?" Philip bumped Harry to get his attention, his buddy staring off in space.

"No, only that she had something she needed to do, and it would run into her shift. She seemed excited but not enough to say exactly why."

"And you didn't think to ask?" Lane asked, surprised.

"No, it's not like we were friends. She works a few hours a day for me. She was just an employee." Harry ran his fingers through his hair. "Sorry, that sounded cold."

"Was she excited? Like maybe she was going on a date?" Lane ventured.

"That's not the impression I got. Heck, it probably was something for the church. Maybe she had a youth group function she was doing. I honestly don't know." Harry smiled weakly as he stood up. "Sorry, I'm not more helpful. Guess I'm really tired."

"Well, if you think of anything." Philip stood as well.

"Yeah, of course. I, uh, ...I better go upfront. I don't like to leave Hattie up there too long by herself." Harry headed for the door. Lane and Philip, a step behind.

"Are you going to tell Miss Hattie?" Philip asked as they breached the swing doors and walked out onto the sales floor.

"I'd rather not, but I'm gonna have to, eventually. You know how news flies. Somebody will be in here spreading the gossip before you know it. I'll probably take her home or stick her in the office for now. Shelter her as much as I can." Harry straightened a haphazard item on the shelf as they walked by.

"Mind if I ask her some questions first?" Lane was trying to keep pace, the width of the aisle preventing her efforts.

"Actually, I do." Harry stopped, turning to face her. "She's a hundred and two years old, can barely see two feet in front of her, and naps all day. She wouldn't be much help, and I don't want to upset her. She was fond of Stacy."

Lane looked unsettled.

"I'm sorry. I didn't mean to..."

"Ease up." Philip nudged his friend, not unkindly.

Harry nodded and continued down the aisle.

"I don't want to upset Hattie, okay?" Harry reiterated, firmly.

"Upset Hattie over what?" Hattie, her tone curious, suddenly called out from her rocking chair.

"Nothing, Miss Hattie," Philip called back, noting there wasn't anything wrong with the old woman's hearing.

"By the way." Harry looked back at Lane and addressed her in a much friendlier tone, changing the subject, "The apartment is all ready for you to move in. I did some light cleaning and put new sheets on the bed, emptied out the closet for your stuff."

"Good! That also reminds me." She pulled out a check from her notepad and placed it in his hand. "Here is a month's rent, and I'll need a receipt. I assume there is basic cable?"

Harry clenched his teeth and grinned an apology as he picked up his pace.

"There's not even a TV."

Lane dropped her smile and mumbled, "Figures."

"Har, we're heading to the high school, gonna see if we can track Rick down. You haven't seen him lately, have you?"

"He was in here last night buying beer."

Lane lightly grabbed Harry's arm, stopping his motion, and asked eagerly, "What time? How did he look? He didn't say anything about Stacy not being at work?"

Harry thought for a moment.

"Let's see. He came in right around five-thirty, so Stacy wouldn't have been on duty yet. He looked normal and talked about the council meeting this coming Friday. They're gonna vote on the soccer field idea. We only talked for like five minutes. Paid cash. Drove off like normal." Harry shrugged his shoulders and slyly lowered his voice to just above a whisper, "You don't think he might've killed Stacy?"

Philip answered, whispering as well, "He's the obvious suspect right now. Maybe they had a fight? Maybe he was jealous? Who knows?"

Sheriff Lane didn't bother to whisper.

"Mr. Vickers, thank you for answering my inquiries regarding the DEATH OF STACY JENSEN."

"What's this?" Hattie's eyes popped open, and she twisted to peer back at them from her rocking chair. "What's this about Stacy? She died?"

"Whoops." Sheriff Lane fawned an apologetic smile as the trio approached Hattie, Harry aghast and Philip annoyed, the old lady still straining her neck to see them.

Harry rushed to her side, putting a gentle hand on her shoulder.

"I'm sorry, Grams. But yes, she died on Monday," Harry explained, his voice gentle, then lifting in tone, "Now, why don't we—"

"Good... little thief," Hattie spat.

"Grandma!" Harry admonished, shocked, and embarrassed.

"Oh, don't Grandma me, Harry. She was a rotten thief, and no good comes to someone who steals from the hand that feeds them. I told you a long time ago you needed to get rid of her." Hattie shook her head in disgust.

Lane came around to the front of the rocking chair and offered her hand.

"Miss Hattie, I'm Sheriff Lane."

Hattie gave a warm, cherub wrinkled smile as she squeezed it.

"Nice to meet you," Hattie said, sweetly. "A female sheriff... how... how very... nice."

"We didn't mean to upset you by this news," Lane continued gently, ignoring the slight barb at her being a woman.

"Oh, you didn't upset me! Not in the least. Though death is never pleasant." Hattie made a face, wrinkling up her nose.

"No, it's not," Lane agreed. "You were fond of Stacy?"

"Heavens no! She was stealing cash out of the till and not ringing people's full orders up. Or she'd double-ring their items sometimes and take the extra cash. Saw it with my own eyes. Just because I'm sitting here looking out this window all day doesn't mean I'm not paying attention. I see Harry counting and recounting that till every morning after she works, and I hear him asking where certain things have gone. He never does it when Missy works." Hattie rocked her chair in agitation.

Harry put a firm hand on her chair, stopping the motion.

"Now Grandma, you're confused. Would you like

to go watch some TV back in the office?" Harry asked, and then added in a coaxing voice, "I can bring you a nice hot cup of cocoa."

"Oh, that does sound nice." Hattie's face lightened, returning to the sweet little old lady with rosy cheeks. "That sounds nice, indeed. Hot Cocoa time."

She eagerly began to work her way to the edge of the chair, using the arms of the rocker for support as Harry hurriedly made his way around, politely shouldering Lane out of the way. Helping her stand, he shuffled Hattie to the back office, giving a casual goodbye over his shoulder as he left the remaining pair standing up front alone.

"Hmmm." Lane followed Philip to the door, stopping short to flip the sign back to Open. "Hattie is fond of Stacy? I don't think so."

CHAPTER 11

Principal Ford escorted the new sheriff, with Philip in tow, through the long halls of the high school arriving at the gymnasium floor where a large group of boys was running laps.

"Coach Hanes?" the principal raised his voice, practically drowned out by the sound of stomping feet, and managed to garner the attention of Rick Hanes, dressed in the typical gym teacher attire of shorts, a polo shirt, and windbreaker.

With a curt nod of acknowledgment, the baseball coach took the whistle from around his neck and gave it a loud shrill, sending the sweaty group of boys to the locker room as the principal and his guests made their way across the gym floor, their footsteps squeaking behind them.

"Morning, Rick." Philip extended his hand to be

shaken. "Can we talk in your office?"

"Don't see why not? Morning." Rick smiled at Lane as he gripped Philip's hand, giving it a hardy, manly squeeze.

"Appreciate it." Philip slightly winced as Rick let go and watched as the gym teacher gave Sheriff Lane a once-over glance before shooting a quizzical look at the principal, who gave a short shrug of the shoulders.

Reaching the gym's double doors, the coach popped the top bar, and both swung open, the trio following as he walked through.

"My office," he chuckled, as they walked onto the sunny baseball field and across the green to the metal bleachers. "I, uh, I see you have a sheriff tagging along." He politely nodded towards Lane in acknowledgment. "Has one of my boys done something? Baseball batted somebody's mailbox? Got caught drinking in the woods?"

Clearly, the coach was more concerned about the effect the listed transgressions would have on his team's baseball season than the wrongs which may have been committed.

"No, no," The principal quickly interjected. "All is right with the team. We're still state bound." Principal Ford smiled widely at Philip and Lane, pulling his belt buckle up higher on his waist in pride. "Looking for a repeat this year."

Lane stepped up and brandished her leather

notepad.

"Mr. Hanes, I am Sheriff Lane, and I'd like to ask you a few questions regarding Stacy Jensen. Would that be alright?" She smiled and then continued, "Is it true that you are in a relationship with Miss Jensen?"

Of all the questions Lane could have asked, it was clear Rick had not been expecting them to be about his girlfriend.

"Yes, we've been dating for about six months. It's not extremely serious, but it's not casual either." He looked over at Philip and added, "She's over eighteen."

With a curt nod, Philip acknowledged he was aware of the fact.

At the comment, Lane arched an eyebrow and gave the coach a hard look and a quick summing up.

Full of himself, most likely a hothead. Roughly forty-two or forty-three years old, holding his good looks steadily. Starting to lose his hair. Nothing a good comb-over wouldn't hide for a few years, though. Womanizer.

She cleared her throat, taking a step closer.

"Mr. Hanes, when was the last time you saw Stacy?"

"Why? What she'd do? Rob a bank or something?" Rick snorted, and then laughed at the idea, pausing to catch everyone's eye, hoping they'd join in his amusement. When no one laughed or smiled in return, he continued, "Um... Sunday. Sat behind her at church. What's this... what's this all about?"

"You sat behind her and not with her?" Lane clarified.

"That's correct." His face turned serious. "Is she in some kind of trouble here?"

Rick's good boy humor was fading.

"I am very sorry to inform you, Mr. Hanes. Stacy Jensen was found deceased Tuesday morning."

Rick looked at the sheriff blankly as a steady color of red climbed his neck up to his semi-thinning hairline.

"My Stacy? Gone?" He placed his hands on his knees and steadied himself. "She killed herself?" Shock and awe were clearly edged in his voice.

"I take it you'd be surprised to hear she committed suicide?" Lane asked.

"Well, yeah. She's a real chipper kind of girl. Always active, always running around doing something." He got up and walked over to Principal Ford. "Her girls are going to be devastated."

The principal, his face somber, nodded in agreement.

Lane flipped a page on her note pad and continued, "Mr. Hanes, Stacy didn't commit suicide. Her body was found in the Rockfish National Park with her throat slit. She was murdered. Do you know of anyone who would want to cause her harm? Anyone, she was concerned about or frightened to be around? A stalker, perhaps?"

"Murdered?" Rick walked himself back to the bleachers and plopped down, clearly in disbelief.

Philip offered his condolences.

"Sorry, man. I know this is a huge shock."

"It's unimaginable."

Lane persisted, "Can you think of anyone she was frightened of? Or was upset with her?"

"No... I mean. She was always drawing someone's eye. She was a knockout. But she never said anything about being stalked or scared of anyone."

"What about Monday evening? She had made plans. Do you know who she was with or what she was doing?"

Rick shook his head in the negative. "Youth group, maybe?"

"And you and her, everything was going well in your relationship?"

"Yeah, of course!"

"Then I need to ask why you didn't realize she was missing Tuesday morning?"

"Missing? I never dreamed she'd ever be missing!"

"I'm sure. However, when you didn't hear from her, you weren't concerned?"

"No. I mean... she's a busy girl."

"I understand that. However, I am sure you spoke on the phone quite often or even text messaged? You didn't find it odd that you hadn't heard anything from her since Monday afternoon?" Lane insisted.

Rick, his eyes growing wide, looked panicked.

"Normally, yeah. I probably would have been. But we were squabbling. Nothing big! Just a little lover's spat."

"About?" Lane inched closer.

"She would've gotten over it eventually." Rick hedged, looking embarrassed.

Lane continued to stare with an arched eyebrow, expectant of an answer.

"She caught me talking to Sue Carter." Rick pointedly looked at Philip and Principal Ford. "You guys know Sue."

Both nodded they did.

Sue Carter, always on the prowl for another husband... or plaything, was the rich widow who owned the antique shop on the island.

"So, she was jealous of this Carter woman?" Lane wrote the name down.

"She was the jealous type, period."

"Was that because of the difference in your ages?"

"What does my age have to do with anything?" Rick blustered.

Lane had obviously hit upon a sore spot.

"Miss Jensen was a little over twenty years younger than you, sir. She may not have been as mature as some women your age. Possibly, she felt insecure dating an older man? Was she super needy? Clingy?"

"No. she wasn't. She was a very mature twenty-two-year-old. She had a lot going on for her. Besides, I'm not the first older man she ever dated."

"And who was that?"

"I don't know, I never asked. It just came up once in conversation."

"So, she sees you with Sue Carter, and then what happened?"

"I told you, she got jealous. Said if I wanted a wrinkled-up prune, like Sue, then I was welcome to it and stormed off."

"And she was currently giving you the silent treatment? Is that what you're alluding to, Mr. Hanes?"

"She wouldn't even let me sit with her at church," Rick sighed, his shoulders slumping under the weight of regret. "But she would have gotten over it. I mean, she hadn't asked for her house key back, so I knew she wasn't going to break it off."

Philip broke in.

"You have her house key?" He gave Lane a meaningful look. "We'll need to borrow that."

"Sure." Rick stood up and dug into his front pocket for his keys. "I'm telling you. I didn't hurt her, and I don't know who would."

"As a matter of routine, Mr. Hanes, I'll need you to walk me through your actions of Monday."

"Sure... I got up Monday morning. Tried to call Stacy but she didn't answer. Didn't really expect that she would. Figured she was still upset but didn't think it would hurt to try. I came to the school at seven, taught all day. School got out at two-thirty, and then I came straight here for practice, umm, which got over at five something? Then went to Hattie's, bought a six-pack of beer. Went straight home and drank myself out of beer. Don't know exactly what time I went to bed, but it was after eleven."

"I can vouch for most of that." Principal Ford laid his hand on Rick's shoulder in solidarity.

At hearing Rick Hanes had a whole baseball team as alibi witnesses for Monday afternoon, Lane shut her notepad with a slap and thanked him for his time.

CHAPTER 12

"Well, her car is missing." Philip frowned as he peered through the rain-speckled window at Stacy Jensen's home, Lane's patrol truck blocking the gravel driveway.

"It could be in the garage." Lane shut the engine off and peered past his shoulder.

Philip shook his head. "Nah. If you parked in the garage, nobody would know you were home."

Lane laughed. "There's a thing called a doorbell."

"You don't understand small-town life, Sheriff. People don't call ahead, and they don't get out of the car if they don't have to. If the person you want to see has their car out front, then you know they're home. If it's not... then you wait five minutes for them to show up or you come back later." Philip opened the truck door and got out, leaning his head back in. "It's called being neighborly."

Lane simply rolled her eyes.

"Do you know what she drives?" She hopped out herself.

"Red Jeep Wrangler." Philip was already halfway across the short drive, hunched over, searching the gravel for footprints or signs of a struggle.

"Missing car?... I have a theory," Lane called out, pulling her yellow parka hood over her head.

"Oh, yeah?" Not finding anything of interest, Philip stopped where he was and waited.

"I bet you if we look at her computer, we'll find she met someone online. I mean, she's mad at the boyfriend, right? So, she decides to look for romance somewhere else. She agrees to meet with this on-line boyfriend and invites him to the island." Lane yanked the parka hood further down. "She picks him up at the ferry, and deciding to show him the wonders of the island, takes him out to the park. There he has her all to himself, and he kills her. Then he takes her Jeep and heads back to the mainland."

"That's an excellent theory except for one thing."

"What's that?" Lane reached the safety of the eaves and started to shake the excess water from her parka as Philip dug out Rick's key.

"The island doesn't have internet."

"Seriously?"

"Seriously." Philip turned away, the corners of his

mouth twitching. "No internet means no internet dating." He put the key into the lock.

"The whole island? How's that even possible in this day and age?" Lane yanked on the back of his coat, trying to draw his attention. "You've got to be pulling my leg."

Philip twisted and glanced down at her hand, still grasping his coat, then met her eye, a slow smile drawing across his lips.

"Yeah, I am."

Lane blinked and bit her lip, stifling a smile as Philip turned back around.

"That's not funny, Ranger."

Placing plastic booties over their boots and snapping on latex gloves, Lane gave a severe knock on the door before Philip gingerly turned the knob and pushed the door open, giving a casual call of "Hello?" Upon no response, the two stepped through the door into a clean and tidy hallway.

A small kitchen was to the left of the entrance and on the right was an open living room furnished with a leather couch, chair, a well-worn coffee table, and TV, with a large brick fireplace built into the wall. Past the kitchen was a short hallway with a bathroom at the end and a room on each side, one storage, filled with odds and ends, and the other, the master bedroom.

"Nothing looks amiss," Lane reported, her voice

raised as she looked around the neat bedroom, the bed made, dresser drawers in place, and closet doors closed. "No struggle in here."

Philip gave a grunt from the living room and she continued on, walking around the room in a large loop, stopping to stoop and peer under the bed.

Finding nothing but dust bunnies, she then turned to the dresser, it lined with picture frames, and selected one with a gold border, a picture of Stacy and the cheerleading team.

"So, this is her."

The cheerleading coach, who had a body any woman would kill for, was wearing a tank top with a plunging neckline showing off her perky bosom, with little to no makeup, her long, pretty blonde hair tossed up in a messy bun. She was beyond stunning and was smiling a "cheer grin," the forced happy smile cheerleaders keep on their cheery faces while waving their pom-poms.

It differed drastically from the bluish-white corpse Lane saw earlier and she shivered, putting the frame down.

Philip's voice carried from the living room.

"She left the central heating on, and the mail from Monday morning has been opened and left on the counter."

Lane moved to the closet and opened the mirrored doors.

"No empty hangers... Got a few empty duffel bags and a large suitcase still in the closet. It doesn't look like she packed to go anywhere." Lane closed the closet doors and faced the room again. "Found the computer!" She walked over and picked the small laptop off the edge of the nightstand.

Philip's voice carried down the hall. "The cheer schedule is pinned to the fridge, and she's got Monday canceled out. Oh, and she's got a youth group schedule here too. Nothing planned for Monday." Philip opened the refrigerator and looked inside. "Looks like she did some grocery shopping recently. Plenty of wilted lettuce and ripe fruit on the counter." He walked back to Stacy's bedroom and found Lane sitting on the edge of the bed with the small laptop opened on her knees.

"Too much to hope for. It's password protected." Lane shut the laptop with a snap and scanned the room again. "Looks like she went with whoever took her without a struggle and I don't see any signs of foul play... at least, not inside the house." She put the computer down on the bed. "Let's check the garage."

Together, they walked outside and entered the separate two-door garage by a door on the side of the building, finding it dark and empty. Not only was the Jeep missing but to Philip's disappointment, there was no blood splatter, no shell casings, no broken zip ties, no clues of any kind.

"Let's check the backyard," he sighed as they walked out, heading towards the house and the small backyard surrounded by dark forest. Once again, nothing seemed out of place. No broken flower pots, no overturned yard furniture, ...not even a muddy footprint under the window sill.

"It's strange she didn't have a dog or cat," Lane mused as they made their way back into the house. "Most single women do."

"You don't," Philip pointed out. "Besides, she wasn't like most single women. She really was on the go all the time."

Philip took a seat at the kitchen table and watched as Lane went back to the bedroom to retrieve the laptop and power cord.

"I just don't see any signs she wasn't planning on coming back." Philip lightly flipped through the stack of opened mail.

"You don't see an itinerary? If she was so busy, maybe she had a day planner?" Lane's voice carried closer as she came down the hallway.

"Probably all on her cell phone... which I don't see."

Lane sat at the kitchen table as well. "And there wasn't one found at the discovery site either." She glanced around the kitchen, noting all the knives were in their wooden block holder. "Alright. Let's think this through. She leaves her house as usual.

Nothing here indicates there was anything amiss or she was grabbed from home."

"By a stranger," Philip corrected. "If it was someone she knew, she'd just follow them out the door."

"So, someone she trusted? Okay. They come up to her door and leave in her car. Drive all the way out to the park, kill her, and then take her car to make their getaway." Lane began to leaf through the open mail herself. "This is interesting." She held up an open business envelope. "Did she fancy herself a model or actress?"

Philip frowned and squinted at the piece of mail, shrugging, as Lane pulled out the contents.

"She was extremely good-looking. Especially for our little island. She might have."

"Hmmm." Lane's eyes scanned the document. "Looks like a photography invoice. Yeah, she had modeling headshots done. Maybe she wanted to be an actress?" Lane placed the envelope and invoice on top of the laptop. "We'll take these with us."

CHAPTER 13

"We're running out of people to interview." Lane sighed as the patrol truck rolled to a stop, the tires hitting the curb.

"Are you kidding? We've still got a squad of cheerleaders to tackle."

"Oh, I'm not holding out much hope of them knowing anything." Lane threw the vehicle in park and leaned heavily upon the steering wheel, staring out at the white-steepled church.

"Why is that?"

"Teenagers, girls, in particular, can be self-consuming. Not the greatest observers, unless it has to do with make-up or clothes." She suddenly sat up straight and nodded towards the building. "Hey, is that him? The pastor?"

Philip followed her gaze across the parking lot

and spotted the Baptist preacher, dressed in jeans and a polo shirt, walking up the sidewalk from a back building.

"Yup. That's him."

"He looks awfully young. How old is he?"

Philip squinted and tilted his head to the side in consideration.

"Late twenties, early thirties?"

"Handsome too."

"Yeah, people like him."

"I'm sure they do." Lane yanked the keys from the ignition, her tone turning suspicious, "I can see why Stacy volunteered to be the youth group leader."

"He's married." Philip twisted to face her and knocked his thermos to the floor, the cylinder rolling to a stop at his foot.

"Doesn't mean his wife trusted him to be around—" Lane paused, her eyes still on the pastor as she suddenly unbuckled her seat belt, the strap snapping back, her next words barely a whisper, "Someone she trusted..."

"What was that?" Philip asked as he bent over, his fingers barely brushing the cap, just shy of gripping the container.

"Come on. I want to rattle his cage and see what tumbles out," Lane announced as she abruptly hopped out of the truck and slammed the door behind her, Philip still stooped over.

"You wanna do what?" He popped up, thermos in hand, the cab empty.

Lane was already making her way across the lawn. "Mr. Adams?" Lane called out, "Pastor Adams, may I have a moment of your time?"

The preacher turned at the sound of his name and gave a warm smile, his eyes darting from Lane to the pickup truck in the parking lot.

"Hello, can I help you?"

"Yes, sir. I think you can. I'm Sheriff Lane." She tapped her badge and continued, "I'm looking into the murder of Stacy Jensen."

Pastor Adams's welcoming smile faded and he shook his head, his expression dampening into a polite frown of dismay.

"Oh, yes, my wife and I heard about Stacy from Mrs. Barnes at the funeral home this morning. We're all grieving at the loss."

"I'm sure you are," Lane said, her tone dry. "I understand Stacy was in charge of your youth group program here at the church?"

"Yes, she, uh... Well, hey there, Phil!"

Out of breath from jogging the length of the lawn, Philip joined them, his eyes darting anxiously from one to the other, the sheriff giving the young preacher the stink eye.

"Pastor Jonas, back to my question?" Lane, her notepad in hand, tapped it impatiently with her pen.

"Oh, yes. I'm sorry. She was, to answer your question, and such a blessing too. She ran the youth group every Saturday evening from 2p.m. to 5p.m. and then Sunday school for middle graders and high schoolers from ten-thirty to eleven-thirty Sunday mornings." He smiled down at the sheriff, who steadily continued to frown back. He suddenly turned, smiling upon Philip instead. "That's after she attended the early service and listened to my sermon at the 9a.m. service."

"Very devoted, I see." Lane tapped her notepad, her eyes slitting. "Since she oversaw Sunday school and the youth group activities, I assume you and Stacy worked closely together?" Lane's tone lent to the insinuation of something improper.

The pastor's smile faltered.

"Well, yes. We met each Wednesday."

"So, you had a weekly standing appointment?" Lane wrote the day down in her notepad and looked up, adding, "Anyone else present during these meetings?"

Philip could almost see the air quotes around the word "meetings."

"No. It was just Stacy and me." The pastor's face reddened. "Our meetings weren't very long."

"I bet they weren't," Lane said under her breath, but loud enough to be heard.

"I beg your pardon!" Pastor Jonas said, shocked.

"Nothing, Pastor. I'm sure you noticed Stacy was a very attractive, and well-built young lady. Your wife didn't mind you meeting with her... alone?" Lane emphasized the last word, Philip moving un easily beside her.

"My wife and I have a very loving and trusting—"

"I'm sure you do. However, it's my understanding Stacy and her boyfriend Rick were on the outs. She may have come to you for some advice? Possibly for some kind of comfort? Did you comfort her, Pastor Jonas?" Lane looked the pastor directly in the eye, challenging him to deny it.

"What exactly are you insinuating, Sheriff?" he asked appalled.

"Insinuating? I think it's fairly clear!" Lane raised her voice, her fake smile dropping.

Philip quickly stepped in front of Lane, placing himself between her and the pastor.

"Listen, I think we may have gotten off course here."

"No!" Lane gave Philip a light shove, and he stumbled to the side, off-balance. "No, I think we're on the right path." She squared herself with the preacher. "Pastor Jonas, I put it to you like this. I think you and Stacy were having an affair. She wanted more than you could give and to keep her quiet... to keep her from telling your wife and the whole congregation of your lusty affair, you killed her!" Lane abruptly tucked her notepad into her back pocket and pulled out a pair of handcuffs.

"I... We never... I wouldn't..." Pastor Jonas, at a loss for words, turned crimson.

"Okay, okay." Philip held up his hands and once again, stepped between the floundering pastor and the yellow parka-wearing sheriff.

Lane, herself stepped back, this time allowing him to intervene.

"Sheriff, can I talk to you for a minute?" Philip practically hissed in her ear as he forcefully grabbed her arm and started walking Lane back towards the truck. "Excuse us for a moment, Jonas." He gave a quick glance over his shoulder and polite nod towards the pastor then leaned in close to Lane as he hurried her across the lawn. "What do you think you're doing?"

"Allowing you the opportunity to question a suspect. Now, go have fun playing 'Good Cop'." Lane gave him a sly smile before jerking her arm free from his grip, making a show of it, and then yelled loudly for the preacher to hear, "Fine! I'll wait in the truck, but you tell him I'll be back AND with a warrant if I have to! I want the truth!"

Shocking Philip with a devilish grin, she left him and stalked across the lawn to the patrol truck, giving the door a good slam once inside.

Philip, stunned, stood rooted to the spot, torn between amusement and annoyance before running his fingers through his hair in exasperation and starting his way back to the clearly distraught pastor.

"I'm so sorry about her, Jonas." Philip jerked his thumb in the direction of the sheriff's truck. "She's a little tightly wound. New to town... trying to prove herself." He put his hands in his jean pockets and rocked back on his heels. "You, okay?" he asked, kindly.

The pastor's shoulders, tight and tense, stooped with relaxation.

"Oh, yes. I... I was just surprised at what she was saying, is all. There was never anything inappropriate between Stacy and me."

"Oh, I'm sure there wasn't. It's only... you have to be careful in a small town like this. Rumors start flying, gossip is suddenly truth, and scandals flare. You can see why the sheriff's department might look at you closely?"

The youthful pastor nodded his head.

"I suppose. But truly, we were just friends."

"Was anyone else in the church, other than Rick, sweet on Stacy?"

"A few of the teenage boys had minor crushes. Nothing of any concern, I suppose. She tried to be a big sister to them."

"Did the ladies of the church like her?"

"Oh, yes. Though she wasn't close to anyone in particular."

"I figure, you being Stacy's pastor and all, you out of anyone would probably have known her best. You'd be able to give us some insight on who Stacy was." Philip smiled and stepped closer. "What was she like?"

"Stacy was a very warm-hearted soul. She had a real interest in the young people."

"Well, she wasn't all that aged herself, Pastor," Philip pointed out.

"That's true. Her youth sometimes was very apparent. She still struggled with living an adult Christian life and setting an example for the younger kids."

"Such as?"

"Well, I don't want to gossip." The pastor straightened, his shoulders rigid.

"Jonas, this isn't gossiping. This is helping in an investigation. Anything you share with me is kept confidential. Besides, it looks better if you're seen working with the sheriff's department and not against it." Philip nodded his head back towards the truck, the sheriff still giving out a death glare from behind the steering wheel. "It might actually go a long way."

"You do have a point."

"Did Stacy ever come to you for help? For advice? Did she have any concerns?" Philip stepped to the right, giving the pastor a clearer view of the scowling Lane.

"Only once. She had found herself in a love triangle." Pastor Jonas moved to the side uneasily, using Philip's chest to block the view of the seething small sheriff.

"With who?" Philip stepped closer.

"She never said." Pastor Jonas looked him in the eye. "He was a married, older man I gathered. She wanted advice on what to do. If she should continue with it or end it."

"And you told her?"

"I told her she needed to end it. Nothing ever blooms from a dying vine. And that the honorable thing to do was to let the man end his marriage or fix it, whatever he may decide. That she had plenty of years to find love, and though this man professed he'd leave everything behind for her, she had to consider his family. They might not want to be left." Pastor Jonas smiled sadly. "I also mentioned if she continued to live that lifestyle, I couldn't allow her to work with the youth group any longer. Needless to say, she took my advice."

"Did you have any guesses to who the man might have been?"

"Oh, no. I figured no one from my flock. An affair is hard to hide in a small congregation. But then... if one is used to deception," Pastor Jonas mused in his thoughts. "That's all I can really tell you, Phil."

"Thank you, Jonas. I'll make sure to tell Sheriff

Lane how helpful and cooperative you've been. You'll let me know if you think of anything else?" Philip offered his hand. "You've got my number?"

Pastor Jonas took the offered hand, nodding that he had Philip's number and then started down the walkway, back to his welcoming church.

CHAPTER 14

"Well, that was fun." Philip shot Lane a bright smile as he hopped into the patrol truck.

"What did you find out?"

"That questioning suspects gives me an appetite." He snapped his seat belt on and nodded in the direction of the parking lot exit. "Go down two blocks and park on the right. I'll treat you to lunch."

The town's only sit-down restaurant, the Royal Fork, was busy and short-handed, as indicated by the sign posted at the hostess stand directing patrons to seat themselves. Following instructions, Lane and Philip maneuvered through the crowded tables to a corner window seat, where they sat down and were greeted by the lone waitress on duty.

Lane smiled at the pregnant young woman, guessing she was six months along and noted the mother to be, had recently been crying, her eyes red and swollen.

Taking an order of two turkeys on rye with coffee, one with and one without cream, their waitress scrawled the information down and sniffed, stating she'd be back shortly.

"Okay, let's get started."

Lane pulled out her notepad and placed it on the table, flipping it open, the corners curled from the constant wear and tear of her back pocket.

"Think you got enough notes?" Philip asked, pointing at her notepad, the crisp paper now crinkled with scribble marks visible all over the page, the chicken scratch handwriting suspected to be some form of shorthand.

Lane ignored him and deftly moved her notepad aside as their waitress returned with their promised coffees and sniffled away again.

"So, let's hear it." Lane eagerly leaned in. "Did he squeal like a baby?"

"Whoa, whoa. Have some decency! The man is a pastor." Philip took a sip of coffee and looked at her sternly over the rim. "He squealed a little."

"Soooo... What did he say?" Her pen was to paper.

"Stacy was having an affair with a married man before she started dating the baseball coach."

"Who?"

Philip shook his head in the negative. "No clue.

Jonas apparently never asked, and she didn't divulge a name."

"Believe him?" She took a sip of her own coffee.

"Yes. I think he has his guesses, but he would consider that gossip. He'd only come forward with a name if he felt it was absolutely necessary."

"Anything else?"

"Only she had come to him on how to handle the situation, as the lover was promising to leave his family and just needed her to stick it out a bit longer. She felt bad about it, and Jonas told her they had no real future. She took his advice, ended the affair, and apparently started to date Rick right afterwards."

"If Stacy and Rick have only been together for six months, then we can assume this was around November of last year? Maybe October? Any scandals around that time?"

Philip started to answer, but spotting their waitress, sandwiches in hand, sat back from the table, allowing clearance for her to set the plates down.

"Two turkeys on rye." She announced, her eyes resting on the gingham tablecloth. "Need anything else?"

"Don't think so."

She continued to linger, her eyes still set on the table.

"Thank you, Lacey. I think we're good." Philip gave her a warm smile, his voice gentle.

Lacey nodded, distractedly so, and wandered back

to the kitchen.

Lane watched the exchange impatiently and leaned in, determined to stay on track. "No gossip running rampant at that time?"

Philip frowned over his sandwich in thought. "I'm not really the one to ask. I'm out at the park all day. Not exactly gossip central."

"Good point." She took a bite and then asked, her mouth full, "So, what do we know about Stacy so far? She was a thief."

"Allegedly."

"She was the jealous type."

"If we take his word for it."

"She was the type of girl to date a married man."

"Or be seduced by one..."

"She liked being around young people."

"She WAS a young people. Remember, she was only twenty-two."

"She thought herself attractive."

"Everyone did."

"Fine. Who do we have that would want to kill her?"

"You're assuming now, it's someone who knew her. I still like your internet date theory."

"Well, let's start with who it could be locally. We can work on the mystery person aspect later. Who might have had it out for her?"

"Honestly, no one comes to mind, and it's not

Harry. I know where you are going with this."

"You have to be objective, Ranger. Now, if she was stealing from him, maybe she pushed it too far. He wasn't at the grocery store at the time of her murder."

"He was taking Hattie home."

"Only his word for it."

"Moving on..."

"Then there is the rebutted lover. Maybe he can't get over her? Maybe he doesn't like that Stacy is dating Rick, and if he can't have her..."

"No one can. Yeah, do you watch a lot of television?"

"Or perhaps, it's the pastor? She's come to him for love advice, and he, having seen her as this perfect angel, realizes she's nothing but a hussy. He's overtaken by his own dark lusting wants and kills her."

"Wow. Reaching, aren't ya?"

"Why? Because he's a pastor?"

"No. Because he's a nice guy."

"I don't know that. I don't know any of these people. That's why I can look at them objectively."

"And I can look at them realistically. Jonas isn't a murderer, and neither is Harry."

"Then there is you." Lane popped the last bite of sandwich in her mouth and smiled.

"And there's me? What is that supposed to mean?"

"You said it before. You could have lured her to the park. Killed her, knowing the perfect spot where a bear might stumble across the corpse, and then taken her Jeep. Hiding it deep in the forest. Probably up one of those old logging roads or something."

"You're not being serious?" Philip asked warily.

Lane tilted her head and stared at him for a moment.

"No, I don't believe you did it. But I wouldn't be doing my job if I didn't seriously consider it. There's also the possibility you helped Harry hide the body. That I haven't quite ruled out yet."

Philip chuckled and leaned back in his chair, pushing the empty plate away.

"You're something else, Lane."

"So, I've been told. You trying to make a point?" She straightened and pushed her plate back as well.

Philip smiled and took another sip of coffee.

"You've got a chip on your shoulder. But I suspect, I'm not the first to tell you that."

"No," Lane said, without a smile.

"Why's the chip there?"

She turned towards the window, considering how to answer.

"I'm the only girl in a family of four boys. All who are either in law enforcement or the military... and all decorated. My father was also the police chief of my hometown. It's expected I succeed in all that I put my hand to." She returned her blue eyes to his. "And I plan to."

Philip held her gaze, his facial expression blank.

"Must have taken some big-time ribbing from your brothers over the years?"

"Let's say I didn't grow up playing Barbie." She gave him a small smile.

"Gotcha. Tough exterior... chewy center?" Philip asked, basically comparing her demeanor to a toot-sie roll lollipop.

"Something like that." Lane gave him a slightly bigger smile and then changed the subject, "I think we need to split up for the rest of the day. It would probably be best if I interviewed the cheer squad without you."

"Be my guest."

"How would you feel about tackling some town residents and getting the scuttlebutt from the streets? I'm sure you know most of them." Lane finished her coffee, wishing the waitress would have swung by their table. She'd felt like a second cup.

"Yeah, I can do that. I'll walk over to Hattie's and ask Harry if I can borrow his truck."

"Then we can meet at the high school around four and compare notes?"

"Sounds like a plan. But we've got to do one thing before we leave."

Lane was in the middle of stuffing her notepad back into her pocket.

"You want me to leave the tip?" she offered.

"Nope. Need to interview our waitress."

And with that, Philip offered the emotional pregnant woman a seat at their table.

CHAPTER 15

"Lacey, you were close to Stacy, weren't you? I remember seeing you two around town quite a bit." Philip asked and handed her a table napkin, tears instantly rolling down her cheeks.

"We've been best friends since third grade," she half-sobbed. "Our teachers always got us confused because our names were so much alike. Lacey... Stacy." She sniffled as Philip nodded that he saw the comparison and she continued, "I just found out this morning she's dead."

"Why didn't you call off work?" Lane asked as the girl was clearly distressed.

"No one to cover my shift." Her hand went to her swelled belly. "And I need the money."

"Lacey, maybe you can help Sheriff Lane out here? She's needing to know some of Stacy's more personal details of life. Relationships and such." Philip indicated for Lane to take over the conversation.

"Yes! You could be a great help to me in finding the person who did this to your friend. I've heard rumors... rumors Stacy was dating a married man about six months ago or so?" Lane peered over at Lacey, her eyes kind and prompting. "Can you confirm this?"

Lacey bobbed her head up and down.

"Yes, but she wasn't with him for long."

Lane scooted closer to the girl. "Can you tell me his name?"

"She never told me. Said she had to keep it a secret so no one would get hurt. I told her there were no secrets between best friends, but she said he had made her promise, at least, until he left his wife. Though I'm pretty sure he was the dad of one of her cheerleaders. Oh, I don't know..." Lacey broke out into fresh sobs.

Lane waited patiently as Philip handed over another napkin.

"Why did you think that?" Philip asked once the sobs subsided.

"Stacy said it was awkward to run into him at events with his wife. I sort of assumed she meant cheer. I... I had just found out I was pregnant and was distracted with my own personal issues to push her on it." Lacey stared down at her belly, almost in shame.

"Did she tell you if he was upset when she ended the affair?"

"She didn't end it." Lacey stared down at the crumpled napkins in her lap, slightly shaking her head. "He did. The guy just stopped calling her. I know she was hurt and upset about it, but then she took up with Rick. She was getting over him."

Lane put a hand on Lacey's arm, pulling her eyes to hers. "You said he might be the father of one of her girls on the cheer squad, but you don't know which one." Lane smiled encouragingly. "Any guesses?"

She shook her head.

"Like I said, I was distracted with my own changes going on."

Lacey distractedly rubbed her belly again and then turned her head at the sound of the front door opening, quickly dabbing her eyes.

"Oh, I better get back to work."

"We'll let you go." Philip gingerly helped her up and out of the chair. "You've been a big help. Thanks, Lacey."

He watched as she half-waddled to the next table, greeting the new patrons with a sniffle.

"Well," Lane watched the girl. "That puts a new light on the jilted lover theory and the pastor's recollection."

"Yeah. Guess interviewing the cheer squad might

be more interesting now than it was a few minutes ago?" Philip placed a heavy tip on the table. "See you at four to compare notes."

CHAPTER 16

Seated at the patio table closest to the sidewalk, Philip smiled in appreciation as he looked up at blue skies.

The weather, drizzling rain moments before, had seemingly decided to cooperate, the temperamental rain clouds having parted and the sun reappearing, making Philip sitting outside with a cup of gelato not so odd to find.

Pleased with himself, he sat back and patiently waited.

The Italian deli was a great place to bump into fellow islanders since almost everyone either walked into it or past it, as a general course of events when coming downtown.

The first person to "bump" into Philip's table was Martha Barnes... George Barnes's gossipy wife.

"Hello, Phil! Haven't seen you in ages! In fact, I was just plum disappointed to have missed you this morning at the funeral home. George told me how you had come to... identify the body."

Martha always spoke in a wave of rushed sentences and whispered endings. Which, one assumed, she developed from working at the funeral home. She shook her head. "Poor Stacy. So young."

Philip casually pulled out a chair for Martha, whose smile widened, and she promptly sat herself down, putting her shopping bags on the ground.

"You hear about these kinds of things happening in Seattle, but on our little island? It just frightens me to the bone to think we might have a killer on the loose... or even worse... possibly a serial killer." She leaned back and eyed Philip, searching for any kind of reaction.

Looking at her blankly, he took a spoonful of gelato and patiently waited for her to continue.

"Of course, it would have to be somebody crazy because everyone just adored her. Always driving around town in her bright little red Jeep. I can't tell you how many times she sped her way through town. Though, I heard she hit Jerry's dog a few weeks back and him being a veterinarian and all. But with her having to rush here or there, I guess something like that was bound to happen. And you know, she was so good with the youth group and absolutely did wonders for the cheerleading team. I did hear a few of the mothers didn't quite approve of her dating the baseball coach," her voice lowered. "Him being so much older than her and all. Bad influence on the girls... But then again, they say love knows no bounds. The principal was saying Mr. Hanes was all sorts of distressed when he was told about her being killed. He actually thought it... was suicide... at first."

"Which is silly, because even if I didn't know what I know, I would have never thought she'd committed suicide. That girl just had too much energy, and there was no stop button on her! What with the church, the cheer team, a dating life, and a part-time job? It's a wonder she even had time to get killed!" Martha broke into a cackle and then caught herself, realizing how inappropriate she was being.

She continued, rushing through her embarrassment, "Oh, it is sad. I just don't know what Harry and Hattie are going to do without her. However, I do have to say this, she wasn't the best grocery clerk. You know, she'd sometimes ring me up twice for one item, and I wouldn't even catch it till I got home. Then I'd have to come back the next day and get Harry to give me a refund. I guess her mind was always a blur. Just wasn't paying attention. Of course, if she'd ever put down those glamor magazines and actually paid attention to what buttons she pushed on the cash register, that would have helped quite a bit. But then... you can't blame her for dreaming. She was such a pretty girl. I'm sure she could picture herself on the cover of one of those magazines... though coming from a small island like ours, she was more likely to find herself on the cover... of a smut magazine... than Vogue. But, that's just my opinion. Oh! And how awful to think she won't have the opportunity to even try... so sad." Martha finally paused to take a breath, and becoming bored with the subject of Stacy, decided to move on to something else.

"George said he met our new sheriff." She lowered her head, trying to make contact with Philip's eye line. "I hear you've been showing her our town. She a nice lady?"

Philip nodded his head.

"That she is."

"Oh, I'm so happy to hear that. Because Nancy at the church said she had seen the sheriff... yelling at the pastor... earlier today." She stopped and waited for some kind of acknowledgment of the fact.

Philip simply smiled back and tilted his head, encouraging her to go on.

"I'm asking you because Nancy also mentioned you were there. Does our new sheriff have an issue... with the church?"

"Don't think so." He put his gelato down and leaned in, his voice conversational. "Martha, can I ask you a question?"

With an eager smile, she suddenly sat up straight and scooted forward in her chair. "Well, of course! What is it?"

"Be it, you kind of have your thumb on the heart-beat of our town. I was wondering if you..."

"Oh, you mean since people call me the town gossip?" Martha smiled, somewhat proud, and tried to act offended.

"Now Martha, I think we both know gossip spreads itself, it's no one person. But..." He leaned in closer. "There are those who know gossip and then, those who know the truth."

Martha leaned back with a pleased smile. "Well, I will agree with you there. I'm not one to tell lies... I just pass on the curious fact from time to time."

"That's what I'm needing. Now, any odd events happen late last year? Anything come to mind, town-wise, which might've ruffled some feathers?"

"Last year? Regarding Stacy?" Martha's eyes lit up.

"No... not necessarily. Just in general," Philip corrected.

"Well..." Concentration caused her forehead to crinkle. "The football team was AA State Champions, but this was considered good news. There was some clucking when they suggested tearing down some trees for a soccer field, mostly by the baseball coach, and that's still to be decided."

Martha was mainly talking to herself, the influx of her voice staying neutral.

"And then we had the poor girl who drowned in the park last year. Silly thing dove and hit her head on a rock. But... that was later in the summer, August? I can't remember." Martha shook her head, dismissing any more consideration. "Mr. Peters died of what some called strange circumstances in late October. Personally, I think the old drunk passed out and burnt his own house down. Oh, then there was Bert's husband leaving. He just up and left everything behind. But I suppose you know all about that." Martha gave Philip a sly look, which surprised him. "And then Mr. Hyles sent those naughty text messages to one of his students. However, he's moved, and so has the student."

"That's more of the line I am looking for. Anything of the... carnal nature?"

"Affairs?" Martha started to gather her things and abruptly stood up. "Now, that is gossip, and I wouldn't even know where the truth lies."

Philip stood up as well, his good manners and upbringing having programmed him to do so, and watched as Martha walked off in a hurried huff.

He'd forgotten the town's current rumor mill was that Martha and the part-time attorney, Mr. Allister, were more friendly than friends.

Disappointed, he sat himself back down and was

about to toss his half-melted gelato away when Sue Carter slid into the seat across from him.

"Bout time the gossipmonger left. I've been waiting to talk to you." Sue gave Philip an almost lioness smile.

"Then I'm glad you did. How are you, Sue? How's business?" Philip grabbed the deli employee's attention, who was cleaning off tables, and asked him to bring out two Italian sodas.

"Business is getting busier by the day. You know, when I bought the little place, I never dreamt it would become the draw it has for this little island. My dear Henry, rest his soul, he'd left me just enough to buy the place, and now, with my wits and knack of good style, I've built a reputable antique shop I can be proud of. I'm actually planning another trip to England later this week." She leaned in, her blouse falling open. "There are a few auctions I want to hit. But you know, I hate traveling abroad alone. The world... it's not as safe as it was and I miss having a man to... keep an eye on me." Her eyes grazed over Philip and a flirtatious smile spread across her red lips.

Philip, in turn, nodded his understanding and pretended to not notice the come-on.

Cougar Carter, as the town had dubbed her, enjoyed being a flirt and did it without shame.

Philip realized early in meeting Sue that it was best to play dumb to her advances, having learned the hard way that if you rebuffed her, she thought you were playing hard to get and simply tried harder. Because of this, most of the men on the island worked diligently to avoid her altogether.

Not because Sue wasn't a good-looking woman, she was, very much so, and it wasn't because she was slightly over the "hill" in her early fifties. Nor because she'd bragged about her plastic surgeries, making her older than one originally thought. No, it was her blatant tactics that reeked of desperation.

Philip wondered if maybe this wasn't on purpose. Sue liked to toy with the men, but she didn't necessarily want to keep them.

"Maybe you'll meet someone on your travels?" Philip lightly patted her hand and gave her a naïve smile.

"Possibly. No luck in this small town. Of course, all the handsome and ruggedly good-looking men are all snatched up." She stuck out her bottom lip in a playful pout and then smiled carnivorously. "How is Bert, by the way?"

Bert was Sue's only real competition business-wise on the island.

"I hardly ever see her, being her shop is ALL the way down at the docks." Sue's smile turned sour, knowing the ferry riders spent a good portion of their money at Bert's Supply Shop before even getting into town.

"I guess we're not much of a secret, are we? You're the second person to ask today." Philip had the good graces to blush.

"Well, not really. There are so few single men in this town, it's easy to keep track of you all, and let's face it, you all are pretty set in your ways. For example, ..." Sue nodded towards Hattie's General. "Harry... he goes straight home to take care of Hattie every night. Once in a blue moon, he'll go bowling or something, but he's a homebody. Boring."

Philip chuckled, agreeing with her assessment.

"Our butcher, he'd rather be around the dead things of this world than the living, and our town veterinarian, he's still got it bad for his ex-wife in Seattle. Mr. Chang, he only lives and breathes his business and well, Mr. Allister, we all know where he spends his afternoons, even if Mrs. Barnes is at home in the evening." Sue's eyebrows raised in a "You know what I am talking about" arch. "Then our attractive baseball coach was smitten by Stacy, and he wasn't the first... Sad thing about her death though."

"Yeah, yeah," Philip said, dismissively, more interested in her prior statement. "Who else was smitten?" He felt as if he was finally getting somewhere.

Sue looked at him, wholly surprised.

"Well, it's just a guess. Though, I'd have thought you would've known by now."

Philip chuckled, not having a clue what she was

talking about.

"I guess, I don't."

"I suppose not... You know, I think I may have said too much. It's not really firsthand knowledge. Only an educated guess." Sue started to get up, taking the Italian soda with her.

"Won't you tell me, guess or not?" Philip stood up with her, his voice somewhat pleading.

"Now, don't look at me with those big puppy brown eyes, Phil! I just melt." Sue slowly ran her hand down the length of his arm and added, "Besides, it's not MY story to tell." She paused and tilted her head, a wrinkle suddenly forming between her brows, then lightly shrugged her shoulders. "Tell Bert I said hello."

CHAPTER 17

Lane found herself sitting cross-legged on the back-field of the high school baseball diamond surrounded by eight teary-eyed teenage girls. All who were currently holding hands, chewing gum loudly, and dabbing their eyes with their sweater sleeves when needed. One, a girl by the name of Darby, had her head on Lane's knee. On the other side, a girl by the name of Taylor had her head leaning up against Lane's shoulder, sobbing. As they sat in the circle of misery, Lane could hear their teenage bemoaning thoughts spoken out loud.

"Great, I'll never get my round off right!"

"Ol' Brewster will take over now."

"There goes cheer camp!"

"Who's going to write up our routines?"

"She was going to do my hair for prom!"

All were self-concerned thoughts, spoken out loud, and yet, Lane could tell the girls had loved their coach.

Taking the group in collectively, she wondered if she should have taken a different approach on letting the squad know their cheerleading coach was dead. She had blurted it out, all matter of fact, honestly assuming Principal Ford had relayed the information already in some comforting way. Or possibly, even the school's gossip grapevine had broken the news. But the principal had instead sent the baseball coach home on a sick day and kept himself locked in his office, not breathing a word to anyone on staff.

"Sheriff, ma'am. Do you think we should wear our cheer outfits for the funeral? You know, in honor of her?" It was Darby who asked the question, and all eight heads bounced up to hear the answer.

"I don't think that would be appropriate... er, necessary. Typically, people wear black to funerals, but it might be a nice touch to bring a photo of the team to the service," she suggested instead.

"I can bring one from home," Shelby croaked, her dangling earrings swinging side to side as she wiped her eyes, her mascara smearing.

"I know I've shocked you, girls, with this news, and I'm so sorry. However, I do need to ask you some questions, if that's okay? I'm hoping you might be able to help me in the investigation of her death."

At the word "death", the girls broke out in sobs again, and Lane gave them a good five minutes to settle back down to sniffles.

"Do any of you know what she had planned last Monday?"

The girls looked at each other, and then, one by one, shook their heads.

"She didn't share with you anything she was excited about or possibly, someone she was hoping to meet?"

More head shaking.

"I suppose you all knew Miss Jensen was dating Coach Rick?"

Lane watched all eight heads bob in agreement.

"Did anyone know if she dated anyone else... before or after Coach Rick?"

She scanned the girls as quickly as she could, but eight sets of eyes were hard to read, especially with smeared mascara. She almost got the feeling the red-head Bridget had somewhat tilted her head towards where Lisa, Shelby, and Trisha were sitting.

"It wouldn't have to be anything serious. Maybe even someone you knew who liked her and she didn't like them back. Or maybe she hadn't even realized they liked her?"

This time the girls in unison sort of shrugged their shoulders in a united "I don't know" movement. Lane bit the inside of her cheek in frustration...

Teenage girls. She scanned the group again, looking for anything telling. Maybe Lacey had been wrong about it being a dad of one of the girls?

"Do any of you go to the same church as Miss Jensen or were in her youth group?"

Only Shelby raised her hand. "We go to the same church, but I work at my family shop. I don't have time for youth group activities."

"Yeah, she's lucky her mom even lets her do cheer," Darby muttered, and then asked aghast, "Do... do you think any of us are in danger? That it could be a lunatic who has something against cheerleaders?"

"I strongly doubt that. But, if any of you remember anything or see anything strange, you make sure you call me." Lane disentangled herself from Darby and Taylor by standing up, thus breaking the grieving circle, and pulled out her business cards, passing them out as she looked each girl in the eye, giving a reassuring smile.

Parents had started to arrive in the school parking lot, followed by Philip, driving an old beat-up beast of a brown truck, assumed to be Harry's. He had hopped out and was busying himself with shaking hands as the girls ran up to their parents in tears, relaying the news of the death.

"Excuse me," a gruff voice sounded from behind.

Sheriff Lane turned, finding herself facing a man of roughly sixty-three years of age, Darby sobbing in the crook of his shoulder.

"Yes?" Sheriff Lane smiled at the sharply dressed man. "Can I help you?"

"Am I to understand you questioned my granddaughter about a murder case, WITHOUT her parent's permission? You realize nothing they've said can be used in court, and you've violated their constitutional rights."

"You must be Mr. Allister, the town's lawyer?"

"Your assumption is correct. Now, did you or did you not question my granddaughter and her friends?"

"Sir, I informed the young ladies of the sad passing and asked a few simple questions regarding the cheer coach's last known plans. No questions were asked which would implicate or entrap any of these minors. I know my job, Mr. Allister, and it's to keep the town people and their children safe."

"Well, as much as I appreciate that... Everyone, regardless of age, deserves to have knowledgeable counsel. If you want to talk to any of these girls again, you come and see me."

"Do you have a card?" Sheriff Lane's smile was steelier than friendly this time.

"Certainly," Mr. Allister snorted and then roughly reached into his suit jacket, pulling out a business card. "I'll be keeping an eye on you, Sheriff," he warned, and then gently patted Darby on the top of the head, encouraging her to move with him towards the parking lot.

"You make friends where ever you go, don't you?" Philip walked up beside her, and Lane's shoulders drooped, the tension leaving her stance.

"Is he always that crotchety?" she asked, stuffing the lawyer's business card into her notepad before dusting her pants and watching the remaining number of parents and kids wander to their vehicles. She was relieved to see Mr. Allister wasn't stirring up a mob and had already driven off in his Mercedes-Benz.

"Oh, he's just a lot of bluster. Probably misses his court drama. He was a big-time trial lawyer once upon a time, and now... he handles small claims, mostly land dispute stuff. He's harmless... sort of."

Lane grimaced at the, "sort of."

"Got a call through to Stacy's parents and Missy Dean on the mainland." She decided to change the subject as she tucked her notepad into her back pocket.

"Parents on their way back?" Philip waved at Shelby, the teenage girl walking towards them.

"No, surprisingly. They're having her remains cremated and sent down to Arizona. They've asked me to board the house up till they're back from their trip. They indicated there would be a nice donation in it for the sheriff's department if I helped them in this..." Lane finished in a posh tone, "small matter."

"What did Missy have to say?" Philip lowered his

voice, Shelby almost in earshot.

"The same as everyone else. Didn't know why Stacy needed the night off. Couldn't think of anyone who would want to do her harm." Lane added from the corner of her mouth as Shelby bounced into their circle. "Extremely unhelpful."

"Hey, Phil! Could you give me a ride home?"

"Where's your car, kid?"

Shelby tilted her head, causing her ponytail and earrings to swing back and forth.

"At home. I'm still grounded until Saturday." She tugged lightly on his sleeve. "Please. Darby was supposed to give me a ride home, but I guess she forgot, and Mom will freak if I'm not home by five. It's almost that already."

"Really?" Lane glanced down at her watch. "Four forty-five! Shoot. I gotta get those boots over to the mainland. Mind if we swap notes later?" Lane started for her truck, stopping short and motioning Philip to follow.

He asked Shelby to wait by Harry's truck and jogged over, Lane already walking and talking. "I want to check out the discovery site again tomorrow morning. How early can you meet me at the park?"

"6 a.m. too early for you?" Philip suggested.

"So, you're wanting to sleep in?" Lane's tone was terse and he looked at her warily, unsure if she was joking or not, until she smiled, clearly teasing him.

"See you bright and early then."

"I'll bring coffee." He waved her off with a smile of his own and headed for Shelby and Harry's truck.

CHAPTER 18

"You sure had one heck of a day." Bert peered over the rim of her wine glass and took a small sip. "Eat up."

Philip eagerly cut into the plate of steak and potatoes in front of him and paused long enough to give Bert a grateful smile. He took a huge bite and gave a friendly wink to Shelby, who was playing with her food in teenage morose.

The three were seated at Bert's dinner table, just off the cabin's small kitchen, Bert having graciously invited him to stay after bringing Shelby home from cheer practice.

"This hits the spot!" Philip happily cracked open the beer placed by his plate. "You didn't have to ask me to dinner, but I'm sure glad you did."

"We have plenty of food. I'm always making too

much."

"Yeah, because she's still cooking for three instead of two." Shelby sighed heavily and suddenly flopped back in her chair. "Can I be excused?"

"Guess you're right, Shelby." Bert let out an embarrassed chuckle. "Old habits die hard, and no, young lady, eat a few more veggies first."

"Mom, I'm not five." Shelby scooted back up to the table and stabbed her carrots, much like a pouting five-year-old would do.

Bert and Philip exchanged a look across the table, and Philip cleared his throat, a humored smile on his lips as he asked, "How long had Stacy been cheer coach, Shelby?"

Philip returned to cutting his steak.

Shelby shrugged her shoulders as if to say, "I don't know." but answered, "This was her third year."

"She seemed to like it?" He dipped his fork in a generous helping of steak sauce.

The shoulders shrugged again and then, "Yeah, she was always coming up with new routines for us to try. She'd even let us pick the music... She was cool."

"Shelby, honey. It's been quite a shock today, hasn't it? Why don't you take one more bite of veggies, and then you can go to your room? I'll check in on you later." Bert reached over and gave her daughter's arm a loving rub.

Shelby nodded, but scooted closer to the table,

suddenly wanting to talk.

"She was really helpful when it came to giving advice. Kind of like a big sister. She even tutored Darby a little last quarter in math so she could stay on the squad."

"That was nice of her," Philip said, in an easy-going, yet coaxing voice.

"And she was soooo pretty. She should have been a model. People use to tell her that all the time."

"Do you think she wanted to be a professional model?" Philip prompted.

Shelby's shoulders once again said, "I don't know." Shelby, instead, said, "I suppose. She had all those photos taken before..." The young girl suddenly looked over at her mother and broke down into tears.

"Ohhhh. Okay, baby. Come here." Bert leaned across the table and wrapped her distraught daughter into her arms. "It's been a tough day, sweetheart. Here, let's get you out of your cheer whites, and I'll bring you a nice bowl of ice cream to your room. That sound good?"

Shelby, tears freely flowing, nodded her head yes and got up from the table as Philip cringed, having apparently upset the girl with his questions.

"Night, Shel," he said, helplessly.

"Night, Phil. See ya later," Shelby answered in return, not seeming to hold him to blame.

For the next twenty minutes, Philip shamelessly emptied his plate, finished his beer, and wished for another while he waited for Bert to return.

When she did, he jumped up from the table.

"Bert, sorry. I didn't mean to upset her. I should have been more considerate."

She waved for him to sit down and lightly shook her head.

"Don't worry about it. She's a teenage girl, and she has been super emotional since her dad left. This thing with Stacy pushed her over the edge. She's crashed out now. I'm sure she'll be fine in the morning. She just needs rest."

Bert began to pick up the dishes from the table, and Philip winced, realizing he could have done that himself.

"Aren't you going to finish your dinner?" he asked, lamely.

"I'm not hungry anymore. Want another beer?" Bert called over her shoulder as she carried the plates into the kitchen.

"Sure, I could do with another."

"Great. Go ahead and get comfy in the living room. I'll be out in a second."

True to her word, Bert returned with two ice-cold beers for him and a full glass of wine for herself. Philip scooted over so she could settle down beside him on the couch.

"How are you doing with this whole... finding a dead body thing?" Bert lightly put her hand on his knee and left it there.

Philip, suddenly feeling warm, shrugged his shoulders much in the way of Shelby. "I'm doing all right, I guess. Still see her when I close my eyes. All mangled and...," he paused in thought, and then continued, "Do you know Sheriff Lane actually suspects Harry?" He decided to change the subject.

"What! Poor Harry doesn't have a mean bone in his body!" Bert gasped.

"I know! That's what I keep telling her!" Philip smiled at Bert and then gave her a quick peck on the lips. "Missed you today." He slipped his arm behind her.

"Missed you too." She smiled back and patted his knee. "Now, why does Sheriff Lane suspect Harry? I'm curious."

"It's dumb. It's all because he didn't mention Stacy had missed her shift the night she was killed. But he didn't think to mention it because Stacy had apparently gotten Missy to cover for her at the store."

"That sounds right. That's what Stacy told me." Bert took a sip of her wine.

"Hold on." Philip sat up and faced Bert. "When did you talk to Stacy?"

Bert looked somewhat startled. "Oh... I'm so stupid. I should have told you this the other day, but then... I didn't know it was her who was missing! She was in my store on Monday afternoon."

"Doing what?" Philip grabbed a pen sitting on the coffee table and then Shelby's school notebook sitting beside it. He flipped the pages till he found a blank one and began writing.

"Clothes shopping. She was in a great mood. She'd picked out a whole bunch of various outfits. A few winter coats, a few windbreakers, tops, shorts, even bought some climbing boots."

"Did she say if she was going hiking or going somewhere special?"

"Noooo... not that I remember. I didn't really think to ask. We were sort of busy at the time, and I had one of my migraines coming on. I sort of just tuned her out. When I was ringing her up, though, I remember saying something about needing to stop by Hattie's to pick up some milk, and she mentioned she wouldn't be working that night."

"She didn't seem alarmed, nervous, agitated, overly excited?" Philip asked, scribbling down Bert's recollections.

"No. She was her typical upbeat normal self." Bert shook her head, amused as Philip flipped the notebook page over and looked at her eagerly. "What exactly is your part in all of this, Phil?" she suddenly asked, curiosity mingled with her amusement.

"Oh, well... I'm just helping out the new sheriff

a little." Philip flinched at the question, once again, caught playing detective. "Nothing official."

Bert smiled sweetly over her wine glass. "Anything else you want to interrogate me about?" she asked playfully.

"Did Stacy talk to anybody while in the store?" Philip questioned, not picking up on Bert's flirtatious cue.

"I don't know... Why don't you see for yourself on the shop's video?" she suggested flatly as she stood up from the couch and walked out of the room, deciding she needed more wine.

CHAPTER 19

"She had all those photos taken before...? Before what?" Lane asked, slightly out of breath, tripping over a tree root.

She was trailing behind Philip as he led her to the discovery site, listening intently as he recited his findings from the night before.

"Before Stacy died, I guess." Philip glanced back, curious to why she was wondering.

"Is that what you thought she was going to say?" she hollered at him, jumping a log, trying to keep pace.

"Well, what else would she have said?" He stopped and let Lane catch up, the sheriff coming to a halt behind him.

"She might've said something else, is all."

"She's a teenager. Most of her vocabulary is... Um, like why, I guess so, and I don't know." Philip gave his best teenage girl impression and started walking, slowing his pace.

Lane frowned at his back, knowing he was probably right.

"You should ask her," she persisted, and not hearing a response in return, followed it up with, "What else?"

"I wrote it all down on the paper I gave you." Philip halted. "Whoa. Hold up. We're here."

Stopping, the two stood in silent reverence and took in the swept area, where a young life had been taken only a few days before.

Calm and serene, the spot was now free of the yellow barricade tape strung from tree to tree, and the numerous generators, bright lamps, and tents. The forensic team, having done their best to leave the site free of debris, except for the splatters of plaster, where various footprints had been cast.

If one did not know better, as Philip and Lane did, one would think they'd stumbled across a small, lovely clearing with a convenient dead stump to sit upon and nothing more.

"I didn't expect it to be all torn down," Philip said rather surprised. "What are we doing here?"

Lane circled the fallen log and stump, where the body had laid, and noticed the recent rains had churned the blood-soaked soil into brown mud once again.

Completing the rotation, she handed him her mini-mart coffee and faced the stump.

"Well, as you and your friend pointed out, there was no real way of keeping the crime scene clean and secure. Forensics did all they could and then let nature go back to her normal self."

Lane, without warning, suddenly jumped atop the stump and let out a high pitch, blood-curdling scream, startling Philip, who grabbed his chest out of pure reflex and swore, almost dropping her coffee.

"Sorry." Lane apologized, a smile cracking her lips. "I wanted to see how loud it sounded out here."

"Well, you about gave me a heart attack! Here, let me help you down." Philip offered his hand, but Lane pointedly ignored it and hopped off on her own.

His chivalry rebuffed, he let his hand drop to his side with a slow smile.

"Would've been muffled pretty good by these trees, is my guess?" he ventured. "Think that's why the killer picked this spot?"

Lane circled around the clearing again as Philip sat down on the stump to think, still holding her coffee.

"It is off the beaten path, but obviously not too physically exhausting to find."

"And not a lot of people to come and see you go. But then again, because of that, you've got a bigger risk of being noticed AND remembered."

"But that didn't apparently happen..." Lane frowned.

"Yeah, I guess not."

"So, our killer somehow gets Stacy out here. Willingly? Tricked? Conscious? Unconscious?"

"You know, maybe we've got this wrong."

"How so?"

"Well, what if Stacy's plans for that night got canceled? She's got the night off from work, no back-up plans, and she's pissed at the boyfriend. She just bought herself some new outdoor threads, maybe she decided to go for a hike to fill up her evening... and stumbled across a stranger."

Philip flashed Lane a thumbs-up sign, hoping for her approval.

"Ehhh... the honey on the body strikes me as pre-meditated, not spontaneous. Also, she wasn't wearing any of the clothes Bert mentioned she bought earlier that afternoon." She gave him a thumbs-down.

"It was a thought."

Lane smirked and gave him another thumbs-down, this time adding a "Thfftppttt" sound to the motion.

"Hey, not as dumb as your suicide theory."

"We'll call it a tie," Lane conceded.

"Think we should look into who bought some honey recently?" Philip rubbed his nose and stifled a sneeze.

"There couldn't have been more than one or two small bottles used. Anybody might have that in their own kitchen cupboard. It's not like they used a bucket full."

Philip stood and wandered over to a large splatter of plaster.

"What did they get back as far as the boot castings?"

"Well, after discounting our footprints... They did find another set coming from where you are standing, but they mysteriously disappeared once they reached the clearing." She joined him, reclaiming her coffee.

"What do you mean, disappeared?" He bent down and peered at the prints, the plaster having all but obliterated them.

"According to the unofficial report..." Lane moved, heading towards where the forest growth was thickest. "Someone or persons, wearing size twelve boots, came in from this direction. Just a little further south than where we entered. Now, if they had stepped into the clearing, the bears and the commotion with the body wiped out those prints. Ours were on top of the bears so it was easy to see them. Our victim was wearing canvas shoes, and as we talked about before, there was no mud found on them. Which means she didn't stand in them... at least, not on this soft ground." Lane walked in a small circle, thinking out loud. "The tech did wonder if two people might have been wearing the same type of boot and size. He thought some of the impressions were deeper than others as far as where the heel or toe sank, but he couldn't be sure."

"If that's the case, we could have had two guys haul her in and dump the body." Philip looked at the clearing again, trying to picture the scene. A look of concentration furrowed his brow. "I don't know. If two people dragged her in, they would've dragged her in dead. Stacy was a flirt, but she was a smart girl. She wouldn't have gone into the woods with two strangers. Maybe one, if she met him on the internet and thought she sort of knew him, but not two."

"I agree, it doesn't fit and once again, there were no signs of a struggle at her home. I don't think she was abducted, killed, and then dumped."

"So, maybe the two-guy theory is just two hikers who happened to be in the area and not really of any relevance to the murder?" Philip scratched his head. "Could have stumbled across the body and then hightailed it out of here?"

"That's a possibility, or the tech is wrong, and those boot prints are the prints of our murderer... as in one."

"Well, if they are, our killer had enough common sense to wear hiking boots in this weather, and Stacy didn't... and she should of."

"Wait... wait..." Lane stopped, suddenly turning to face Philip, her blue eyes bright. "Didn't Roberta say something about Stacy buying boots that afternoon?"

"Holy Sh..." Philip held his tongue in front of the lady. "Yes, she did!"

"I wonder what size?"

CHAPTER 20

"Can I get you guys anything before the movie? Popcorn, Red vines, Milk duds?" Bert joked as she cued up the shop's video surveillance tape.

"No thank you, Roberta." Lane was busy digging through the store's receipt records, looking for Stacy's transaction.

Philip waved his hand, catching Bert's eye, and mouthed the words, "Milk Duds." Which caused Bert to giggle and Lane to look up.

"It's nothing. Keep looking," Philip reassured her, and then scooted his chair closer to the monitor. "So, I just turn this round knob to make it go forward and backwards?"

"Yes. Sorry, it doesn't have sound, but it is in color." Bert sat back and let Philip try his hand at the controls.

"Found it!" Lane held an extremely long receipt up in the air.

"Great. What time was the transaction?" Philip asked.

She scanned down to the bottom.

"1:33 p.m."

"And she shopped for a good forty minutes before I rang her up." Bert moved, making room for Lane to join them and view the monitor.

"Okay, let's see." Philip twisted the knob, the video fast-forwarding, the time stamp spinning until it displayed 1:15 p.m. He let go, and the tape played at normal speed, showing the shop, four people milling around the sales floor.

The version of Bert on the screen stood by the register, busily tagging items on a stand not far from two ladies, who were sifting through stylish climbing wear on a round rack, the two apparently interested in the same pair of leggings. The last patron, a young man, was browsing in the back corner, checking out fishing lures and tackle. All four circulating the shop independently, not paying attention to one another. Just visible through the windows, a red two-door vehicle pulled up, and forty-three seconds later, Stacy Jensen walked into the store dressed in the yellow tank top and cut-off jeans Philip had found her in, her hair up in a messy bun, wearing white canvas shoes on her feet.

Upon entering, the girl quickly scanned the shop and, spotting Bert, gave a friendly wave before walking straight toward her, her arms extended, the two women embracing with smiles. Stacy looked happy and in a good mood with no sense of panic or concern to be traced.

Bert ended the hug as Stacy leaned back, her head tilted as if asking a question. TV Bert in response, pointed to various places within the store before returning to her task.

For the next several minutes, Stacy proceeded to shop, the pretty blonde piling clothing item after item over her arm and, at one point, creating a pile by the register.

While Stacy shopped, the two ladies in the rock-climbing area had grabbed a few items, paid, and left. Philip focused on the young man in the fishing department, whose full attention was no longer on the lures and tackle, but on the gorgeous blonde. He seemed to watch her as she moved between clothing racks and had been slowly starting to make his way closer when she took her final pile up to the register.

Bert, busy ringing and bagging her items, paused as Stacy appeared to ask another question.

"This is where she wanted my suggestion on men's boots." Bert gestured at the screen. "I pointed her to the section and told her they were all good brands."

On the screen, TV Bert suddenly pointed in the

general direction of the shoe section and Stacy quickly went over and started looking at sizes. She paused and seemed to call back, asking another question. Bert, in response, shook her head in the negative, and Stacy shrugged her shoulders in return, taking the box she had in hand up to the register.

Meanwhile, a couple had walked in, making their way over to the climbing wall in apparent awe.

"What did she ask there?" Lane leaned past Philip and looked at Bert.

Bert sat there, frowning in recollection before answering, "I think... If the boots came in any other color?"

"Okay, she's got her stuff," Philip said excitedly as he noticed "fish guy" had moved closer to the door.

Stacy proceeded to wave goodbye before glancing at her wristwatch and heading out the door with two very large paper shopping bags.

"Time?" Lane asked, pen to notepad.

"1:37 p.m." Philip paused the tape. "Two hours before..."

"Keep rolling." Lane nodded for him to go on with the tape. "I wanna see who leaves next."

The young man browsing followed Stacy out the door a minute later, not having bought anything. This left only TV Bert and the rock wall couple in the store, the latter moving to the men's section. In the corner of the screen, TV Bert had started to straighten the clothing racks while absentmindedly moving her hand to her forehead, occasionally pausing in her work.

"This is when my migraine started up," Bert explained.

The tape rewound suddenly.

"Sorry, I want to see what "fish guy" is driving," Philip apologized, as the two ladies shook their heads at the screen's rapid reversal.

"Fish guy?" Bert asked. "Who's that?"

"The man shopping in the fishing section, who left without buying anything," Lane answered for Philip. She had noticed him too.

"Yeah, he left right after Stacy." Philip stopped the tape, and they all three leaned towards the screen.

Through the store window, they could see the red of Stacy's Jeep and next to it, a blue vehicle.

"Is that a Ford?"

"Might be." Lane squinted. "Looks like a four-door SUV."

They watched as the blue vehicle followed the Jeep out of the camera's view.

"Wait a minute..." Philip suddenly stood up and wrestled his hand into his jean pocket, pulling out his cell phone. He quickly started to scan through his photos. "Yup!" He looked up excited. "Ford Escape BLUE SUV!" He turned the phone towards Bert and Lane so they could see the phone screen.

"This car was in the Park and Ride lot the day I found Stacy's body. It was one of the cars I didn't recognize on the dock."

"You've got the license plate?" Lane took her cell phone out and started to make a call.

Philip practically yelled the combination of letters and numbers in his excitement. Cringing at the volume, Lane nodded as she scribbled the information down in her own notepad and got up from her chair.

"We're going to have to take the tape," she told, more than asked, and then said into her phone, "Jenny? Hey, this is Sheriff Lane. I need you to run a license plate for me."

Lane indicated she was going out to her patrol truck and left the small office.

"What... what just happened?" Bert's smile looked confused, clearly missing the point. "Did you just catch the killer?"

"Maybe?" Philip paused and decided there would be no harm in sharing. "See, our theory is whoever killed Stacy also took her Jeep, driving it back over the ferry, on the account, we've not been able to find her car still." Philip ran his hands through his hair and blew a big puff of air out in relief.

"And then left his own car at the Park and Ride? But it's not there anymore, right?" Bert asked, her confusion deepening.

"Which means he must have come back and got

it or it was towed," Philip explained his reasoning.

"But... If he drove off after her and, I guess in theory, followed her?" Bert was starting to follow along. "How did his car get back to the Park and Ride?"

"Well, depends on where Stacy went next. He might've bumped into her, played himself off as real charming, and convinced her to take him somewhere—"

"Somewhere being the park! Where he kills her and then drives her Jeep back over the ferry! Phil, you're brilliant!" Bert jumped up from her chair and wrapped her arms around his neck, giving him a big kiss.

Stepping back into the small office, Lane stopped short at the sight of the kissing couple, who were wholly immersed in each other's arms. She noisily cleared her throat and not waiting for them to separate, began to refer to her notepad.

"Well, our blue Ford Escape was reported stolen the day before Stacy went missing," she stated loudly.

The two quickly broke apart, Bert lightly wiping her mouth and adding in an excited hush, "Which gives more credence to this guy stealing Stacy's Jeep!" She clapped her hands together in excitement and gave a small jump.

Lane eyed Bert, her lips thin, and continued to read from her notes, "It was stolen from Issaquah. Owner didn't realize it for two days as they were out of town." She closed the leather flap on the note-pad. "I'll have them pull the ferry's video so we can see when this guy arrived and roughly when he left. Hopefully, we'll catch him driving a red Jeep somewhere in the middle."

"That's great!" Philip, quickly sitting down, re-wound the tape all the way to when "fish guy" had walked in. "If we've got a good enough shot of his face, you could put it out on the news, and maybe someone will recognize him."

"He's definitely not a local," Bert confirmed.

"Look! There... right there." Philip played with the knobs, the video zig zagging and then pausing. "He's stealing fishing line... right... there." Philip's big finger smudged the screen as he pointed out "fish guy" slipping a few spools of fishing line under his jacket.

"Son of a gun! I didn't even notice," Bert complained, a scowl on her face.

"What would he want with fishing line?" Lane asked, noting it in her pad.

"I don't think this guy was really a fisherman." Philip played with the video some more.

"Think he snatched it for binding purposes?" Lane looked up from her pad and added doubtfully, "It wouldn't be the ideal thing to use."

"Maybe, but Stacy didn't—" Philip started to say.

Lane cleared her throat and spoke directly to Bert, "I'm sorry. We're going to need to have this conversation privately. I'm sure you understand, Roberta."

Bert looked surprised, then annoyed. She shook her head musingly as she stood up and placed her hand on the door knob.

"I'll go up front," is all she said as she walked out of her own office and firmly shut the door behind her.

"What did you do that for?" Philip stood up, starting to fold up his chair. "She's only trying to help."

"I know, and I appreciate it, but she's not in on this... YOU are. I need your full attention here."

Philip started to say something smart, thought better of it, and instead unfolded the chair, flopping down onto it.

"Alright. So, do you think we found him? I mean, could this be the guy?"

"It's hard to say. I'm hopeful. However, until we identify him and know a little more about him..." She sat down in Bert's vacant chair. "Check out this shopping trip of Stacy's. It's kinda weird." Lane pulled the lengthy receipt out of her pad. "See here, she bought duplicates of things, but in different colors... and it was all charged to the store on credit. I mean, she didn't technically pay for any of these items. Roberta let her use store credit. Is... is that normal?" Lane handed him the receipt.

"I suppose? I didn't know Bert offered store credit. As far as what she bought, maybe she was going to take them home and try them on?"

"The shop has dressing rooms."

"Maybe she was on a time crunch?"

"Possible. She did look at her watch before she left," Lane admitted, then shook her head, dismissing it.

"Or maybe they were gifts?" Philip said, next.

"The boots were size twelve and men's... so your gift theory might not be off the mark. Stacy was a size six in shoes and a size four in clothes. I noticed when I looked in her closet. All the sizes on those clothes seem to be about right, except for those boots."

"Which matches the boot size at the crime scene." Philip shook his head. "This could all mean nothing. Especially if "fish guy" is our stalker, slash killer."

"Philip, we've got to look at all the possibilities."

"Listen, I think you've already figured it out, Lane. She meets a guy online, okay? They've arranged to meet, so she does some shopping. Maybe she's not quite sure what she wants to wear? Who knows how girls think? But she does know he needs hiking boots. Hell, could be a hiking date? I don't know. Whatever the case, she decides to pick him up a pair. NOW... either "fish guy" is Mr. Internet and since she didn't notice him in the shop, they meet and..." Philip knew he was reaching.

"We've always said this was not an abduction case." Lane took the receipt back from Philip and put it in her notepad. "We are either right... or we are really wrong."

"There was no fishing line at the scene or on the body," Philip said, more to himself than Lane.

"Nope," Lane answered him anyway.

"We still need to follow it up, though... just in case."

"I concur. We've finally got an official suspect. That's worth a corn dog, don't you agree?" Lane offered her hand as she stood up and helped haul Philip from his chair.

"A corn dog? You don't like—" Philip's mouth twitched into a smile as he realized Lane's intentions. "Oh, from the new mini-mart."

CHAPTER 21

"Hello, Mr. Chang. Doing some redecorating?" Philip lightly called as he and Lane walked across the parking lot to find the mini-mart's owner painting over graffiti on the outside of his building.

Mr. Chang, perched on his ladder, twisted, and gave them a welcoming smile, dropping several dots of paint on the sidewalk in doing so.

"Got tagged last night, the little shits." Mr. Chang dipped his already soaking paint roller into the paint tray.

"Do you happen to know who it was?" Lane stopped and looked at the wall, trying to decipher the bits she could see through the first coat of paint.

"Nah, no cameras on this side of the building."

"Ah... speaking of cameras." Lane took a step onto the sidewalk next to the ladder, being careful not to step in the blots of paint.

"I'm sorry, Sheriff. I already told you. I don't want to get involved," Mr. Chang's voice ended gruffly. "Sorry." But politely.

"So... how's business been?" Philip gave Lane a "let me give it a try" look, and she took a step back.

"Slow."

"Yeah..." Philip looked towards the empty gas pumps. "Looks it."

"But summer is coming in a few months, so it should get better." Mr. Chang smiled, his voice sounding hopeful.

"Normally, yeah. That would probably be the case." Philip shook his head as if to say for shame and then gave a dramatic sigh.

"Normally? Why wouldn't it be this year?" Mr. Chang was taken aback by the opinion.

Philip put on his best surprise face.

"Well, the murder!"

The mini-mart owner shook his head, not understanding how the two things, summer tourist season and murder, had anything in common with each other.

Philip continued, "There's been a murder or... as rumor has gotten out, a bear attack. Which to the nature-loving tourist is just as bad. Neither is a drawing point for summer fun." He looked behind him and over to the docks. "Nah, this tourist season is most likely already shot."

"That's too bad." Lane eyed Mr. Chang, and see-

BLACK BEAR ALIBI · A ROCKFISH ISLAND MYSTERY : I

ing he wasn't quite convinced, added, "You know, the big news conference in a couple of days probably isn't going to help either." She grabbed onto the ladder and peered up at him, shaking her head. "There will be nosy reporters everywhere, and I bet it'll be the top story of the evening news. Nothing but bad press! Oh, and reporters... Ugh. They will work a story like this to death! Basically, just telling everyone to stay away!" She looked over at Philip, changing her shake to a nod. "I think you're right, Ranger. I doubt people will be hopping the ferry to come over here anytime soon. You said it, all right. It just doesn't sound like summer fun."

"Well... maybe next year. See ya, Mr. Chang." Philip turned to leave, signaling for Lane to follow.

"Wait!" Mr. Chang began to climb down the ladder, paying no attention to the paint roller smearing across the front of his shirt. "What if you solve the case?" He looked between the two eagerly. "You know, find the killer?"

"Weeeelll..." Philip looked at Lane and made a face of uncertainty. "I'm guessing things would go back to normal? Bad guy behind bars? Maybe even a little bit of notoriety to the place?"

"Imagine, Mr. Chang. If your video surveillance tape actually helped lead us to the culprit. The community..." Sheriff Lane shook her head, the idea leaving her speechless.

"They'd be grateful!" Mr. Chang finished the thought for her.

"I'd say so!" Philip confirmed. "Practically free advertising as well!"

"That for sure couldn't hurt business." Lane gave a light chuckle. "But I understand if you still don't want to get involved."

Mr. Chang plunked his paint roller down with a splash.

"Sheriff, I'd like to help."

CHAPTER 22

"You're going to get sick if you keep eating those," Lane complained, watching Philip toss another corn dog stick upon his growing pile.

"I never turn down free food," he mumbled through a full mouth, then swallowed. "Got anything?"

Lane had been painstakingly watching the small, black and white, fuzzy television in the mini-mart's breakroom for the last thirty minutes. Even without color, it had been easy to spot Stacy's Jeep leaving the Outdoor Supply Shop, heading to the gas pumps straight from the store. The Ford Escape, however, appeared to have driven past the mini-mart, heading downtown.

As the blue SUV passed, the surveillance video showed Stacy standing outside her vehicle pumping gas, the pretty blonde periodically checking her reflection in the side mirror and her cell phone twice, responding to at least one text message. After putting the pump hose back, she had jumped into her Jeep, took another look at herself in the rearview mirror, and headed towards town.

Lane leaned back from the tiny screen and stretched her back.

"Well, no signs of "fish guy", other than him driving past." She grabbed the small bag of chips she'd been munching on and found the bag empty. "I wonder who she was texting?"

"Maybe whoever she was supposed to meet?" Philip took a long and loud slurping pull from the straw of his thirty-two-ounce slurpy.

Giving a side-eye of disapproval, Lane picked up her own drink, an eight-ounce coke, and found it empty as well.

"We need to find her phone."

Snatching up the trash, she rose from the table, but Philip pulled on her sleeve, dragging her back down.

"Hey, keep watching. He still might show up," Philip let out a burp, then at Lane's disgusted look, said "Pardon me," picking up another corn dog.

"I'm telling you, you're gonna get sick!" she warned, exasperated, and leaned back into the small monitor.

"Wait! Did you see that?" Philip grabbed the television and turned it towards his chair, completely blocking Lane's view.

"See what?" Lane yanked it back.

"Rewind it a tad. Behind pump three. Watch the road." Philip used the corn dog stick to track the small blur that looked a lot like a Ford Escape driving down to the docks.

They held their breath as they watched the SUV park in the Park & Ride section, a dark figure climbing out and making its way to the awaiting boat.

Lane gave a frustrated sigh. "Just in time for the three o'clock ferry. He went back to the mainland on foot."

"Damn. He ditched the car." Philip tossed the half-eaten corn dog violently onto the small pile.

"Okay. Let's not get disappointed here. We now know for sure the last time Stacy was seen was at the gas station which was at one forty-five. She didn't meet anyone at the ferry dock, so that's out. What did she do with her time after getting gas? Did she go home? Did she drive straight to the park? Did she meet someone somewhere else?"

"I guess we can wait to see if she met anyone at the four o'clock ferry? Coroner said time of death was between three and four. If they left the docks straight away...?" Philip scratched his head, furiously thinking.

Lane wearily nodded her head. "No stone unturned," she agreed, and then leaned back into the small monitor, not holding her breath.

CHAPTER 23

"Hey, Kody. Wanted to check-in. Anything turn up on the Jeep trails? Over." Philip leaned his head against the truck's headrest, closing his eyes.

Lane was still in the mini-mart using its facilities.

"Hi, Phil! No. All roads were clear, and gates still padlocked. You might like to know the wild-life department was here today and tagged the cubs. Derrick says for you to give him a call, that is, if you feel up to it."

"Man, is it Thursday already?" Philip said to himself, but over the two-way, "Will do."

"Oh, and I had the tow truck up here again for another tow. Guy left his lights on while climbing The Mole Hill. I put it in the daily report."

"Another tow? Someone get their vehicle towed on Wednesday?" Philip watched as the yellow parka clad sheriff said her goodbyes to Mr. Chang and started to make her way to the patrol truck.

"No, on Monday night." Kody slurped loudly from one of his power drinks. "It's in the log."

"Hold up, Kody. I didn't know a car got towed on Monday." Philip tried to keep his voice level.

"I told you Tuesday night before I went home for the day. The tow guy had driven up because of all the cop cars and thought there was an accident. Remember?"

"Yeaahh? I remember. But that's not talking about Monday, Kody!" Philip didn't hide his frustration this time.

"Like I told you on Tuesday. The tow driver said to give him a call, in case we had ANY MORE breakdowns in the park." Kody took another large slurp. "It's in the report, Phil. Don't worry."

Lane opened the truck door and climbed in, only to have Philip signal for her to stay quiet.

Good job, kid. But, back up a little. Tell me about the car towed on Monday night."

"Um, okay. I was doing the nightly go through and spotted a vehicle with its lights on and hood up. There was a note on the dash saying the owner had walked to town on foot. I'm guessing, they couldn't get cell service. So, I called the tow truck for them. It was no big deal, Phil."

"And what kind of vehicle was it?" Philip looked

at Lane and mouthed the words as they came over the two-way.

"Jeep Wrangler."

CHAPTER 24

"I could just kick Kody!" Philip huffed, slamming the two-way back into its slot. "I could just kick myself."

"No. It's both our fault. As soon as we knew her car was missing, I should have checked with the island's tow company." Lane glanced over at him as she took the road heading out of downtown. "We had tunnel vision and assumed someone had driven her car onto the ferry."

"Yeah, but Kody should've mentioned it. Especially after I asked him to check the Jeep trails."

"He did." Lane grimaced as soon as she said it. "Kind of..."

"The time we've wasted!" Philip vigorously began rubbing his forehead and cracked the window, letting cool air hit his face, a headache suddenly coming on.

"Slow down. Go down this road here on the left and then take the second right." He suddenly shook his head, and repeated, disgusted, "Just wasted!"

Lane, understanding the frustration, let Philip stew in silence until they arrived.

"Well, there it is." She parked the truck and stared out at the crowded towing lot. Barely visible was the grill of a bright red Jeep parked in the back row, half-hidden by two impounded yachts. "Not easy to spot behind those boats." She let out a loud sigh. "What is the tow driver's name again?"

"Edgar Rowles. Rowles Towing." Philip began to climb out, his shoulders slumped.

"Hey, Phil?"

He paused, and turned back, meeting her eye.

"Yeah?"

"This could be the break we need," Lane encouraged, adding a smile as she pulled the yellow parka hood over her head with a tug. "Don't lose heart."

The two stepped out into the late afternoon drizzle which had suddenly come along. Dodging the rain, they made their way hastily to a small building with a chain-link fenced lot in the back, the Rowles Towing truck parked inside, a small Honda Hatchback strapped to the flatbed.

Reaching the stoop and finding the OPEN sign lit, the two walked into the dingy office entrance, the room smelling heavily of cigarette smoke.

"I don't see anyone..." Lane spotted a silver desk call bell on the Formica countertop and gave it a good smack, sending a loud ting across the room and into the living quarters in back.

A tall and unkempt-looking man, wearing oil-smeared overalls, came upfront from the living quarters and gave them a crooked tooth smile.

"Evening, folks." Edgar offered his sweaty, greased stained hand to Philip.

"Evening, Edgar. This is Sheriff Lane." Philip gave Edgar's hand a hardy pump and let it go, fighting the urge to wipe his palm on his pants leg.

"Evening, Sheriff." Edgar offered his hand to her as well, but the sheriff looked at it blankly and took out her notepad instead.

"Hello, Mr. Rowles. We've come to ask you a few questions about the tow you did on Monday night. The one out at the National Park?"

"Oh, yeah. The red Jeep I've got sitting out back. Your deputy... I guess you'd call him, gave me a call. Told me there was a broken-down rig to come get. So, I did."

"And what time was this?" Lane looked around the office walls, noting the calendar was two months past due and the clock five minutes late.

"It's in the logbook. I'd say, around 6p.m.? But let me look." Edgar rummaged around the front desk and then pulled out a dirt-smudged logbook. "Yup, hooked her up at 6:20 p.m."

"What kind of condition was the vehicle in?" Philip leaned over the counter and peered at the log, making sure it indeed stated six-twenty.

"When I pulled up, lights were on. Hood was up with a note on the windshield saying the driver had hoofed it back to town." Edgar, noticing Philip's glance, placed the logbook up on the counter and turned it so both he and the sheriff could see.

Philip took the opportunity to also see what Edgar had written down from 3 p.m. to 4 p.m. the same day.

"What was wrong with the Jeep?" Lane copied the log into her notepad.

"Nothin'," Edgar answered as he moved the book back onto his side of the counter. "Keys were in the ignition, and it turned over just fine."

"That's odd. You didn't feel you should have reported this to anyone?" Sheriff Lane looked up from her notepad and gave Edgar a level stare, though he towered over her.

"No. I called the insurance company as there was a card in the glove box. Car wasn't reported stolen or nothin', and there was a note. I figured they'd come looking for it eventually."

"So, you knew it was Stacy's vehicle, then?" Philip questioned. "From the insurance card?"

"Name on the insurance card is Larry Jensen," Edgar said, confusion in his voice. The big man paused, frowning deeply. "He's in Arizona, according to his insurance company."

Philip rolled his eyes and said to Edgar as if talking to a child, "Larry Jensen is Stacy Jensen's dad. The Jeep must be in his name instead of hers."

"Mr. Rowles, this is a small community. You must have heard about the death of Stacy Jensen by now. Why didn't you let someone know you had her Jeep in your lot?" Lane took a step closer to the tall man.

Edgar looked down shyly at his hands.

"S'pose I didn't put two and two together."

"Mr. Rowles, try again," Lane suggested firmly. She wasn't buying the dumb, backwoods, don't know better act.

Edgar scowled and then mumbled, "Business hasn't been so great. I need the lot fee."

"Mr. Rowles, are you saying you KNOWINGLY kept information from the authorities in hopes of collecting a fee for storing the Jeep at your facility?" Sheriff Lane's voice was hardened steel.

Edgar's pretend shame turned into defensive petulance.

"They can afford it. At eighty bucks a day and with them not coming back from Arizona till May, it would've helped me out quite a bit."

"Especially if the Jensens don't claim their car after a certain period of time, isn't that, right? You can sell it at auction, can't you, Mr. Rowles? But before you do, by law, you must put a notice in the newspaper. Of course, knowing the owners are in Arizona and now, most likely will be staying longer, they probably wouldn't see the notice. Is that what you were hoping for?" Lane's glare grew steelier by the second. "That would be a heck of a lot more money than a couple months of lot fees," Lane speculated, outraged at the idea.

"I didn't think of it that way, ma'am," Edgar's eyes dropped to his shoes as he pulled out a handkerchief to wipe his sweaty palms.

"Not to mention, I think you know, Mr. Rowles, if you had reported the vehicle to the sheriff's office, it would have been towed to the mainland. Where it would have been kept in the evidence lot instead of yours. Then you wouldn't have even had the lot fees, would you?" Lane slapped her notepad against the counter, drawing Edgar's eyes back to hers.

"No, ma'am. I s'pose I wouldn't," Edgar practically growled his answer.

"Edgar, have you cleaned the vehicle? Touched it at all?" Philip quickly asked as he lightly stepped sideways and bumped Lane's arm, causing her to drop her eye contact with the greasy tow driver.

He was getting worried the small sheriff was going to push the big man a little too far, and though Philip figured he could take Edgar on, he'd rather they did this the nice way.

"Just when I hooked it up. I didn't sit in it. Only leaned in and turned the key over." Edgar turned to his right and pulled a set of keys from a large peg-board, handing them to Philip. "She's just like I found her. Except lights off and hood down."

"Do you still have the note found with the vehicle?" Philip handed the keys to Lane, the pair dangling from a "Cheer is Life" keyring.

"I tossed it in the glove box."

"Mr. Rowles, we're going to take a look at the vehicle now. I'll also be calling into the station to have it towed to the mainland for inspection." Lane jiggled the keys at Edgar. "I expect to find that neither the insurance company nor the Jensens will be billed for your services. Correct?"

"Yes, Sheriff," Edgar answered sourly.

He swung open the waist-high swing door and allowed them to follow him through to the back part of his office/living quarters and out into the tow yard, where they got a full look at the red Jeep.

Philip groaned in dismay.

"You left the top off?"

"I told you, I left it as I found it," Edgar said, sullenly. "Thought you'd be happy to see it that way."

"Mr. Rowles, when you moved this vehicle, was it raining?" Lane asked, deflated.

The Jeep's doors and wheel wells were caked in mud, along with splatters of dirt on the inside windshield and dash.

"No. It was a clear day." He frowned at the question.

"Since then, have you moved the vehicle while it's been raining?"

"Yeah, I hooked her back up. Had to maneuver it a couple of times to get it behind the boats. Got it stuck for a second, but I got her pulled out just fine," Edgar said, curious as to why it mattered. He started to walk around the Jeep, checking for damage. "What's the problem? There's no dents and I didn't scratch the paint neither."

"Mr. Rowles, if you move a vehicle while wet... will dirt and grime get on it?" Lane waited for him to answer, and when he didn't, she continued, "The problem, Mr. Rowles, is that even though it rained, we could have still lifted fingerprints off this vehicle. But now... now that the vehicle is dirty and muddy... and grimy..." She took a deep breath in an attempt to keep her anger under control. "You've probably destroyed any helpful prints which might have been left behind."

"I don't see how a little bit of dirt or mud is gonna make a difference," Edgar argued.

"You don't? Mr. Rowles, we have oil in our skin, and that oil doesn't go well with water. So, when you touch a smooth surface, say a metal hood... or a car door. Even though it's been exposed to water, like rain, for instance, your fingerprint remains on that surface. But when you throw dirt, mud, sand, grit onto the same surface, it distorts the latent print. In other words, the arches, loops, and whorls are now ruined." She stopped at the utterly confused look on Edgar's face. "Are you following me?"

She'd lost him at arches, loops, and whorls.

"You know what? I don't have time to give you a lesson in Forensics. Just take my word for it. You've most likely destroyed evidence which could have helped find the person who killed a beautiful, young girl." Lane shook her head, completely disgusted.

"Didn't do it on purpose." Edgar was shame-faced.

It was the first time he'd shown any kind of re-morse for his actions since the conversation had started. Philip almost felt bad for him... almost.

"I think we've got it from here, Mr. Rowles. We'll check in with you before we leave." Lane waved him off, clearly at her wit's end.

"Alright, then. Have fun," Edgar said dismissively and headed back inside.

"This is a mess," Lane said, as she opened the driver's door, a trickle of water running down.

It was obvious the Jeep had been sitting in the off-and-on rain for the last three days. Philip opened the passenger's door, stepping back as well, and looked down at the wet floor mats, then up at the myriad of rain droplets standing on the leather seats.

"Mr. Jensen wouldn't have gotten much of a car

back, especially if Edgar let it sit and rot out here until they came back from Arizona." Philip popped open the glove box.

"Don't touch anything yet." Lane handed him a small flashlight from her duty belt. "Let me grab a couple of gloves from the truck."

She jogged to the fenced gate and headed towards her vehicle.

Using the flashlight, Philip peered into the glove box, bobbing the beam back and forth, and spotted, as Edgar had promised, a crinkled piece of paper. Behind it was an ice scraper, a folded map of the island, the ferry schedule, and a small flashlight.

His curiosity satisfied, he shut the glove box to keep everything dry, a steady stream of raindrops pelting the vehicle's interior, and glanced up at the grey heavens, suddenly finding himself wishing he had a yellow rain parka of his own.

When Lane returned, the rain had picked up and turned into a downpour, the numerous raindrops hitting the Jeep's metal hood, creating a monotone xylophone.

"Here." Lane handed him a pair of examiner's gloves and a large evidence bag. "Just put everything that's in the glove box in there. In a few short minutes, we'll be soaking wet."

Philip gave a hurried nod, and using as much of his frame as he could, he shielded the dash and popped the glove box as Lane opened the driver's side and climbed in.

"Seat hasn't been moved. I can touch the pedals," she reported, climbing out and moving the bucket seat, looking down at the floorboards. "Here's what looks like a vanity case of cosmetics and a gym duffel bag."

Finished with emptying the glove box, Philip pushed forward the passenger seat and peered behind. "Nothing much on this side. Roof cover is stuffed under the seat."

"No cell phone?" Lane started shoving her hand down and around the seat cushions, feeling for anything which might have fallen between them.

"No... but we should ask Edgar on our way out. Strikes me as if he's pretty hard up for money. May've found it and then tried to hock or sell it." Philip pushed the bucket seat back into place with a small bang.

Lane did the same, and then they shut the doors.

"Let's check the back."

Philip pulled the latch next to the large spare tire, and the door swung open. "Ya know, I never realized how much it rains here," he muttered under his breath and then, unexpectedly, yelped in triumphant as he held up what looked to be a bright pink, dripping wet cell phone.

"Found the phone!"

CHAPTER 25

"Where to now?" Lane turned the engine over and cranked up the heat, having stuffed the two wet bags between them, the heating vents directed towards the soaked items.

"Hattie's. We need to buy some rice for the cell phone, and I need coffee."

Philip held up the plastic evidence bag containing the note and squinted at the contents, his arms moving back and forth as if playing an invisible trombone, unable to read the small print. He covertly pulled out his readers, shooting Lane a side glance, and then tried again, letting out a soft "Ahhh," before reading aloud, "Car won't start. Heading to town. Get a tow truck." Philip frowned, sliding his readers off. "Block lettering." He slipped off the glasses and tucked them into his shirt pocket, adding, "Our killer didn't take her Jeep. They abandoned the rig and let the tow company take care of disposing it for them. Clever."

"You don't think Stacy left the note, and somebody found her walking?" Lane asked, a curious lilt in tone.

"Edgar said there was nothing wrong with her car," Philip pointed out.

"Yeah, that's what Edgar claims. But we know we can't fully trust anything he says." She slowed the truck down, an idea beginning to form. "Phil, Edgar could be our guy. He's out, prowling for cars to tow. Sees the red Jeep parked in the woods with a pretty blonde in the driver's seat. He makes a pass, gets turned down... probably unkindly. Loses his temper, kills her, and hauls her off into the woods. Then leaves the note, knowing he'll be called in to tow her Jeep away. He then hides it in his own lot!" Lane pulled up to a red light.

"Except..." Philip tilted his head in her direction, giving her an arched brow, predicting her next words.

"Except he seems to have an alibi." Lane shot him a look, taking in his pleased smile, before returning her eyes to the road.

"Exactly. According to his log, he was changing two flat tires for Sue Carter at 3:30p.m. in town on Monday," Philip recalled from his memory of the logbook.

"Two flats? Come on. One I could buy, but two?" Lane was shaking her head in disbelief. "Probably falsified the log."

"You don't know Sue Carter! She likely had one flat and then let the air out of the other tire, just to keep Edgar's attention. It's easy enough to check up on."

"Edgar is our strongest suspect so far."

"I feel a 'BUT' coming on." Philip wrestled with the seat belt, twisting to face Lane.

"BUT, for the damn honey. Edgar doesn't strike me as the brightest bulb. I can see him doing all the things I said... I just don't see him having the foresight to pour honey all over her body to attract wildlife to it."

"Unless he's done it before and gotten away with it," Philip said somberly.

The truck was quiet for a minute as they waited on the red light.

At the sight of it turning green, they both seemed to come out of their thoughts.

"And that brings up something else I wanted to talk about. I've been thinking... you pour honey on the body in hopes the park's wildlife will come and devour the evidence, or at least, strew it halfway across the forest. But you leave the murder weapon behind? Why leave the bowie knife? I mean, it's not like the bear is going to eat that too!" She gave out a small snort. "Like Yogi the Bear is gonna come along and toss it into his picnic basket."

Lane suddenly felt she was rambling, the wetness of the cold day and the lack of sleep from the night before catching up with her.

"Left by accident, maybe? The way I see it, if this murder was planned, you've got a lot of working parts. You've got to somehow lure your super busy and active victim out to the middle of basically nowhere without her telling a soul... AND without being seen in this small town. Then you've got to either carry or convince them to follow you into the woods. Murder them, smother them in honey, walk yourself back out of the woods, probably honeyed and bloodied yourself, then make arrangements for the victim's vehicle to get towed, and THEN manage to find your own way back into town without being seen. One might forget to leave the murder weapon behind." Philip shook his head. "Forget the coffee. I need a beer."

CHAPTER 26

"You two look—" Harry yawned mid-sentence. "As tired as I feel. Have a seat and get off your feet." He directed them to the picnic table with a nod of his head, and then returned to what he was doing, his attention focused on a poster.

"I want to grab a few things first, Har," Philip called over his shoulder, the ranger heading towards aisle seven.

"What are you doing, Mr. Vickers?" Lane watched Harry, the poster in hand, stroll to the front door.

"Made a 'Help Wanted' sign." He placed the poster below the open sign. "And letting folks know the temporary change of store hours. Missy isn't able to work all the night shifts, and I have to be home to keep an eye on Hattie. So, until I find somebody, I'm gonna have to close the place down in the evenings." Harry pressed the tape down and stood back to make sure the sign wasn't crooked.

"That's probably rough on your business." Lane stifled a yawn, getting up to make her way to the coffee machine on the left wall.

"If I don't find somebody by next week, it will be."

"Find what?" Philip plopped a box of instant rice, a plastic cereal container, coffee creamer, and a six-pack of beer on the counter.

"Clerk for the night shift." Harry walked over to the register and began ringing up the items. "How are things going?" he whispered, looking over Philip's shoulder to make sure Sheriff Lane was still standing at the coffee machine.

"Good, but not great. If I can get this thing to work again, we might actually find out who did it." Philip ripped the plastic wrap from the empty cereal container, then popped an opening into the rice box, pouring the rice and a bright pink cell phone into it, tightly sealing the lid. "The phone records are taking forever to come in from the cell company."

"That still might take a few days." Harry, doubtful it would be any faster, motioned towards the container.

"Well, it's all we've got right now." Philip gave him a twenty-dollar bill, signaling at Harry to keep the change for the donation box. "You closing up shop early?"

"In a few. Sit, get warmed up, and have some coffee. I'll give you a ride home." Harry handed him the paper bag filled with the six-pack of beer and coffee creamer. "I'll be just a minute."

Philip, picking up the rice-filled container, shuffled to the picnic table where Lane was sitting, already sipping on a hot cup of Joe, and sat in front of the coffee waiting for him, creamer already added.

"Bless you." Philip gratefully gripped the cup, warming his hands.

"Hope you get some sleep tonight." Lane blew on the molten surface of her coffee, having already burnt her tongue on the first sip. "You don't want to be catching a cold."

"I've worked in wet weather before. Don't worry about me," Philip complained, not liking to be mother-henned. "I'm just tired. Which feels stupid since we really haven't done anything too physically exerting."

"It's brain wariness. My Dad used to say it came from thinking too much... happens to cops all the time. You keep turning things over and over in your head, and you never shut off your mind. It can be very fatiguing." Lane plopped the small make-up and gym bag on top of the picnic table.

"You gonna look at those right now?" Philip asked, surprised.

"No. Not where the whole town can gather outside the window and watch," Lane admonished.

"You've forgotten. I'm fifty paces away from my new abode."

Philip nodded his head.

"Welcome home then."

"See you in the morning?"

"Bright and early."

"Bring coffee."

Lane tiredly got up and snagged the yellow parka on a bent nail, stopping short and off balance. Philip grabbed her elbow and helped her off the bench. This time she didn't jerk away.

He smiled... progress.

CHAPTER 27

Lane tiredly made her way up the rickety stairs that clung to the backside of the general store, the steps steep and thin.

Even though she was in good shape, she found herself quickly out of breath, and upon reaching the top, let out a puff of air, making a "woooooo" sound as she did so.

She set her bags down, careful to not knock over the potted flowers, the clay pots precariously balanced on the small railing of the mini landing, and took a cautious glance over the side, down into the alley. It was higher than she thought.

Having caught her breath, Lane dug out Harry's key from her parka pocket, once again grimacing at the sight of the rabbit foot dangling from the keyring.

"Poor bunny," she whispered to herself, feeling

sorry for the footless rabbit.

Putting the key in the lock, she heard the heavy deadbolt click over and pressed on the apartment door, it barely budging. She gave a harder nudge, forced to use her shoulder to shove it open, wide enough to bring her luggage through the door.

Seeing the whole of the tiny apartment clearly from the doorway, Harry having left the kitchen light on, she took three steps in and found herself standing in the bedroom. Turning to her right, she took ten more steps and discovered the minuscule kitchen. She then walked the thirteen steps back to the front door and heaved it shut, making sure the bolt was turned.

"Home, sweet home." She flopped her suitcase onto the bed.

This was indeed going to be home, sweet home for the next month, and as depressing of a thought as it was, the place also felt surprisingly homey. The light from the kitchen was warm and welcoming, and the cheerful yellow drapes matched the feather-down comforter on the twin bed, two fluffy pillows at the head, and a white crocheted quilt at the base.

The small apartment had only two windows, one in the kitchen facing the back side of the building and a larger one on the same side of the apartment stairs. She instantly took a liking to the only picture hanging on the walls, a vase full of sunflowers, circa 1973.

There was even a deer head mounted over the bed.

She decided to name it Merl.

Lane opened the small closet, sandwiched between the tiny bathroom with a shower and the front door, finding barely enough room to stuff in her suitcase and hang a few clothes. Luckily, she hadn't brought much. A few changes of uniform, a t-shirt, and a pair of jeans, for if she got a day off. Her suitcase was mostly filled with books which she stacked by the small nightstand. She figured if there was no television, she'd have to occupy her time somehow.

After unpacking, Lane familiarized herself with the kitchen cabinets, stocked with the bare necessities, and peeked into the refrigerator, finding she'd need to visit Hattie's and do some grocery shopping of her own. But until then, what was she do with herself?

Swinging the fridge door closed, she grabbed a folded TV tray found leaning against the wall and sat down on the only chair in the apartment, pulling the TV tray apart and using it as a makeshift desk. She then snapped on a pair of latex gloves, shook open a brown paper evidence sack, placing it on the floor by her chair, and picked up the make-up bag she had found in the Jeep.

There wasn't much of anything she hadn't expected to find. Eyeshadow, foundation, birth control, a couple of lip glosses, nail polish. Lane zipped closed the small satchel and placed it carefully inside the evidence sack.

Next, she placed the gym bag on the tray and unzipped it. Moving the sides apart, she found unfolded and previously worn clothes. A workout bra, a white t-shirt, yoga pants, and an oversized hoodie sweatshirt. She placed each article of clothing in its own clear Ziplock baggie and then rummaged the various small pockets of the duffel bag, ultimately discovering a stick of ChapStick, and a white envelope with a receipt partially sticking out.

Excited, she removed the opened sleeve and placed the duffel bag aside, pulling the contents from the envelope, laying them separately on the TV tray.

Inside was a small note with a paper clip still attached, a paystub from Hattie's, dated a few months prior, and an ATM deposit receipt dated the same day as the paystub.

Lane's eyebrows slowly came together as she examined her find, a crinkle forming in the middle of her brow.

"Nooo, this isn't suspicious at all..." she said to an empty room and carefully placed the envelope and its contents into a Ziplock baggie, slipping that between the bindings of her book resting on the small nightstand. She then got ready for bed.

On her first night on the island, Lane slept with

the kitchen light on, and the door barricaded, the chair jammed under the doorknob. Just in case someone had a key...

CHAPTER 28

"Thanks for the ride home, Harry. Sorry to make it a habit this week." Philip climbed into Harry's old brown pickup truck and leaned across the seat to unlock the driver's door for his buddy.

"Hey, no problem." Harry slid in and then hand-cranked the window down two turns, explaining, "I know it's chilly, but this keeps the windows from fogging up."

Philip chuckled.

"When you gonna break down and buy yourself a new truck, man? Aren't you saving any of your money?"

"She's still got life in her," Harry said, giving the steering wheel a loving pat.

"Oh, that she does," Philip acknowledged. "But you're over forty-five, and pretty soon, if she rusts up anymore, you'll have to climb through the window to get in. That's tough on an old man."

"You wanna walk home, Bud?" Harry threatened.

"I'll shut up." Philip smiled and looked out the window, the tree line whizzing by.

"So, what do you think of her?"

Philip didn't need to ask 'who' Harry was referring to.

"She's nice, once you get past the brittle exterior. She's smart, got a good eye for detail, and she doesn't know how to back down."

"Feisty!" Harry wiggled his eyebrows up and down. "I like that!"

"Too feisty for you, my friend," Philip warned.

"You calling dibs?" he asked, a slight tone of seriousness creeping into his playful demeanor.

"No... didn't say that. I just think she's not interested." Philip looked out the window, the forest growing thicker.

"That's what you said about Bert," Harry pointed out, and lightly bumped Philip's arm.

"I know, and I'll say it again. I didn't have plans for Bert and me to get together."

"I know that's what you SAY. But you also said it was too soon after her husband left for me to make a move on her... and yet."

"I'll remind you, good buddy. She was the one who made the moves on me."

"I'd thought she'd have better taste," Harry teased, pulling into Philip's driveway and bringing the rig to a complete stop.

Ignoring the barb, Philip cracked open a beer, handed it to Harry, and then opened one for himself.

"And you better hope I never ask Bert for her side of the story." Harry eyed his friend, taking a swig to hide his smile.

Philip laughed. "Ask away, my man. Ask away."

They brought their beers together in a light aluminum clink.

"So, you found Stacy's cell phone, huh? Think it will help?" Harry suddenly asked awkwardly.

"Yup." Philip lightly kicked the rice-filled container at his feet.

"Anything else?" Harry ventured.

Philip stared down at his beer, considering if he should tell Harry about finding Stacy's Jeep but thought better of it, as he didn't think Sheriff Lane would appreciate his loose lips. The one thing he didn't want to do was jeopardize their working relationship, and he thought it better not to give Lane any excuse to send him packing.

"Was Stacy a good employee?" Philip asked, instead.

"Hey, don't pay any mind to what Grandma Hattie said. She's starting to fade... ya know?" Harry looked out the driver's window, into the dark, and sighed,

"That Stacy. She sure was a looker." He suddenly glanced down at his beer and took a hurried gulp.

"She was practically a kid," Philip said, surprised at his friend's comment.

"Nah, Phil. She was a woman. A beautiful woman!" Harry lifted his can into the air and toasted, "To Stacy." Then finished off the beer and handed the empty to Philip. "Should I pick you up tomorrow?"

"I'd appreciate it."

"See ya in the morning." Harry wished Philip a good night as he climbed out of the truck with his things.

From his front lawn, Philip watched as his best friend drove off and suddenly wondered, if maybe, Harry didn't hold a small grudge against him.

CHAPTER 29

Lane was already dressed and sitting at the make-shift TV tray desk writing in her notepad when Philip knocked on the door. She got up, peered outside the window facing the stairs, and gave a wave of acknowledgment.

"I brought coffee as requested," Philip said when she opened the door. He handed Lane an extremely large thermos and stepped into the small apartment.

"You're joking." Lane unscrewed the cap and peered inside, the deep aroma of coffee hitting her senses.

"A full day's supply," Philip pointed out, walking to the kitchen cupboard and pulling out two coffee mugs.

"Were you by chance in the Boy Scouts as a kid?" Lane teased.

"Be prepared IS our motto." Philip gave the Boy Scout salute and held out the coffee cups so Lane could pour.

"Thanks. This will count as breakfast." Lane screwed the top back onto the thermos and took the offered mug from Philip, indicating with a nod for him to take a seat on the freshly made twin bed, then sat herself down behind the TV tray desk. "Get comfy. We need to talk."

"You find something out?" Philip sat down, placing his mug on the nightstand, and broke open a small creamer, pouring it into his mug. "Is that a list?" He indicated to Lane's open notepad, laid out flat on the TV tray.

She flipped the leather flap closed, blocking his view, and took a deep breath. "I need you to have an open mind on what I am going to show you." She produced the plastic baggie with the white envelope, its contents on display.

"Sure," Philip agreed, taking a hurried sip of his coffee before putting the mug down on the night-stand and accepting the plastic bag from her hand.

"I found the white envelope in one of the side pockets of Stacy's duffel bag. That's its contents. What conclusion do you draw?" Lane watched him closely, willing herself to see the gears moving in Philip's head.

"Weelll... the envelope, which was sealed, has Stacy's name handwritten on the front. It's been ripped open by hand. The long piece of paper looks..." Philip stopped and grabbed his readers from his shirt pocket. "Like a paystub from January of this year. The smaller piece of paper was probably torn from a blank notepad... almost looks like receipt paper. It's got a paper clip still clipped to it." Philip brought the plastic bag closer, squinting even with the readers, the cramped handwriting on the note, difficult to decipher.

"The note says..." Philip read out loud slowly, "This is all I have." He shrugged. "Then it's signed with the letter H." He dropped the bag onto his lap. "And then there's an ATM receipt for eighteen hundred dollars on the same day as the paystub."

"But the paystub was only for three hundred dollars," Lane pointed out eagerly, hoping Philip would come to the same realization she had.

He snatched up the bag and looked at the paystub, this time more closely.

"Okay, I see what you're implying." Philip put the bag down on the bed and leaned his elbows onto his knees, looking over at Lane. "There was fifteen hundred dollars cash, paper-clipped to the note, stashed in Stacey's paystub envelope, and you think... what? This indicates a bribe or rather, a blackmail payment?"

"Don't you?" Lane stood up, pacing the small room. "I know Harry is your friend, but you have to admit that's a bit odd, and he really doesn't have an alibi for the time of death. He was close to the victim and would have been able to concoct some kind of story to get her to meet him. Especially if she was blackmailing the guy." Lane turned to face him. "I just think it's strange he didn't tell us he was giving her large amounts of cash."

Philip looked at Lane, blankly, not giving any indication of his thoughts.

"Don't you think he might have had a reason to get rid of her?" she persisted.

Philip shook his head, dismayed, and stood up, grabbing his coffee mug in one hand and the plastic evidence bag in the other.

"You know what? Let's go ask him."

CHAPTER 30

At the general store, Hattie was happily rocking in her chair, entertaining two elderly gentlemen over coffee.

The two men, who sat on opposite sides of the picnic table, were in a heated debate. Something to do with fishing lures vs. fishing chum, the trio, so engrossed in their discussion that they failed to notice Philip as he blew through the front door, Lane right on his heels.

"Morning, Hattie. Morning, Dub. Morning, Glen." Philip gave each a friendly tilt of his coffee mug. "Is Harry back in his office, Hattie?"

Surprised, Hattie blinked up at Philip and nodded her head as he briskly walked past and strode down aisle one. Lane, a step behind, desperately trying to keep pace.

"Philip, wait a minute," she called out.

"Hey, Harry!" Philip bellowed as he banged on the swing doors and hollered, "You've got company!" He breezed through the doors, causing them to violently swing back and forth.

Lane paused a moment as the doors swooshed back towards her and then pushed her way through as they swung forward.

"Phil, hold up a second!" she tried again. He kept walking, steadily ignoring her. "Ranger Russell, please stop!"

Philip paused by the empty freezers, two still lit and one dark, with an impatient stance.

"I can tell, I've upset you," she whispered harshly as Harry gave a welcoming bellow from his office.

"Upset? No. I just want to get this cleared off your plate so you can stop this nonsense about Harry and REALLY focus on finding the true killer," Philip whispered back fiercely. "You've been on Harry's back since the beginning. It's a waste of time!"

"Not without apparent reason, Ranger. I told you. I'm looking at this objectively."

"And I've known the guy my whole life. I KNOW him, Sheriff." Philip stepped back and took a deep breath, rubbing his forehead. "I admit... it looks... bad. But you'll see in a few minutes you've jumped to the wrong conclusion. Again."

"Again, huh? Well, then I guess the laugh will be

on me!" Lane gave Philip a hard glare and brushed past him, heading towards Harry's office.

CHAPTER 31

"Hello, Sheriff! What do I owe this pleasure... Hey, Phil!" Harry cut his morning greeting short upon seeing the scowl on Philip's face. "What's going on? Something wrong?"

Lane ignored his question and politely asked Harry if she could have a seat.

He eagerly offered her his chair and took the La-Z-Boy for himself, Philip declining to sit, placing his back against the door jamb.

Lane started the conversation off with a warm smile. "Mr. Vickers, we located Stacy's Jeep yesterday afternoon, and were able to retrieve a few of her personal items left in the vehicle."

"You found her Jeep? Yesterday afternoon?" Harry gave Philip a confused look as his friend hadn't mentioned it the night before when asked.

"That's good news then!" He suddenly smiled, giving Philip a thumbs up and frowning when his friend didn't respond.

"There are a few things we found in the Jeep that we wanted to get your take on," Lane continued.

"Sure, sure. Whatcha got?" Harry scooted himself closer to the edge of the Lay-Z-Boy.

Lane looked at Philip, who waved impatiently for her to go on.

"Can you tell me what this means, Mr. Vickers?" She produced the plastic evidence bag with the white envelope and papers and watched as Harry took hold of the bag and brought it close to his face. Reading the paper-clipped note, Harry's face immediately fell, his color blanching.

"I can explain this!" he blurted, looking scared out of his wits, his face ashen and his hands trembling, the plastic bag shaking with them.

"Aw, Harry. What did you do?" Philip practically crumbled in the doorway and leaned up against Harry's desk for support.

"Nothing!"

"Nothing? Come on, man. You're as white as a sheet! What the hell did you do, Har?" Philip raised his voice and took a step towards his friend, his hands balled into fists.

"I didn't kill her if that's what you're thinking!" Harry briskly stood up, his hands clenched, knuckles white.

"Okay... Okay!" Lane stood up herself, stepping between the two men and nodding towards Philip, directing him to back off, the ranger shaking, out of anger or fear, she couldn't tell. "Please, everybody. Just calm down."

Philip stepped back but kept his eyes on his shaken friend.

Lane faced Harry, who was glaring at Philip as well, his hands still clenched.

"Go on. Sit down, Mr. Vickers," she said firmly, and then more softly, "Please, Harry. Sit down."

Harry nodded, picking up the evidence bag which had fallen to the floor, and took his seat on the Lay-Z-Boy, meeting Lane's eye.

"I didn't kill her."

"That's not what we are thinking at all," Lane lied smoothly.

Unconvinced, Harry handed her the plastic bag, then eyeballed Philip before closing his eyes and taking a deep breath. "I didn't, Phil," he insisted.

Philip ignored him and sat down on the edge of the desk.

"Tell us about this note, Harry." Lane lightly put her hand on top of his, drawing his eye.

"She needed some money. I was helping her out."

"Money for what?" Lane prompted, and after a minute of him not responding, prodded, "Why did she need money? What did she tell you?"

"Stacy said she was pregnant." Harry put his head in his hands, his color slowly returning.

"Who did she say was the father?" Philip asked, sitting to attention.

"Me." Harry pursed his lips together and looked up at his friend. "She said it was me, Phil."

"Wait, what?" Lane was shocked. "You two were involved!"

"No, not exactly." Harry leaned over and shut the office door, swatting it closed and leaning back on the La-Z-Boy. "It started last October on Halloween night. I'd forgotten to bring the Halloween candy home from the store, so I came back here to grab it. Stacy was working and she was just about to shut the place down." Harry turned to Lane. "I don't keep the store open late on Halloween. I have them close down as soon as it gets dark."

Lane nodded.

"And, when I got here, Stacy seemed real upset about something. You know, not her normal bubbly self. So, when she was in my office putting away the till for the night, I asked her what was wrong." Harry ran his hands through his hair in a nervous gesture. "She started telling me about a guy who had given her the brush off." Harry held a hand up. "And before you ask, no. She didn't say a name, and I didn't bother to ask. I told her the guy must be insane because she was the most beautiful girl I knew, and you know... said stuff to make her feel better. Then..." Harry took a deep breath, dropping his hand down to his lap. "One thing led to another."

"You became lovers," Lane finished for him.

"It only lasted a few weeks. She seemed to lose interest pretty fast."

"And started dating the baseball coach," Philip added.

Harry tossed his head side to side with a shrug.

"I guess so."

"So, when did she tell you she was pregnant?" Lane had covertly taken her notepad out and was taking notes.

"A month later. She showed up with a positive pregnancy test and told me the baby was mine. I started to give her money to buy the things she needed. A crib, baby monitor, diapers..." Harry's voice trailed off.

Philip, eyes pinned on his friend, took a wild guess. "She wasn't really pregnant was she, Harry?"

"No," Harry admitted. "She was faking."

"How did you guess that?" Lane looked at Philip, surprised he'd figured it out. She hadn't told him about finding Stacy's birth control the night before.

"Simple. Harry's got a big heart which makes him easy game. Stacy claiming she was pregnant seems to have happened around the same time Lacey told

us she found out she was pregnant. Made me wonder if she swiped Lacey's positive pregnancy test and
tried to play it off as hers. I bet you if we asked, Lacey
would tell us how much Stacy spoiled her with gifts
for the baby." Philip put his hand on Harry's shoulder. "Must have been a big disappointment."

Harry nodded his head, his eyes downcast, focused on the floor.

"And not something you want to brag about.
Even to your best pal."

The two men made eye contact, and Philip nodded his understanding, adding, "Stacy eventually
would've said she lost the baby or... asked for abor-
tion money, and you'd hopefully be none the wiser."

"So, if she took you for all of this money, why
did you let her continue to work at the store?" Lane
asked, confused.

"Because when I confronted her about the fake
pregnancy and asked her to pay all the money back.
She threatened to tell people I was sexually harass-
ing her at the store." Harry turned toward Philip.
"You know this town, Phil. Gossip like that would
fly and Stacy... the youth group leader, cheerleading coach, ...and me? Ol' single and lonely Harry?
People would've believed her in a heartbeat."

"And she kept stealing from you, taking money out of the till, ringing customers up twice, taking
product home after the store closed. Knowing you

wouldn't do anything about it," Philip sneered. "What a piece of work."

"Why didn't you tell us this from the start?" Lane asked, crossly.

Harry was taken aback. "Because it has nothing to do with her murder. What she did to me has nothing to do with what happened to her. I promise you."

"But Harry, it says a lot about her character. This whole time we've been thinking she's this sweet innocent kid... and in fact, she was a conniving, extorting, lying little whor—"

"Don't speak ill of the dead, Phil," Harry said sternly. "She was young and foolish and yeah, she got away with a lot of stuff because of her looks. But she didn't deserve what happened to her."

"That's not what I was saying, either." Philip put up his hands in a placating manner. "It just changes the optics a bit, Harry."

"I know. You're right. I should have told you. Sorry."

"It's all right, man. It's all right."

CHAPTER 32

"I guess we were both right?" Lane suddenly spoke, lowering her head with a friendly smile, trying to catch Philip's eye.

The two were currently sitting at an outdoor patio table in front of the Gelato Deli, the last ten minutes spent in silence, Philip staring at his feet.

He only grunted.

"I'm sorry I thought Harry might have been a homicidal murderer," Lane offered, scrunching up her shoulders and holding her hands to the side in a helpless gesture. "There, I said it. Feel better?"

Philip rolled his eyes, lightly shaking his head.

"I don't need your apology. Harry did have something to hide. You were right."

Lane mumbled under her breath, "I know."

"But!" He pointed at her, giving his finger a violent shake. "I knew he wasn't a homicidal murderer."

"I said, I was sorry."

Lane flagged down the waitress and ordered a couple of salami sandwiches.

"So, where do we go from here?" Philip asked, his stomach growling.

Lane pulled her notepad out and flipped to the middle. "I made a list of questions that have been bothering me. Maybe we can find a new direction there?"

"Worth a try," he said, not seeming convinced.

"A couple of these we've already talked about." Lane cleared her throat and read from the list.

1. Why was the bowie knife left behind?
2. Why was the victim scalped?
3. Who was the married man?
4. Why did Stacy use store credit at the Outdoor Supply Shop?
5. What happened to the clothes Stacy bought there? (Not at her house or in her Jeep.)
6. How did her cell phone get in the trunk?
7. Why did Stacy buy boots in men's size twelve?
8. Why did she buy so many same sizes, but different colored items?
9. Does Kody have an alibi? Does he wear a size twelve boot?

"Wait!" Philip put his hand on Lane's notepad and pushed it down to the table. "What was that last question?"

"Now, don't get all upset again. It's only a question. I'm being objective."

"That's what you keep telling me," Philip sighed. "So, why's Kody on your radar?"

"Well, that Monday you'd gone home already for the day and Kody had the whole park to himself. What if he made a date with Stacy? Meets her, kills her, hides the body, and calls a tow truck. You said it yourself, when he mentioned it, he only said it in passing. He must have realized it was Stacy's Jeep as much as anyone else. I mean, in just the few days I've been driving around this town, I've seen the same eight cars three times a day. A red Jeep is bound to stick out."

"You forget. Tourists come and go through the park all the time. Not to mention, this is the Pacific Northwest. Jeeps are a dime a dozen," Philip countered.

"I'm just being obbbbjjjjectivvvve," Lane said the last word slowly for emphasis.

"Don't be a smart ass," Philip warned, and then said, "Okay, it was dumb of him not to figure it out. But he's a good kid, Lane."

"I know he's a good kid, Phil, and you live among good people, but someone on this island might be a killer."

"It might not be a local," Philip suggested, stubbornly.

"Do you honestly think after how dishonest she was with Harry? Or, with her supposed affair with a student's father, that there might not be more skeletons in this girl's closet we haven't discovered yet? That she didn't make a few more enemies on this small island?" Lane suddenly mumbled under her breath, "Makes me want to talk to that Pastor Jonas again."

"Hey, folks," Their waitress awkwardly interrupted. "Here's your order."

They mumbled, "thank you" and took the hoagies.

"Need anything else?" she asked, looking as if she didn't have a great desire to oblige.

"No, we're good for now. Thank you." Lane smiled and handed over the few dollars from the change as a tip.

"Okay," was all the waitress said as she pocketed the money, and wandered off.

"I think we need to dive into the cheerleader dad aspect again." Philip began to unwrap the sandwich, ignoring Lane's mumbled Pastor Jonas comment.

"Agreed." Lane unwrapped her hoagie and pulled out the tasseled toothpick, pointing it at Philip and stating, "Darby."

"Divorced. Dad lives on the mainland."

"Taylor?"

"Same." Philip took a bite and held up a finger, quickly chewing. "Same goes for Bridget, Lana, and..." He looked up at the sky, trying to recall the girl's name. "Sara."

"A lot of single women on this island," Lane noted. "Trisha?"

"Parents still together. Dad is the History teacher."

"Kind of rules him out."

"How so?"

"I think instead of telling Lacey it was awkward seeing him at events, Stacy would have said at school. I could be wrong, though. Who else?"

"Lisa. Her parents are still together. Dad's a fisherman up in Alaska at the moment. He was home in October, I believe."

"Might explain why she was so upset he stopped contacting her? Shelby?"

"Dad is out of the picture."

"Yeah, tell me about that. I don't quite understand. Does she ever hear from him?"

"No, I mean the guy just walked out. Vanished into thin air and hasn't been heard from since."

"Did Roberta report him missing?" Lane used the toothpick to pick at a stubborn piece of lettuce, stopping when she saw Philip's amusing stare.

"Well, since he emptied out all their bank accounts, she didn't think he was actually missing. Figured he got tired of life on a small island and took off for the big city." Philip picked up his own toothpick and stuck it in the corner of his mouth, chewing on the minted splinter.

"When was this?"

"Last fall." Philip busied himself wrapping the rest of his uneaten sandwich.

"Last fall as in October, November?" Lane proffered, her tone questioning.

Philip paused in thought, the sandwich half-wrapped. "Yeah, now that I think about it. It was around October. Huh, that's a coincidence."

CHAPTER 33

"I see you've still got your shadow," Bert whispered in Philip's ear, walking past him as Lane followed her into the shop's office and storeroom.

Philip gave a small grunt, holding the door open for both ladies.

"Mrs. Esten, I appreciate you taking the time to see me again." Lane turned on her heels. "I just had a few questions and was wondering—" Her eyes swept past Philip and out onto the sales floor, spotting Shelby at the front counter. "Oh, Gee... Would it be alright if I talked to your daughter for a second? Since she's not with a customer."

Lane began to walk back through the door and Bert took a protective step, blocking the way.

"Why do you need to talk to Shelby?"

Philip put a light hand on Bert's arm, giving his

best-disarming smile.

"It's okay. The Sheriff just wants to ask Shelby some basic questions. Mostly about the girls on the cheer squad. Nothing serious."

"Well, I guess that's all right." Bert stepped back and let Lane through the doorway. "But... try not to upset her." She smiled lovingly at her daughter, who was busy folding t-shirts. "Shelby's been really emotional ever since she found out about Stacy."

"Of course," Lane promised and closed the office door behind her, offering at the last second, "I'll just give you two some privacy."

As soon as the office door latched shut, Lane made a straight beeline to Shelby. She figured she had about ten minutes to talk with the teenager while Philip kept her mother occupied in the back.

She had insisted on being the one to speak with Shelby, arguing the girl might be more open if her mother and Philip weren't hanging on her every word. She also decided it would be best to divide and conquer instead of questioning each woman separately together. Philip had begrudgingly complied.

Having set the plan into motion, it was now Lane's job to get the typically non-verbal, shoulder-shrugging teenager to talk. Doing her best to appear as casual as possible, Lane took a pretended interest in one of the t-shirts Shelby was folding.

"What does that say?" Lane touched the shirt the

young girl had in hand.

"This one? It's got Big Foot on it. Hide and Seek Champion. Like it?" Shelby held it up against herself to show it properly.

"Actually, I was thinking of it for my dad. His birthday is coming up," Lane lied, his birthday being over a month ago.

"What size is he?"

"X-Large."

Shelby started digging through the sizes while Lane looked back towards the office to make sure the door was still closed.

She tried to strike up a conversation.

"I sure miss my dad. He lives in Montana. I don't get over there much to see him." Lane casually started to pick through the other unfolded t-shirts on the counter. "I bet you miss yours too. I'm assuming your parents are divorced?"

Shelby shrugged her shoulders. "Separated. Here's an extra-large." She handed over the item.

"Thanks! This will make a nice birthday present." Lane laid it casually over her shoulder and started to help Shelby fold the pile. "My parents divorced when I was about your age. My mom remarried and moved back east. I ended up staying with my dad and brothers."

Shelby looked at Lane and asked shyly, "Did you see your mom very much after she moved?"

"No. She sort of forgot about us." Lane could hear the bitterness in her own voice and quickly looked up, giving Shelby a reassuring smile. "But I turned out okay. What about you? You get to see your dad?"

Shelby's baseball-capped head swung side to side in the negative, leaving her earrings to dangle with it.

"Kind of mad at him at the moment, huh?" Lane volunteered, trying to advance the conversation.

Shelby shrugged again.

"Sort of..." And then pouted, "He's been gone almost half a year and hasn't even bothered to call me."

"You worried about him?" Lane asked tenderly, seeing tears well up.

"Mom says he's traveling and just hasn't been able to call. You know, going to all of these out-of-the-way exotic places."

"Must be pretty exciting for him."

Shelby's shoulders quickly lurched up and down.

"Yeah, guess so."

Lane handed Shelby a small folded stack of shirts and motioned for her to move the larger pile her way to fold.

"Mind me asking what your dad does for a living?"

"He's a wildlife photographer."

"Nice. Are all of these pictures his work?" Lane pointed to the various wildlife prints placed sporadically on the shop's wall. Shelby perked up and smiled fondly.

"Sure are! He used to drag me along with him and I'd help carry his gear. I liked it because at the end of the day we'd go down to the waterfront and feed the seals. It was fun."

"Sounds like fun! He ever help here at the shop?"

"Nah, it wasn't his thing. He didn't like being cooped up. Mom and him use to fight about it because sometimes his photographs didn't sell." Shelby bent her head and whispered so a lady standing close by wouldn't hear. "Grandpa left a lot of bills. Mom says it's from remodeling this place before he died. It stresses her out."

"I can imagine." Lane quickly calculated what the climbing wall might have cost and the water feature trickling through the store. It most undeniably hadn't been cheap.

"To make extra money, dad started taking school pictures. ASB cards, team sports, elementary class pictures. That sort of thing. He hated it."

"Did your dad ever do headshots? Like for actresses or models? Maybe for people in town or on the mainland?" An idea had popped into Lane's head.

"Just once that I know of. He did our team cheerleading photos, and Stacy asked him if he'd be willing to give her a good deal on some modeling shots."

"And did he?"

"Yeah, they spent a few afternoons each week for about a month going to various places on the island."

"And did you get to go along and carry the gear for him on those photo ops?" Lane smiled, her face saying she expected to hear a yes, but knew she'd hear a no.

"Nah, he said he didn't need me for something so easy. I helped mom out here instead," Shelby explained, her attention focused on putting the sizes in order.

"Did Stacy like the photos he took?"

Shelby shrugged her shoulders.

"I don't know..." Lane waited a few seconds figuring Shelby would add more to the comment, which she did. "He left a week after they finished."

"Oh, then did your dad see much of Stacy right before he left?"

Shelby shrugged and then took a deep breath.

"When he picked me up from practice after school and at church on Sundays. The only good thing about him being gone is I have his car now." She placed the last shirt on top of the folded bunch and smiled at their work. "Thanks for your help, Sheriff. I can ring you up now."

CHAPTER 34

"I don't think she likes me." Bert frowned at the closed office door. "To be honest, I don't think I like her either."

"Well, I like you." Philip wrapped his arms around Bert and gave her a small squeeze.

"I like you too." Bert leaned against him and put her head on his chest. "You wanna come over for dinner tonight?" She peered up at him and smiled. "I'm making my world-famous meatloaf."

"Bert's world-famous meatloaf! How can a guy say no to that?"

"He can't!" Bert tilted her head up for a kiss, which she duly received.

"Mind if I ask you a question?" Philip let go of Bert's waist, letting her return to organizing the stockroom, the chore she had been doing before they'd arrived.

"Not at all." Bert smiled and handed him a large box to hold.

"The day Stacy came in and bought all those clothes... Sheriff Lane noticed she got everything on store credit."

"Yeeeaaah?" Bert said casually, stretching up on her tiptoes to reach further back on the shelf.

"I didn't know you gave out store credit?" Philip asked lamely, not knowing how else to word his question.

Bert grunted and pulled a hanger down from the shelf. "Well, as a general rule I don't."

"Then why did you for Stacy?"

"Oh, well, that's easy. Because Tim owed her money." Bert snagged the hanger onto the shelf and went back to pulling another box down.

"For what?" Philip asked, surprised.

"She'd paid him for some modeling shots he took but never gave her." Bert turned around and stacked a new box on top of the box Philip was already holding. "I guess I wasn't the only one he screwed," she said, sarcastically.

Philip couldn't help but wonder if that wasn't exactly the case.

"So, you're paying off Tim's debt by giving her free clothes from your store?"

"Yup."

"Why didn't you just let her file collections against

Tim himself?" Philip handed Bert the top box when she motioned she was ready.

"And what would that have taught Shelby? That you can just run away from your commitments? Not be a person of your word?" Bert's voice was strained.

Philip couldn't tell if it was from the weight of the box she was pushing or from the emotion of the conversation.

"I'm now raising that girl on my own, Phil. Somebody has to be a good role model."

"Anybody ever tell you, you're amazing?"

Philip moved past Bert and placed the last box on the shelf.

"Not recently." Bert smiled up at him and then frowned when there was a light knock.

"Everybody decent?" Lane called softly into the room, cracking the door open.

Bert smirked at the question but instead said, "See you at six for dinner."

CHAPTER 35

"I need to drop you off somewhere. I'm heading over to the city for a meeting. Just got the call," Lane said, as they climbed back into the patrol truck.

"Meeting? Anything serious?" Philip looked concerned.

"No. Just going over some results with Coroner Ames." She hurried on, sensing he was going to ask to come along. "Don't worry. I'll tell you all about it when I get back tonight."

"I'll be over at Bert's, though."

"You two having a sleepover?" Lane teased.

"None of your beeswax." Philip picked up a small shopping bag sitting on the seat between them and looked for the opening, wanting to peer inside. "What's this?"

"A t-shirt." She grabbed the bag and placed it

back down on the seat. "Where do you want me to drop you off?"

"Oh, anywhere downtown is fine. I thought I'd go over and see if Sue Carter really had two flat tires last Monday."

"Were you able to ask Bert... err... Roberta about the store credit?" Lane turned the truck away from the docks. Philip's mouth twitched with a quick smile at hearing the slip.

"Yup. Apparently, Stacy had paid Tim for some modeling headshots. He was a photographer... Did I ever tell you that?" Philip frowned, trying to remember. "But he disappeared before she got them. Bert has been paying his debt by giving Stacy store credit."

"Hmm, makes perfect sense, actually. Roberta probably wasn't able to pay the girl back in cash, owing so much on the store's remodel already. Also, it explains why Stacy ordered more modeling headshots. Remember the billed invoice we found at her house?"

"Think Harry's money paid for those?" Philip wondered aloud, glaring out the window.

"Maybe. Either way, we can cross the question off the list." Lane almost sounded disappointed.

"Why was it on your list anyway?" Philip asked, suddenly curious.

"I just thought it was odd is all." Lane avoided Philip's eye contact and went on, "Shelby opened up a bit. I think it's safe to say Tim was the married dad sleeping with the cheer coach."

"Go on..." Philip twisted in his seat, his usual riding position.

"Well, Shelby use to go with her dad on his photo expeditions all around the island. However, when it came to shooting the modeling shots for Stacy, he had her stay home. He also used to pick Shelby up each day at cheer practice, and since he has seemingly hightailed it out of town without a word to anybody, it would explain Stacy being upset he gave her the brush off."

"It does seem to fit," Philip agreed.

"It's also another dead end."

"I don't agree. For all we know, Tim could have gotten back in contact with Stacy, arranged to meet her in the park, and then slashed her throat."

"Why? What's his motive?"

"Maybe because she wouldn't run away with him? Maybe she found out where he was and threatened to tell Bert? Or maybe she tried to pull the same thing on him as she did with Harry? Point is... Tim could have come back to the island!"

Philip leapt at the new theory.

"Or we're going down another rabbit hole." Lane's mouth scrunched into a disappointed pout. "Did you know Roberta told Shelby her dad is traveling the world, and that's why he hasn't called her? Because he's so remote he can't get to a phone."

"No, but what else is she going to tell the kid?"

"The truth," Lane said, sharply.

"I don't think it's all that easy," Philip countered. "He might very well show up later in life."

"And you'll have taken his place. Might be awkward," Lane warned. "What does Shelby think of Roberta dating so soon after her dad has left?" She pulled into the parking spot in front of the antique shop.

"I don't know. I think she likes me. Don't know if she really considers us dating. More like, I'm hanging out with her mom." Philip grabbed his thermos.

"She doesn't think you're trying to take her dad's place?" Lane asked, surprised.

"No, because I'm not. She's a good kid. We have our own friendship." Philip pulled on the door handle, pushing the truck door ajar.

"And you don't think Tim will be resentful when he comes back?" Lane's mouth quirked.

"I'll worry about it, if or when, it happens. Catch ya later." Philip suddenly hopped out of the truck, not bothering to look back.

"Touchy," Lane mumbled as she reversed the pickup and headed towards the ferry dock. "Very, touchy."

CHAPTER 36

Lane politely cleared her throat, once again knocking on the door frame, trying to make her presence known. The thin coroner, who was sitting at his desk, wearing a business suit and pouring over forms, hadn't seemed to notice she'd been standing there.

"Oh, Sheriff Lane! Come on in and have a seat. I'll be with you in just a moment," he said warmly and returned to his document.

Lane stepped into the stark office and sat in one of the two chairs placed in front of his desk. Not quite knowing what to do with herself, she stared at the older gentleman for a while as he scribbled away intently on the page.

After a few more minutes, she found herself leaning forward to read what he was writing, tilting her head to the side. The coroner suddenly looked up and gave a firm but discouraging cough.

"Sorry." Lane sat back in her chair and continued to wait, casually looking about the room.

Lining the walls were awards, certificates, diplomas, and letters of accolades. Standing by the door was a wooden coat rack holding the coroner's fluffy downed jacket and thermal stocking cap. On the other side of the room stood five large filing cabinets, placed side by side with a wilted plant on top.

"There," Coroner Ames said, placing a stapled bunch of papers onto a stacked filing system and giving the pretty sheriff a warm smile. "You're here for your official report, aren't you?"

"Yes, sir." Lane smiled in return and scooted to the edge of her seat. "Though, I need to give these to you first." She placed a large Tupperware container on his desk filled with homemade cookies. "These are from Mrs. Barnes."

"Oh, how generous!" The coroner exclaimed happily, popping open the lid and grabbing a large handful, placing the cookies on his desk.

"I have no idea how she even knew I was planning on seeing you today." Lane was perplexed. "She was waiting for me at the ferry, cookies already in hand."

"Well, please tell her thank you, and I'll return the Tupperware whenever I need to come back over."

"No offense, Mr. Ames. But I hope it's not anytime soon," Lane confessed.

"Believe me, Sheriff. No offense taken," he said chagrined, a cookie hanging halfway out of his mouth. "Now, let's get to business." He stood and walked to the third filing cabinet, opening the top drawer and rifling through the folders. "Let's see, yours was the Black Bear Alibi Case, wasn't it?"

"Excuse me?" Lane asked, surprised.

"Oh, you'll have to forgive me. I'm afraid I have a habit of titling cases, so I don't confuse them. Believe it or not, sometimes one dead body very much resembles another, especially when they start to pile up." The small coroner stopped suddenly, noticing the sheriff's look of shock. "That must seem very cold and callous. I'm sorry, Sheriff. It's just in this line of work you have to be able to have some self-detachment... but never to the living!" He gave her a warm smile while shaking a fatherly finger.

"I suppose so," Lane admitted, liking the little coroner despite his quirkiness or because of it.

"To be honest, your case has been a breath of fresh air. It's not often a killer uses a wild animal as an alibi." He pulled the report and idly looked it over.

"I'm still not understanding what you mean by an animal giving the killer an alibi?" Lane twisted in her seat, facing the small man as he moved his poor dying plant into the sunlight.

"Well, in this particular instance, your killer killed

his victim in a place and in such a way as to attract wildlife... A black bear to be precise. The black bear being the only big enough animal on the island to consume the majority of the dead body's flesh. Other scavenger animals eventually would have cleaned up the remaining leftovers... foxes, weasels, bobcats. Critters like that."

The little man stopped briefly and stood in a lecture stance. He took a hold of his jacket lapel and continued, "Now, if Ranger Russell hadn't stumbled across the bear and thus discovered the body. We can assume, after a short period of time, there would have been nothing left in the woods but bones. Which after a few seasons, if undiscovered, would have been buried under pine cones and needles, moss, and dirt... Most certainly scattered across the forest floor, having been dragged off by the previously mentioned critters.

And if finally discovered in a skeletal state, any indication of death might well have been blamed on the animals, as all evidence left available would have been bite marks on the bones. So, in essence, if the killer's plan had worked as they had hoped. The black bear would have given them an alibi by being blamed for the murder instead of a human murderer, and the killer would never have had to give an alibi for himself... Because he never would have been suspected in the first place. Understand?"

"In a roundabout way... yes," Lane said, some-what still confused, but understanding the gist of what the coroner was saying.

"Good." He smiled cheerfully and gave the file cabinet door a good shove, banging it closed with a loud clang. "I'm afraid, though. This report won't tell you much more than we discussed a few days ago."

He tapped the report on Lane's shoulder, indi-cating for her to take it from his hand. She did and immediately began to flip through the pages.

"You're kidding?" she said, disappointed. "Nothing helpful to shrink the scope of suspects?"

"I'm afraid not. The fingernail clippings original-ly had promise, but as you'll see in the report, they didn't lead anywhere." The coroner put on his fluffy jacket and sat down behind his desk.

"Do you need to leave?" Lane asked, partially standing and closing the report.

"No, no. Sit. I'm just cold." He opened the Tupper-ware container again and pulled out another handful of cookies.

Lane scanned the report for a minute longer and then flipped it closed on her lap in frustration.

"I'll read the rest later," she said and then shook her head, declining an offered cookie. "What I would like to know is if there is anything you can tell me that you couldn't say in the report?"

"Unofficially?" he asked, wiping cookie crumbs

from the corner of his mouth.

"Any guesses? Hypothesis?" Lane curiously wondered how the small coroner stayed so thin, having such a ravenous sweet tooth to contend with.

"If you and I are speaking completely hypothetically, then I would say your killer has killed before."

"Serial killer?" Lane's heart sped up. The idea petrified her.

"No, I wouldn't venture to that degree. But I don't think this is their first murder. Unless they've taken great pains to think everything out. There were no obvious missteps or mistakes. It's just their poor luck that their black bear alibi didn't pan out."

The coroner popped another cookie in his mouth and said, between bites, "Tell Mrs. Barnes, thank you again, when you go home tonight."

CHAPTER 37

"Sheriff... Lane, isn't it?" Jerry Holmes, his curled mustache hiding some of his smile, hopped onto the barstool next to hers at The Royal Fork. "Almost didn't recognize you out of uniform."

Dressed in the oversized Big Foot t-shirt and a pair of jeans, Lane swiveled on the barstool, giving him a brief once over. She suddenly smiled in recognition.

"Mr. Holmes, good evening."

"Call me, Jerry." His smile widened. "What you drinking? Looks... fruity." He waved for the bartender.

"Oh, this?" Lane picked up the glass so he could see it better. "I don't know its name. It was the bar special. It's not that good."

The bartender sauntered over, and Jerry ordered himself a beer.

"You, ah... you want a beer instead?" he offered.

Lane accepted, and Jerry told the bartender to bring a second one.

"I had plans to meet my daughter for dinner tonight. Unfortunately, she just texted to let me know she missed the ferry." He moved the peanut bowl closer, grabbing a small handful.

"Oh, that's too bad," Lane said casually, the bartender deftly removing the fruity drink and replacing it with a beer and a small napkin.

"What brings you here tonight? Meeting somebody?" Jerry popped the handful of peanuts into his mouth.

"The TV to be honest." She pointed at the small colored monitor hanging in the corner over the bar and seeing Jerry's confused expression, explained further, "I'm renting the small apartment over Hattie's General, and it doesn't have a TV."

"You're kidding."

Lane smiled and shook her head.

"I kid you not. No TV and no Wi-Fi."

"And you've lived to tell about it. Amazing," Jerry joked.

"It was a close call. I mean, if I hadn't caught the last five minutes of this infomercial, I would have been a goner for sure."

He looked up at the TV.

"You'll forever be in debt to..." He squinted, making a face. "What are they selling?"

On the small bar TV, a man was demonstrating the many uses for some type of adhesive in a can.

"I don't know. But I can double my savings if I buy in the next two minutes."

Lane playfully reached for her phone and Jerry laughed, suddenly asking, "You hungry?"

She peered at the screen, pausing to consider.

"A little."

"Want to get a table? You can keep me company since my daughter can't make it." He signaled the bartender, indicating they were moving before she could answer.

"Alright." Lane picked up her beer, and Jerry led them to a table close to the wall, pulling out a chair. "Mind if I ask you to trade me places?" she asked, eyeing the other seat.

"Want your back to the wall, so you can face the door, don't you?" Jerry smiled, pulling the requested chair and offering it to her.

"Sorry, it's a law enforcement thing."

"No, no, I totally understand. My brother, he's State Patrol."

"Not Mike Holmes?" Lane asked, surprised.

"Yeah, that's him. The ugly lug." Jerry handed Lane one of the two menus sitting on the table tucked between the salt and pepper shakers.

"Mike is a good guy. We've been to the same conference a few times." Lane browsed the menu. "You know how they make people sit together in focus groups? Well, he's been stuck with me twice."

"I'm sure he didn't complain."

"I wouldn't be so sure about THAT," Lane said, seriously. "So, did you and Mike grow up on the island?"

Jerry shook his head as he put the menu down.

"No, grew up in North Bend."

"Oh, then what brought you here? Your veterinary practice?" Lane looked up as their waitress, an older lady, asked for their order. Jerry chose pork chops, Lane opted for the salmon.

"Actually, my ex-wife. She was born and raised here. When we met in college, I followed her to the island and set up my practice. And then she divorced me, tried to take all my money, almost alienated my kid, and suddenly moved herself to Seattle." He took a deep breath. "But I'm not bitter," Jerry's voice dripped with sarcasm.

"Oh! No, not at all. I can tell you harbor absolutely no ill feelings," Lane teased back. "Sorry to hear it, though."

"It's all good. Got a beautiful, if not, sometimes difficult daughter out of the deal and I love living here. I enjoy the wilderness, like the people, and I get to do what I love. Work with animals."

"And occasionally tranquilize black bears?" Lane took a sip of her beer, a small smile hidden behind the bottle.

"And tranquilize black bears, yes," Jerry admitted, with a light chuckle. "That reminds me. When do I get my boots back?" He suddenly leaned into the table with a confidential manner. "Hope they didn't smell too bad."

"I still have to crack the windows in my patrol truck," Lane confessed, not sounding pleased. "I actually have them in my truck. Just got them back today. I was going to give them to Ranger Russell, so I'm glad you said something."

"How's the investigation going, if I'm allowed to ask?" He kept his voice low, the waitress having arrived with their plates.

After both saying thank you and declaring they didn't need anything else, Lane answered, "Not as quickly as I was hoping. I mean there's progress, but no concrete answers yet."

"I hope you don't mind me asking. I've been thinking a lot about it. I wondered if you'd come up with anything on the bowie knife yet?" Jerry cut his pork chop into a series of manageable bites.

"Why?" Lane didn't volunteer any information. "What about it?"

"I don't know if Phil mentioned it, but knives are kind of my hobby. I collect them. The bowie knife we found... I think I've seen it before."

"Are you talking about in someone's house or

in a store? Part of your collection?" Lane suddenly became very serious, pausing the fork halfway to her mouth.

"No, nothing like that, and not in an outdoor shop either. I want to say it's a knife Sue Carter had in her antique shop."

"Like for sale?"

"Well, it was in a display case by the register. I noticed it because it seemed odd it was there. I mean, the knife on display was newer. There was nothing antique about it."

"You didn't ask Mrs. Carter about it?"

Jerry guffawed. "You haven't heard about Cougar Carter yet, have you?" He reached for the salt shaker, taking note of Lane's expression. "Listen, if you are an able-bodied, single man on this island, and you don't want to be devoured, you hide or run when you see Sue." Jerry salted his baked potato.

"Then why were you in her store?" Lane cocked her head and raised her eyebrows playfully.

"I was dropping off her Pekinese. Better I deliver then get cornered in my office," he said, half-joking and half-serious.

"Guess I'll just have to go antiquing tomorrow and see if a bowie knife is still there."

"Is it terrible to say I hope it's not?" Jerry confided.

"No. I feel the same way." Lane admitted, wearily. "It would definitely be a break in the case if she could tell us who bought it."

"You, uh, you want to talk about something else?" Jerry offered. He noticed the more they talked about the murder, the less Lane smiled, and Jerry suddenly realized he liked her smile. He twisted the end of his mustache, his grin widening.

"Fine by me!" Lane was having a good time and thoroughly enjoying the company. It was a nice change of pace. "What do you want to talk about now?" She took a sip of beer and smiled prettily at Jerry.

"Let's see... got any pets?"

CHAPTER 38

"That... was the BEST meatloaf I've ever had in my WHOLE entire life." Philip announced, leaning back in his chair and placing both hands on his full belly.

"I'm glad you liked it." Bert smiled and motioned for him to hand her his empty plate.

"No, I mean it. That was delicious."

"I'll wrap some up for you and you can take it for lunch tomorrow." Bert put the dishes in the sink and turned on the tap water, rinsing the plates.

"Why don't you leave those and let me do them?" Philip got up from the table and covered his mouth with his fist, a small burp escaping.

"No, I've got it. Sit back down. I'll bring you another beer." Bert waved at him, tiny soap suds flying from her fingertips.

"You know, you're spoiling me, don't you?"

Philip sunk into his chair and looked over at where Shelby normally sat. "Shelby in her room?"

"No. I ungrounded her a day early. She's over at a friend's house. She'll be cruising the island for the majority of the night."

"She's feeling better then?"

"Well, I wanted to talk to you about that." Bert shut the water off and placed the two rinsed dishes into the dishwasher. "The talk Sheriff Lane had with her? She didn't ask her one thing about the girls on her squad."

"No?" Phil played dumb and hoped he wasn't blushing from shame.

"No." Bert shut the dishwasher door with a bit of a slam. "All of her questions were about Tim." She made her way to the dinner table and sat down, looking suddenly exhausted.

"Maybe she was working up to it? Trying to gain Shelby's trust?" Philip offered, knowing full well that wasn't the case. Lane's aim had always been to find out about Tim.

"I think she was just being nosy." Bert stood back up and walked over to the fridge, taking out two beers.

"Possibly." Philip thought it was better to agree than to defend the other woman.

"But if she wanted to know so badly, I wish she would have asked me... or even you! Not my kid."

"Have you heard from him?" Philip was suddenly curious.

"Honestly? After you came into the shop saying you'd found a dead body in the park and I jumped to the conclusion it was Tim? I called his parents to see if they had heard from him."

"And?" Philip took both beers and unscrewed the tops.

"They told me he's living in Olympia. Shacked up with some girl twenty years younger than him and living the high life off our savings," Bert's voice broke, and a tear streaked her cheek. Philip got up from the table and gathered her into his arms.

"I'm so sorry."

"It's not that I still love him." She looked up at him earnestly. "Because I don't... I haven't for a while now. It's... it's just, we had built a life together. We had a child, a home, a business, and he's thrown all of it away for... for a girl barely older than Shelby." Bert roughly wiped her tears away and pulled back. "I'm okay, had a weak moment. It's passed."

"I get it." Philip quickly sat in the chair next to Bert and kept a hold of her hand.

"Can we keep this between us, Phil... I mean, really JUST between us? I'd hate for Shelby to find out, and well, no offense to Sheriff Lane, but I don't think she would keep that quiet."

Philip nodded, cringing inside, knowing he'd just made a promise he wouldn't really be able to keep.

This was information important to the investigation...
or at least to his theory, and he'd have to tell Lane. He
still regarded Tim coming back to the island to kill
Stacy as a plausible solution.

"Do you think he'll ever come back? I mean... to
at least see Shelby and be a part of her life?"

"Ohhhh, I hope not." Bert shook her head sadly.
"Though I know Shelby would love him too."

"Does she know? You know, that he's so close?"
Philip asked, though he already knew the answer
from Lane.

"She thinks he's traveling for his photography."

Philip suddenly took a deep breath and blurted
out what he was thinking, "Bert, was Tim having an
affair with Stacy?"

"No!" she answered, aghast, her head rocking
back, shocked at the allegation. "Not at all! At least...
I don't think so? What kind of question is that?"

Philip, taking Shelby's approach, shrugged his
shoulders and mumbled, "I don't know. I just wondered... is... all," his voice rumbled into silence.

Bert peered at him silently, as if she was trying
to read his thoughts, and then suddenly got up from
the table.

"Ya know, I'm feeling one of my migraines coming on. I think I'm gonna go lie down. Can you let
yourself out?"

Philip quickly stood and let go of Bert's hand,

but not before giving it a light squeeze.

"Uh, sure. I'm sorry you're not feeling well. I can lock up behind me."

"And take some leftover meatloaf with you," she offered as she waved towards the refrigerator, heading down the hallway to her bedroom, leaving Philip in the kitchen, feeling like a complete heel.

CHAPTER 39

"Hey, you back yet?" Philip's voice crackled over Lane's cell phone, the reception lousy in the upstairs apartment.

"Yeah, got in like twenty minutes ago!" she yelled into the phone, hearing her own voice crackling back.

"Good. I'm outside," Philip said, followed by a knock at the apartment door.

Lane punched END on her cell and yelled, "Just a sec," as she walked over and pulled aside the yellow curtain. She found Philip standing on the small landing, and quickly unlocked the door. With some minor difficulty, she managed to yank it open. "Come on in."

"Sorry to stop by so late, but I was in the neighborhood, and... YOU look different!" Philip stopped dead in his tracks and stared.

Lane was in a t-shirt with jeans and barefoot, her long hair loose, flowing down over her shoulders.

"It's because I'm out of uniform," she said shyly, waving for him to shut the door.

"Like the T-shirt. Hide and Seek champion. That's funny," was all he said further and then took a seat on her bed with a heavy bounce.

"Thanks." Lane started twisting her hair into its customary bun. "You, okay?"

"Not really. I upset Bert tonight."

"What happened?" Lane headed for the fridge. "Want a soda?"

"Yes, please." Philip grabbed the book laying on her bedside table and read the title aloud, "Forensic Investigations: Killers Caught." He flipped it over, browsing the back text, adding sarcastically, "I bet this is great reading right before bed."

He lightly tossed the book back onto the nightstand.

"Actually, it is. Here." She handed him a Coke and then sat down herself. "So, tell me, how did you upset Roberta?"

"I flat out asked her if Tim was having an affair with Stacy." Philip took a sip and shook his head, clearly upset with himself.

"And? What did she say?" Lane asked, her eyes instantly roaming the room, searching for her leather notepad.

"Off the record for once, Lane, okay?" He stood up and began to pace. "She emphatically denied it and then basically kicked me out."

"Why would that upset her so much?"

"Well, it didn't help that she had found out you didn't ask Shelby any questions about the squad."

"Did you tell her we got interrupted before I could? That's what I would've said."

"Something to that effect. She thinks you're being nosy."

Lane's mouth dropped open. "I am not being NOSY! I'm not a nosy kind of person! Nosy? Did she say that? Really... I'm simply following a line of inquiry and—"

Philip looked at Lane as if she was nuts.

"I know that! It's Bert, who doesn't."

"Yeah, I guess so, huh."

"I found out Tim is living in Olympia," he continued blandly, pacing closer to the bed.

"How?" She perked up, her eyes wide at the news.

"After Bert thought it was Tim I found in the park, she called his parents. Apparently, he's hooked up with a twenty-year-old girl over there."

"Reeeaaaally..." Lane ignored Philip's previous request and got up, searching for her notepad.

"Which makes me wonder if I am right. He might very well have taken the ferry to the island, arranged to meet Stacy, and well... you know the rest of the story." Philip sat back down on the bed again. "Oh, and she asked me not to tell you, so..."

"Why?" Lane found the leather-bound pad in her uniform pants pocket, hanging in the closet.

"She doesn't want Shelby to know he's so close."

"I don't think that's fair to Shelby. If I were Roberta, I'd—"

Philip interrupted, "Lane, I know. You'd do things differently, but it's her kid, so we've just got to respect her wishes as much as we can."

"Okay, okay. Keeping my opinions to myself." Lane put her hands up in surrender. "Back to the soon-to-be ex-husband. What's his parent's names?"

"Um, I believe it's Ben and Ethel Esten?"

Lane wrote the names down.

"I've got a friend with the Olympia Police. I could ask him to look up Tim, see if he's got an alibi? I'll call OPD first thing in the morning."

"Thanks. That would put my mind at ease. I'd hate to think Bert and Shelby might be in some kind of danger."

"No problem." Lane flipped a few pages back on her pad. "Wanna know what I found out this afternoon?"

"I'm all ears."

"They were able to get some DNA from underneath Stacy's fingernails and ran it through CODIS. No hits yet. Which means whoever she scratched most likely hasn't been in trouble before."

"That's discouraging. So, it could be someone who's never killed before?" Philip's brow wrinkled at the idea.

"Or who's never been caught."

"That's even more so. Anything else?"

"They didn't find any hair samples besides the victims. Also, no fabric samples, carpet threads, or fingerprints. But then again... Even if they did, she was so dirty and mangled, they probably wouldn't have helped much. The bowie knife had been either wiped clean or the perp wore gloves."

"Anything on the laptop?"

Lane's shoulder sank. "Clean as a whistle. No dating sites, no strange internet searches, no weird emails. She apparently used it for cheer and church stuff only."

"Back to the drawing board then, I guess." He let out an exasperated groan and dropped his hands into his lap. "Man, I feel like we're just not getting anywhere!"

"I wouldn't say that. We've discovered Stacy has made some bad decisions and might have an enemy or two. Which lessens the chance of this being a 'no motive' murder. We've also been able to reasonably zero in on a few people who may have had a reason to do her harm, and thus, limit our suspect pool from everyone to a few key people."

"That reminds me. You can scratch Edgar Rowles

off your list. Sue really did have two flat tires. Though I would still bet money, she flattened the second tire on her own."

"So, Sue was able to confirm the time he had in the log?" Lane flipped a few more pages back.

"Well, I didn't actually talk to her directly. She left for Europe today." Philip picked up the forensic book again and started to flip through the pages aimlessly. "I talked to Ricardo. He runs the place for her when she's out of town. He told me she had been late on Monday for a meeting with a prospective customer because she had two flat tires. I asked him the time, and it matched up with what Edgar had in the log."

"Crud," Lane said and crossed Edgar's name off the self-made suspect list. Unbeknownst to Philip, she still had Harry, Pastor Jonas, Kody, Tim, and Unknown written down.

"Speaking of Sue's antique shop. When you were there, did you happen to notice a bowie knife in the glass case by the register?"

"That's an awfully specific location, and no, I didn't."

"Didn't see it or didn't notice it?" Lane asked, a tinge of excitement in her voice.

"Didn't notice it. Sorry."

"Oh, that's all right. We'll have to check it out tomorrow then." She added "Antique Shop" to her "To-Do list" for the next day.

"Where did you get that lead?" Philip finished the Coke and placed the empty can on top of the book on the nightstand.

"From your buddy Jerry. Oh, wait! I've got your boots!" Lane jumped up from her chair and went over to the small bathroom, opening the door. "I had to quarantine them, but here you go." She returned, holding a brown paper bag, it containing Philip's work boots.

"Thanks. If you've got Jerry's, I can drop them off."

"I already gave them to him." Lane closed the bathroom door but not before spraying a spritz of air freshener into the tiny room.

"You did? At his office?" Philip asked, surprised.

"No. Tonight at dinner."

"Hold up. You had dinner with Jerry? Is he like on your list of suspects or something? You keeping something back from me, Lane?" Philip accused, slitting his eyes in suspicion.

"I checked out his alibi the day he gave me his statement. When he was with us at the crime scene? He's cleared."

"Annddd?" Philip motioned for her to continue.

"Well, we bumped into each other at The Royal Fork. He invited me to sit with him and have dinner, so I did. He asked me how the investigation was going, which I didn't divulge anything, and that's when he mentioned he thought he may have seen the murder weapon at the antique shop. It apparently caught his eye because it wasn't an antique. That's it." Lane ended in a rush, patting her bun to make sure it was still in place.

"You had a date." Philip smiled slyly.

"It was NOT a date." Lane stiffened.

"Did he buy you a drink?"

"Yes."

"More than one?"

"It was only two beers," Lane said, somewhat defensively.

"Did he pull out your chair?"

"As any good gentleman would. That doesn't mean it was a date."

"Hmm, hmmm. Did he pay for dinner?" Philip smiled knowingly.

"It wasn't a date."

"It was a date." Philip stood up.

"It wasn't," Lane muttered under her breath and then said loudly, "I'm not having this conversation with you. Good night, Ranger." She started to usher him to the door.

"See ya tomorrow?" Philip called over his shoulder, Lane's hand firmly in the middle of his back, pushing him towards the exit.

"Bright and early," she directed. "And bring coffee."

Her smile widened as she shut the door in Philip's smug face.

CHAPTER 40

Lane blinked at the morning sunshine as she stepped out onto the small porch landing, looking intently at the signal strength on her cell phone. It was a measly two bars which sadly was better than the one bar she barely got inside.

Realizing this was probably as good as she was gonna get, unless she wanted to climb up on the roof, Lane dialed the memorized phone number and propped herself up against the porch railing.

"It's not the Ritz, that's for sure," she said to herself, taking in the grand view of the deserted and dirty alleyway below. "I need to find a new place."

"Olympia PD. Lane speaking." A male's deep voice rumbled over the line, almost over powered by loud yelling in the background.

"Hey! Ya, busy?" she asked, with familiarity.

"Hay is for horses."

"Yea, THAT never gets old," Lane said, sarcastically.

"Nah, I'm not busy. Just a sec." She could hear the mouthpiece being covered and a faint voice in the background yelling something to the effect of, "Keep it down, I'm on the phone!"

"Sorry about that. What's up, baby sister?" Narcotics Officer Kent Lane rolled his chair up to his desk and grabbed a pen from his shirt pocket.

"Need a small favor. I'm investigating a homicide and there's a possible suspect who lives in your city. Was wondering if you could track him down and see what his alibi is for last Monday? Between 3 p.m. and 4 p.m." Lane quickly added, "Pretty please."

"Sure thing, kiddo. What's the guy's name?"

Lane sighed. "Please don't call me kiddo. I'm thirty-five years old, for goodness sakes."

"Yeah, but you'll ALWAYS be my kid sister, kid-doooo." Kent smiled mischievously, knowing he was getting a rile out of her. Ribbing his kid sister was one of his most favorite things to do.

Ignoring him, she said, "His name is Tim Esten. E.S.T.E.N. N as in Nancy. Roughly forty-one years of age. Six-foot, brown hair, brown eyes, Caucasian. He's supposedly been in contact with his parents, a Benjamin and Ethel Esten, who live there as well. Sorry, don't have an address. The soon-to-be ex-wife here on the island claims she hasn't seen him in roughly six months. She also stated her husband had cleaned out their shared banking accounts before running off on her. Apparently, he's now living with a twenty-year-old in your neck of the woods."

"Got it. Who'd he maybe kill?" Kent asked, writing everything down.

"A twenty-two-year-old girl he was sleeping with here locally. A woman by the name of Stacy Jensen."

"Likes 'em young, doesn't he? I'll hop on it, as soon as I can," he promised.

"The sooner the better."

"Tell ya what." Kent waved to his partner, who had arrived at his desk with two cups of coffee in hand. "Why don't you come over to dinner this Sunday and tell me all about it? Mindy's making some fancy Indian dish from her cooking class." He nodded his thanks for the coffee, and then leaned back in his chair, lightly tossing the pen onto his desk. "Kids would love to see you."

"I think I can make that happen. You guys still have dinner at six?"

"On the dot." He took a tentative sip of his hot coffee and then remembered. "You know Jimmy is in Seattle, right? He told you he was coming this week, didn't he?"

Jimmy was their second oldest brother, an FBI agent based in Idaho.

"No!" Lane said, with irritation. "What brings him

to Seattle?"

Her brothers, as a general rule, were always expecting the other sibling to tell her what they were up to and so, no one typically told her anything at all.

"He's giving a lecture at the University on his serial killer case. He's leaving on Wednesday."

"Well, shoot. I would've liked to have seen him," Lane said, sadly.

"You know whaaaaat?" Kent sat up, a sudden idea striking him.

"Chicken butt!" Lane said, as quickly as she could, snorting a laugh.

"Ha. Ha. I'll just make him come to dinner on Sunday."

"Oh, do! Twist his arm if you have to!" Lane stifled a yawn and looked at her watch. "Any word on little bro Alex?"

"Yeah, on my birthday. I got a text saying he was overseas but couldn't tell me much more. You know, top secret stuff."

"I worry about that kid," Lane said, wistfully.

"Don't," Kent admonished. "He's a big boy, and they don't let just anybody be a Navy Seal."

Alex was the "oops baby," nineteen years younger than the rest of his siblings, and by far the wildest and crazy of the bunch. Having caused their father a lot of stress and hair pulling in his teens, the old man had suggested Alex join the military, where the kid flourished. Now he was off seeing the world and doing dangerous, top-secret stuff like Kent had said.

Lane stuck her tongue out at the phone, making a face. She'd worry about him if she wanted to.

"I talked to dad about two weeks ago. He said Clark is actually thinking about going into politics! Can you believe that?" Lane's tone of voice said she couldn't. It was already difficult enough coming from a family where every sibling was well connected in some form of law enforcement or high military standing... and now, she might have a brother move into politics! Lane figured she'd never be able to keep up.

"So, our General wants to be a congressman?"

"That's what Dad says..." Lane yawned again.

"What else did the old man talk about?" The brothers didn't call home as often as they should. But then, Lane only managed to call their father once a month. She was no one to judge.

"He's hating retired life. Doesn't know what to do with himself."

"Uhhh, uhhh," Kent said, with distraction. His partner, standing at the desk across the way from him, had answered its ringing phone and was suddenly motioning the need for a pen to write with. Kent leaned over and quickly tossed him the one off his desk. "But not enough to ever leave Montana," Kent added and then strained to see what his partner was writing down.

"I need to get back there for a visit," Lane said, feeling guilty. "Maybe we can all surprise him for Christmas or something?"

"Hey, kiddo. I gotta cut this short." By the sound of Kent's voice, something important had come up and was requiring his full attention.

"Hay is for horses. Be safe." She ended the phone call with her brother and looked back down at the deserted alley, stifling yet another yawn. Bored with inactivity, Lane figured there wasn't much more she could do with the rest of her morning but wait for Philip to show up with coffee.

CHAPTER 41

The antique shop wasn't at all like Lane had imagined. At least, not in the inside. The outside had an almost New England Cape Cod appeal, its shingled roof, and dark blue window shutters standing out against the white painted wood siding. In large scroll, the word ANTIQUES was painted in bold black letters above a bright red door with a welcome mat at its base. The shop looked clean, crisp, and welcoming with large flower pots lining the sidewalk.

Upon entering the store, Lane was shocked at the amount of... what was to her inexperienced eyes... a whole bunch of junk. The junk, she imaged, was most likely a treasure trove to those who knew better. It clearly wasn't her.

The clutter, for that's what Lane thought of it as,

was wall to wall with hardly any place to sit... or stand for that matter. Scarcely discernible was a small path carving its way through the untidy mass of antiques to the back of the store. There, one could barely make out a large glass case. The glass case itself, apparently showcasing the finer things to be offered.

A little further beyond that was an open doorway covered with a cascading curtain of beads from the 60s. The store, for all of its contents, seemed deserted.

"This place looks more like a swap meet or flea market," Lane whispered out of the side of her mouth.

"The locals treat the place like it, that's for sure. They're always leaving boxes of junk behind the store. Sue just turns around and sells it to someone else. It's like a large yard sale but with fancy expensive old stuff tossed in the mix," Philip whispered back, glancing around to see if there was anyone they could talk with.

Not spotting a soul, Philip and Lane carefully made their way through the cleared path, making sure to keep their arms close to their sides as to not knock anything over. As the two got closer, they realized someone was sitting behind the glass case, propped up on a stool reading a book.

"Hi! Ricardo around?" Philip asked the pretty, red-headed teenager.

"He doesn't work weekends," the girl replied monotone, her eyes glued to the book laying open on her lap.

"Well... maybe you could help me?" Philip suggested politely, almost knocking over a hurricane lamp with his elbow.

"Probably not," the redhead answered blandly, her eyes still glued to the book.

"Why's that?" Philip asked, surprised at her answer.

"Abby knows all the history stuff, and she's in the back," the girl answered, and then suddenly hollered, "ABBY!"

The three waited for Abby to make an appearance, and when after several minutes, she didn't, Philip rapped on the glass case, trying to garner the girl's attention. She still hadn't bothered to look up from her reading.

Lane put a warning hand on Philip's arm as she stepped around from behind. She could tell he was about to lose his temper and wondered if he'd gotten any sleep the night before.

"Hi Bridget, Remember me? I met you at cheer practice?" Lane smiled as the girl slowly looked up at the mention of her name.

Seeing the sheriff, she gave a huff of recognition and yelled, "Never mind, Abby!" towards the back-room and slammed her heavy book shut. "You want to buy something?" she asked, obviously put out.

"Oh, not really. We're just browsing at the moment," Lane answered lightly, looking casually into the glass case. There were no knives on display. "This your after-school job, Bridget?"

"I just work the weekends," the young redhead sighed, watching Sheriff Lane examine the glass case. "Now that I'm eighteen and graduate this year, I'll find a job over on the mainland come this summer. I won't have to stay in this dump."

Lane pretended to listen and continued to peruse the glass counter, Philip having decided to wander off to cool his temper. He found an antique chair and gingerly sat down to wait.

"Did you want to look at something closer, Sheriff? I noticed you eyeing the beaded coin purses," Bridget offered, being helpful and at the same time, sounding completely bored. "They're authentic Pacific Northwest Native American. At least, that's what Abby says."

"Actually, what I was looking for doesn't seem to be here. But maybe you can tell me who bought it?" Lane pulled out her notepad and used her "official" voice as she continued, "There was a large bowie knife in this case. Elkhorn handle, with black stri—," Lane stopped. Bridget had taken a sudden step back and was looking extremely nervous. "Know anything about it?"

Bridget shook her head no, now avoiding eye contact, and busied herself with trying to find her place in the book, clumsily sitting back on the stool.

"Nope."

"Okay? Maybe I'll have Abby come out, and I'll ask her?" Lane moved to walk around the glass case, heading towards the beaded curtain doorway behind the girl.

"No, don't!"

"Oh, you suddenly remember something?" Lane asked, a cocky grin springing to her lips. She signaled Philip to make his way over.

"How much trouble am I in?" Bridget asked, tartly.

"I don't know. Depends on what you did?" Lane answered cautiously. "Do you know what happened to the knife?"

"She knows who bought it?" Philip asked eagerly, joining them.

"No one bought it. I took it," Bridget confessed, sharply, and then quickly added, "Please don't tell Sue or Ricardo." She lowered her voice, obviously not wanting Abby in the back to hear. "It's the first time in my life I've ever stolen anything."

Neither Lane nor Philip believed that for a second.

"What did you take it for?" Philip narrowly missed the hurricane lamp again.

The girl shrugged her shoulders defiantly, and when Lane nodded for Philip to get Abby, she quickly answered, "I took it for a friend."

"Who's your friend, Bridget?" Lane kept her hand on Philip's arm, threatening with one light shove, to send him to the backroom to find Abby.

"I'm not a tattletale." Bridget hardened her resolve. "I can get it back. Nobody has to know." She looked between the two of them, chocked-full of attitude.

"Bridget, listen. It's very important we know who you gave the knife to. I'm willing to look past your bad decision making if you help us out here. Being you are eighteen, as you mentioned earlier, I am within my full rights to bring you in for shoplifting. Unless you want to give me a name. If not... and you're not willing to be co-operative... Well, then my hands are tied." Lane reached for her handcuffs.

Philip knew it was a bluff, or at least, he thought he knew it was a bluff.

"But I can get it back!" Bridget's eyes widened as Lane clicked one of the cuffs open.

"I need a name, Bridget." Lane moved towards the girl.

"It was for Shelby Esten!" Bridget folded, not holding up to the threat of being arrested.

"Shelby!" Philip knocked the hurricane lamp over in his shock, managing to grab it before it came crashing down to the sales floor.

"Why would Shelby need the knife, Bridget?" Lane pushed, not wanting the girl to shut down.

"For protection. You know her Dad's gone, right?" She clearly didn't think they did.

"Yes, your point being?" Bridget's snarky attitude

was grating on Lane's nerves.

"Well, it's just her and her mom at home now, and she doesn't feel safe with him not being there. We're not old enough to buy a gun, so she figured a knife would do just as good."

"You sure? She's not worried a particular person is going to hurt her? She's not in any kind of danger? If she is, you've got to tell us, Bridget," Lane insisted, concern clearly written on her face.

"No, nothing like that. Honest," Bridget promised, losing all her bravado. "It's just for if a burglar broke into the house. She keeps it under her pillow."

"When did you give the knife to Shelby? How long ago was this?" Philip simply held the hurricane lamp against his chest.

"Two weeks ago, maybe? Nobody, but you guys, have even noticed it's missing." She looked down at Lane's handcuffs, still held in her hand. "You still going to arrest me?"

Sheriff Lane and Philip exchanged a look, both wanting nothing more than to snap the sassy young teenager off the stool and give her a good scare.

Instead, Lane said in her best "good cop" voice, "No, I don't think so. No harm done. Just don't steal anything else... AND don't do any more favors for friends, okay?"

CHAPTER 42

"Lane, I have to tell Bert that Shelby has gotten a hold of a knife... even if the kid is only keeping it stashed under her pillow," Philip pleaded as Lane drove, the antique shop in her rearview mirror. "I can't, not tell her."

"I understand your concern, Phil. But it might not be under her pillow anymore. It might be in an evidence bag in the forensic lab," Lane argued with his reasoning.

"That's ridiculous!"

"Why? Because you know her?" Lane asked, an edge to her voice.

"YES!... And the fact she's a sixteen-year-old kid." Philip tried to jerk the seat belt on, but it flew loose from his hand, smacking hard against the door.

"Hey! Watch the truck," Lane gave him a scalding look.

"Sorry," he mumbled, irritated.

Lane rolled her eyes in frustration and pulled off to the side of the road, stopping the vehicle abruptly.

"Listen, whether we like it or not, and whether we are comfortable with it, Shelby has a motive."

"You honestly think she killed Stacy because Shelby found out the cheer coach was sleeping with her dad, and maybe that's why he left her mom?" Philip parroted, refusing to confess he had come to the same conclusion.

"I do, yes." Lane paused for a minute, letting it sink in. "And I fully realize this puts you in a bit of a predicament. So, if you want to walk away from the investigation, I would completely understand." Lane looked straight ahead, over the steering wheel, her face pensive.

"Walk away?" Philip turned and stared at her, a mixture of confusion and anger flickering across his face. "You think I should walk away?" he repeated, indignant.

"That's not what I said. I said IF you WANTED to. I'm not ASKING you to, Phil. I need your help still." She banged the steering wheel in frustration. "Phil, I'm not going to make you do something or say something you can't bring yourself to do. I get it." She looked over at him, her lips a grim line on her face.

Seeing he was still conflicted, she continued, "You're in a tough spot. You've grown close to Shelby and obviously, have deep feelings for her mother, which might cloud your judgment a little. But most importantly...," Lane softened her tone. "If things don't go right, it could really affect your relationship with both of them. I mean, last night you were upset because Roberta took offense to a simple question. What do you think she's going to do if you go in there, and we accuse her daughter of murder?" Lane paused, putting her hand gently on his shoulder. "Let me be the bad guy. If I'm wrong, then you won't take any of the fallout from it."

Philip sat quietly for a second and then said, "You may be right. My judgment might be a little... clouded when it comes to them. But I want to see this through, and well, if we're wrong, then I'll just do my best to get Bert to forgive me. If we're right, then you're going to need me on the inside." Philip put his hand on Lane's shoulder so their arms crossed. "We started this together, and we'll see it to the end together. Deal?"

"Deal." Lane dropped her arm and let out a relieved sigh. "So, how do you want to handle this then?" she asked, glancing over her left shoulder, checking to see if traffic was clear. She waited for a passing car and then pulled out.

"Well, if you don't want to go in with guns blazing and clap the cuffs on her at first sight?" Philip said sarcastically. Lane snorted in disgust.

"It was a bluff," she confessed, referring to her and Bridget's little stand-off.

"I could get myself invited over to the house and do some snooping? If I find the bowie knife, then we tell Bert."

"Think you can find out if Shelby has an alibi for Monday, as well? I mean, without Roberta getting suspicious?" Lane assumed he wouldn't find the weapon.

"I'd have a better chance at it than you would."

"Won't argue with you there," Lane agreed and nodded to his cell phone. "Give her a call."

CHAPTER 43

"Hey, I called to see how your head is feeling? Any better?" Philip asked over the phone, trying to sound as natural as he could with Lane eavesdropping.

"I'm still a little light-sensitive," Bert answered, not sounding as if she was still agitated. "I've got Ernie watching the store for me today."

"Ahhh, Bert. I am so sorry I upset you last night with my stupid question." Philip truly sounded sorry.

"It's okay. I know you didn't mean anything by it, and to be honest, I should have known a migraine was coming on from all the stress this week. It wasn't really your fault."

"Can I bring you anything? Chicken Soup? Aspirin? Sheriff Lane's head on a platter?" Philip teased, eliciting a giggle from Bert and a swat on the arm from Lane, who was sitting next to him in the truck.

"No, I'm okay. But you could just come see me, to see me."

"Really? You up for a visit?"

"For a little while at least. I'll probably need to lay back down soon, but I wouldn't mind a big hug from my guy."

"You're in luck, I deliver hugs. Be there in a few minutes," Philip said suavely and hung up.

Lane snorted and said under her breath, "You're in luck, I deliver hugs. Oh, boy."

"Ah, shut up and drive."

CHAPTER 44

Philip gave Bert's cabin door a light knock and waited for her to answer. He noted Shelby's car wasn't parked upfront, which was usually the case, and counted it as a good thing. He wouldn't be able to snoop much if the girl was home. Of course, she might come back any minute, meaning whatever sneaking around he was going to do, he'd need to do quickly.

Bert came to the door, looking a little worse for wear, and swung the door open. She gave him a weak smile and then peered behind him as if she was expecting to see someone in tow.

"No shadow today," Philip reassured and leaned in, giving her a light peck on the lips.

Convinced it would be best if Bert didn't see the petite sheriff, Philip had made Lane drop him off about a half-mile down the road where she was waiting for him, probably scribbling in her leather notepad and wondering what was taking him so long.

"Come on in." Bert stepped back and let Philip enter.

Even though it was almost one in the afternoon and a sunny day, the house was dark with all the lights off and the window draping closed.

"Wow, I should have brought a flashlight," Philip joked, making his way into the living room practically by feel.

"Yeah, sorry about this. Light makes my migraine worse." Bert put her hand to her forehead and smiled, Philip taking this as a cue to wrap his arms around her, and give her a long, but gentle squeeze.

"You look zonked," he said, in a practical whisper.

"I am. This migraine medicine just about knocks me out, but it's the only thing that will cut through the pain."

"Did Shelby ditch you?" Philip asked, without any rancor. "I noticed her car wasn't in the driveway." The house was also deathly quiet. The teenage girl was definitely not home.

"She gets bored because I won't let her watch TV or play her music unless she's wearing earphones." Bert stepped back from Philip and took a seat on the edge of the couch. "She decided to hang with her friends down at the deli instead of staying home and babysitting mom."

"Spending time with her friends is probably a good thing right now." Philip sat in the large recliner across from the couch. "Get her mind off of things."

"I don't know. I like keeping her close, especially since Tim is gone. You think I should let her out a bit more?"

"A little bit of rope probably wouldn't be a bad thing," Philip concurred. "Just don't give her enough to hang herself. Make sure she keeps her curfew."

Bert snickered at him playing dad and then frowned in pain.

"Sorry. Speaking of Shelby... Sheriff Lane meant to ask her what time cheer practice ended last Monday. I guess they got interrupted?"

Bert frowned further, this time in concentration. "Last Monday? There wasn't any cheer practice."

"There wasn't?" Philip acted as if he didn't already know.

"Yeah no, because I remember I came home early with a migraine and made Shelby stay in her room. She was still grounded."

"Bet she hated that," Philip said, with feeling.

"She wasn't too happy with me, no," Bert admitted, and then said in an apologetic tone, "I think I need to go rest again."

"No problem. Why don't you lay down on your bed? I can bring you a nice hot cup of tea and then

I'll lock up as I leave," Philip offered.

"I don't really feel like tea, but thank—," Bert started to say.

"I read tea is really good for migraine headaches because of the caffeine," Philip ignored her protest and stood up, heading towards the kitchen. "Also, you need to stay hydrated. Now, no arguing. I want my girl back to normal by tomorrow." Philip walked back over and kissed Bert gently on the forehead.

Bert shrugged her shoulders in resignation.

"All right, if you insist."

"I do. Now, go lay down. I'll get the water going and make sure to take it off the stove before the tea-pot whistles," he promised and then lightly pushed her towards the hallway where her bedroom sat at the end. "Now, get."

"I'm going, I'm going." Bert retreated from the room happily.

Philip watched her slowly walk down the hall-way and then busied himself, finding where Bert stashed her teabags. In no time the kettle was filled with water and placed on the cold burner. He then rummaged through her cupboards, locating a large mug which was then filled with water from the tap. He quickly plopped a tea bag in and left the mug sit-ting on the kitchen counter.

Philip cautiously took a step out of the kitchen, checking over his shoulder to make sure Bert wasn't watching him from the hallway or from her bedroom door, which was standing wide open. Seeing the coast was clear, he tiptoed past the small bathroom and then carefully opened Shelby's bedroom door.

Her room was fairly typical of a teenage girl. Everything pink and frilly, boy band posters taped to the walls, and almost every piece of clothing the girl owned piled on the floor.

Philip immediately made his way to the bed and lifted her pillow... no knife. He then reasoned maybe the girl kept it under her mattress. He decided it would be unwise to slide his arm between the mattresses, being he might come in contact with a large, sharp bowie knife. So, as quietly as he could, he lifted the top mattress. Still no knife. He then checked behind the headboard. Not there.

Philip then got on his hands and knees and looked under the bed. Negative. He walked over to her dresser, which amazingly enough still had clothes in it, and looked through the drawers. Nope, not there either. Next, he looked behind the dresser and the mirror attached to the top, to make sure the girl hadn't taped the knife to the back.

For a brief moment, he considered picking the clothes off the floor, then decided against it. It looked to be all chaos to him, but Shelby might realize her stuff had been moved and if Bert was to catch him in the act, he'd have no reasonable explanation to give for himself. Instead, he quietly opened her closet and took a quick look. There were several shoe boxes, most of them filled with either shoes or random pictures and birthday cards. No sharp and pointy objects there and no men's size twelve hiking boots either. It was a complete washout all the way around.

He had managed to make it back to the kitchen when Bert softly called out, asking what was taking so long. Philip quickly placed the mug full of water into the microwave, heating it and the teabag at the same time. Making sure to pop the door open seconds before the microwave's timer went off, he then bobbed the teabag a few times till the water turned a murky tan. He then added a squirt of honey and placed the mug on a tray, hustling his way down the hall to Bert's bedroom.

"You won't believe this! I forgot to turn the burner on!" he fibbed, placing the tray carefully on her lap. "Here you are, Bert. Hope you feel better. Get some rest, and I'll call you tomorrow."

Feeling guilty as hell, Philip quickly made for the front door.

CHAPTER 45

Lane had been sitting in her patrol truck, impatiently drumming her fingers on the steering wheel, when a sudden knock on her window startled her. She turned to see the smiling face of Pastor Jonas.

"Morning, Sheriff," The Pastor said cheerfully, after Lane rolled down the automatic window. "Sorry if I startled you. Was just out for a stroll and spotted you sitting here."

"Hello, Pastor Jonas. You didn't startle me." Lane, hating she was, in fact, startled and not particularly liking the pastor all that much to begin with, forced a fake smile on her face.

"Well, I saw you and thought this might be a good opportunity to give you a warm invite to church tomorrow." He smiled genuinely. "Especially since we sort of got off on the wrong foot. I hope Phil convinced you there was nothing inappropriate going on between Stacy and I."

Only stating the day before her desire to have another talk with the pastor, Lane nodded her head emphatically.

"Yes, he did. And... I want to apologize for my jumping to conclusions." Lane dug her nails into the steering wheel as she gave the friendly pastor false platitudes.

"Oh, it's all right. No harm done." He gave a forgiving smile and then lightly pounded on the door in a goodbye gesture as he started to walk away

"Though, I do have another question you might be able to help me with," Lane added quickly, seeing the pastor physically cringe before taking two steps back to her window.

"I'll try my best to help," he said, with a nervous smile.

"Were you trying your best when you told Ranger Russell you didn't know who Stacy was having an affair with? When in fact, you knew full well it was Tim Esten." Lane smiled. Her blue eyes didn't. "That could be considered impeding an active investigation, Pastor."

Pastor Adams gave a heavy sigh and hung his head. "I didn't know for sure is why I didn't say anything. Stacy never actually said it was Tim."

"But you still knew, didn't you?" Lane pressed.

"I'd caught the glances they'd give each other and noticed how Tim would linger after service or show up early. He had never shown any real interest in the church, and when I at first mistakenly took his actions as wanting to be more involved, Tim basically brushed me off. That's when I started to suspect... but never actually saw them together," the pastor clarified.

"And, when Stacy came to you with her problem, you didn't then tell her you knew or at least strongly suspected who the married man was?" Lane asked, surprised.

Pastor Jonas shook his head. "As a pastor, it's my job to lift people up and sure, to rebuke them when they're in the wrong. Stacy had come to me for advice, which told me she was already struggling with the decision in her heart. I didn't need to pile any additional shame on her with my accusations."

"Were you also aware Stacy faked a pregnancy and managed to extort money on false pretenses?" Lane asked sternly, expecting to see shock and denial on the pastor's face. She was surprisingly disappointed.

"Yes, I knew," he said, a quiet sadness in his tone.

"She tried it on you as well." Lane assumed flatly.

"No! Like I said. Stacy and I were nothing more than friends." Pastor Jonas looked earnestly at the small sheriff. "Truly, I love my wife, and I take my walk with God very seriously."

Lane found herself believing the pastor and maybe, even starting to like him a little. She paused in thought and guessed, "She told you herself?"

Pastor Jonas nodded. "Not willingly. We had just finished one of our meetings, and her purse had accidentally slipped off the pew, tumbling everything on the floor. I helped her gather the items and ended up being the one to pick up the positive pregnancy test. I questioned her on it, and not believing her initial denials she wasn't actually pregnant herself, she eventually confessed to the scheme." The pastor took a deep breath. "I, of course, admonished her and encouraged her to repay the money to the poor souls she deceived."

"Souls? She tried the scam more than once?" Lane asked, in disbelief.

"A couple of times, from what I gathered," Pastor Jonas admitted. "I was going to ask her who she lied to. Unfortunately, we got interrupted, and the subject never came up again."

"And you didn't share this information because?" Lane demanded with irritation.

The pastor was quiet for a minute.

"I had no names to give you and everything had happened half a year ago. I honestly didn't and still don't think it has anything to do with what happened to her now."

"What do you think did happen, Pastor?" Lane was curious, eager for his insight.

He peered up at the clouded sky and took a deep breath.

"I think a horrible person took a shining light. I'm assuming you never got to meet Stacy in the flesh. She... was... beautiful and light-hearted and joyful, with so much energy. She radiated happiness, and though I never fell to her charms, I wouldn't be much of a man if I didn't tell you, I was attracted to them." He looked back down and made eye contact with Lane. "People like bright and shiny things, Sheriff. Some people are content to look at them from a distance. Some people need to touch them and other people, snuff them out in their greed. That's what I think happened."

Lane sat quietly in thought, mulling over his explanation.

"Pastor, one more question," she said, not unkindly. "If you knew Stacy was extorting money from people and having an affair with one of the married men of your congregation, why did you allow her to continue to run the youth group?"

Lane was still baffled by it.

"It seems strange, I know," Pastor Jonas agreed. "Stacy, for all of her flaws, drew people to our small church. The kids really enjoyed her events, along with her energy, and positive disposition. They'd tell their friends, who would tell their friends, and so on. And she always stuck with the lessons I gave her, so I wasn't worried she was misleading the masses." Pastor Jonas chuckled lightly, his mouth turning up at the edges, saddened. "I always hoped she'd turn things around. If I'm being completely transparent and honest with myself, I have to admit, I tried to capitalize on her appeal to the youth to keep the program going."

Lane smiled at the pastor, appreciating his candor. "I can understand that. Anything else you can tell me?" she questioned earnestly, searching his face.

Pastor Jonas shook his head.

"I'm all confessed out. Hope to see you at church sometime." And with that, he strolled off, Lane watching him till he cut off into the woods, in the direction of the church.

A loud rap, this time on the passenger's window, made Lane jump in her seat and yell, "Dammit!"

Philip gave a "whoops" expression and opened the passenger door leaning his head in.

"Sorry. Didn't mean to scare you."

Not in the most forgiving of moods now, Lane snapped for him to get into the truck. Philip obeyed, and she started the vehicle, doing a large U-turn in the middle of the road.

"Well?" she asked, impatiently as Philip snapped on his seat belt.

"No luck. It looked like a bomb had gone off in the kid's room. I didn't find the knife."

"So, either it's not there or it is... and you didn't find it," Lane mused, greatly disappointed.

"She could have it on her?" Philip rationalized.

"Possibly. Though it would be a pretty good-sized bowie knife, and she carries a tiny purse AND wears her clothes tight enough you'd most likely see it on her."

"But I've got good news," Philip added, knowing neither of them wanted the girl involved. "She's got an alibi."

"Thank the Lord. Where was she?" Lane gushed, relieved.

"At home with Bert. She was grounded, and Bert had come home from the shop with a migraine trying to sleep it off. Kid was stuck in her room all night."

"That's not much of an alibi," Lane pointed out, not sounding pleased.

"Maybe. But it still counts. Takes the kid off the hook."

"Far from it!" Lane looked over at Philip and saw he wasn't following her train of thought. "Her alibi is her mother? And her mother was asleep in a separate room? Come on! How do we know Shelby didn't sneak out and Roberta just didn't know it?" Lane took her eyes off the road and shot Philip another quick look. "For all we know, Shelby called

Stacy asking her to come pick her up because she's grounded from her car. She sneaks out her bedroom window and off to the park they go." Lane shook her head, annoyed. "Any Prosecutor worth his salt would blow that alibi out of the water."

"So, what are we saying here? We're putting all our balls in one basket and calling it a game? Shelby is our bad guy?" Philip rubbed his forehead, feeling his own migraine coming on.

"Even as damning as it looks, no. Though, let's face it. She's now at the top of the list."

Lane then recounted her conversation with the pastor, his educated guess that Tim was the one having an affair with the young woman, and the revelation that Stacy had tried the pregnancy scam several times.

"But if Stacy tried it more than once... that would mean?" Philip trailed off, his thoughts deepening.

"There's at least one other suspect out there, Phil."

CHAPTER 46

Hattie, waking up from a nap, sleepily looked up from her rocking chair and gave Philip a big ruby cheeked smile.

"Mornin', Phil. Or is it afternoon? I can't keep track anymore," she said, offering her hand, Philip taking it gently in his and squatting down beside her.

"You're in luck. It's early afternoon, so right in the middle," he said, his tone warm.

"That means it's almost hot cocoa time!" she said, cheerfully.

As Hattie had gotten older, her sweet tooth had become almost insatiable with Harry finding it harder and harder to get anything of nutritional value down her. Especially when she would stubbornly claim she wasn't hungry or was already full. This was until she was offered something sweet, then she somehow always seemed to have room for dessert.

"Have a seat," she offered, nodding towards the picnic table. "You can keep me company for a spell."

"My pleasure, Miss Hattie." Philip walked the few paces to the picnic table and sat on the edge of the bench, facing her, scooting to the right, trying to block the sun from her eyes, which was shining in through the store's front window.

"That pretty female sheriff caught anybody yet?" Hattie asked, putting her wrinkled hand up to her hair, patting her permed curls in place. She had been a very beautiful woman once upon a time and still had a bit of the vanity that went along with it.

"She's working on it."

Harry suddenly came into view, coming out of aisle five on his way to aisle six, and stopped when he got a glimpse of his buddy. Philip waved him off, letting him know he was fine to sit there and keep Miss Hattie company.

"Hope she does!" Hattie sat quietly for a minute. Philip started to wonder if she had dozed off on him when she added, "I remember when we had a murder on the island, back in '31. It was a love triangle." Hattie's half-closed eyes had a faraway look. "I was just a girl at the time."

"What happened?" Philip asked, being polite.

"Two fellers were fighting over the same girl, who in my opinion, wasn't worth the spit to say her name."

Philip snorted at Hattie's colorful opinion.

"Didn't like her much, huh?"

"Well, she'd promised to marry one feller and then got engaged to the other," she explained with disdain.

"Not a very honorable thing to do," Philip agreed.

"No, it wasn't," Hattie said, in a matter-of-fact tone.

Philip waited for her to continue, and when she didn't, he prompted, "What happened to them, Hattie?"

"The one feller got so jealous he took a chainsaw to the other feller. Sawed his head clean off," she said briskly, and then started to rock her chair. "We was a logging community back then, and people had shorter tempers due to prohibition." She nodded with the sway of the rocking chair as she recalled the times. "Sometimes a man needs a stiff drink to set his head straight."

Philip couldn't disagree.

"That wasn't all, though. After he'd sawed the feller's head off, he went looking for the girl. She'd been warned he was a comin' and took to hiding in the old church. Figured she'd be safe there." Hattie sniffled, pulling a handkerchief from her sleeve and wiping her nose, dutifully putting it back.

"Was she?" Philip, now, was truly curious.

"Not a lick. He just broke down the church doors as if they were kindling and chopped her up too... But he used an axe on her."

"Jeez!" Philip said, shocked at the ending. Hattie

gave a small smile.

She enjoyed keeping her audience entertained.

"Well... love triangles are dangerous," Hattie stated, as if explaining the obvious, and smacked her lips together. "Is Harry within hollering range?"

"Yeah, you need something?" Philip got up and walked to her chair.

"Oh, I'm just ready for my hot cocoa."

CHAPTER 47

"Let me guess, you need to borrow my truck?" Harry eyed Philip warily, having been told a favor was required of him.

"I do," Philip admitted. "But I also need you with it."

"You need your couch moved or something?" Harry quietly shut his office door behind them, letting Hattie enjoy her hot cocoa, and The Price is Right game show in peace.

"I want to do a stakeout," Philip said, in a practical whisper, looking both ways apprehensively.

"Oh, you want to use my truck because everyone will notice the sheriff's rig?" Harry nodded, comprehending the request.

Philip cringed at the question and said, "Not exactly."

"What? She doesn't know?" Harry asked shocked, unconsciously lowering his voice.

"Let's just say I'm forming my own line of inquiry. Until I have some kind of proof, I don't want to bring her in." Philip placed his hand on his friend's shoulder. "You in?"

Harry hesitated.

"This is gonna blow any chance I have with her if she finds out," he said sourly.

Philip chuckled.

"I hate to break it to you, buddy. You never had a chance, to begin with." He gave Harry's shoulder a squeeze and then playfully pushed him off. "Give me your truck keys. I'll pick you up at five."

CHAPTER 48

Dropping Philip off at Hattie's, Lane headed for her small apartment above the store. She needed to grab the evidence bags and run them to the mainland before four. She was already late getting them to the forensic team, though she doubted they'd find anything of value for their efforts.

In a rush, she gathered all the bags, putting them atop the small kitchen counter, and took a quick inventory. She was about to stuff the bag containing the "Cheer is Life" keychain into a bigger sack when she had a thought and squinted at the small group of keys attached to the keychain.

"Wait... is it?" she muttered to herself, then dug through her own keyring, removing Stacy's key, the house key still in her possession as she'd be boarding up the place for the Jensens, once the investigation was over.

Lane painstakingly and impatiently compared her key to each of the individual ones on Stacy's key-ring and concluded, that indeed, the house key was missing from the dead woman's keychain.

"Why would they take the house key?" she asked herself out loud.

Her mind whirled.

Was there something Stacy had stowed away? Was she blackmailing someone, and they hoped to find whatever evidence she had against them in the house? Or was it, that they left something behind and needed to retrieve it? Maybe they had stolen the key before the killing, and that's how they gained access to her house? Could explain why there were no signs of a forced entry? Maybe the young woman had been abducted after all?

Lane quickly snatched the bags from the counter and headed for her truck.

Hastily unlocking her vehicle, she gave a fleeting glance into Hattie's storefront. All she saw was an empty rocking chair, the sign "Hattie's chair" swaying gently with it, its occupant having left it a few minutes prior. She briefly thought about going in and seeing if Philip was still around but then noticed Harry's brown beast of a truck was gone and assumed Philip had gone with it.

Lane threw the evidence bags inside her rig and

then herself, making a straight beeline to Stacy's house. It was a short eight-minute drive before she arrived, and Lane smiled despite herself. She was still getting used to it only taking a few minutes to get anywhere on the island, her morning commute, having been at least an hour-long on the mainland.

When she got to Stacy's house, everything looked normal. Except for the crime scene tape, criss-crossed in a large X across the front door, and the legal sticker notice telling people to stay out. She looked at them both closely and tried to determine if they'd been removed or messed with, and had to admit, she couldn't tell if they had.

Lane braced herself, her arm against the door jamb, and put on a set of plastic booties, then a pair of disposable gloves before pulling back the yellow tape and opening the door, using her key.

The house was much like it was when they had left it earlier in the week, barring the fruit on the counter, covered in fuzzy decomposing mold and smelling sickly sweet. Ignoring the rotting odor, the best she could, Lane started her search in the kitchen, systematically opening cupboards and drawers, looking for anything out of place.

Finding a typical kitchen, she moved to the fridge and freezer before migrating into the living room, where she pulled apart the couch and checked between the chair cushions.

Next, she tackled the bathroom, hoping the medicine cabinet might hold some insight, but all she found was aspirin, Midol, and dental floss. She then ransacked the vanity. In a drawer next to the toilet, where Stacy kept some light reading material, was a "What to Expect, When You Are Expecting" book. Lane frowned, knowing Stacy likely used the book as a guide to fake her pregnancies.

She put the book back and moved to the spare bedroom, the catch-all room. There were boxes of winter clothing, high school memorabilia, extra blankets, and various unimportant items. She closed the door and crossed the hall, entering Stacy's bedroom.

Much like the other rooms, things looked the same as when they had left. She ruffled the bed and then remade it before approaching the dressers. After she pulled out and ruffled the drawers, finding nothing, she took a deep breath and another look around the room. The only place unchecked was Stacy's closet. She approached the double doors and pushed one to the side, sliding it behind the other.

"There they are!" Lane quickly took out her cell and snapped a picture.

Sitting on the closet floor, beside a few empty suitcases, were two full shopping bags, each with the name of Bert's Outdoor Supply and Kayak Rentals imprinted on the side.

Finding the missing clothing bags confirmed

Lane's theory. Someone had removed Stacy's house key from her keyring after or possibly before her death and sneaked themselves in, all in an effort to hide the clothing she bought at Bert's shop the day she died.

Done documenting the discovery, Lane ran out to her truck and grabbed a few evidence bags, packing them into the house. She then busied herself with cataloging and sealing everything in the shopping bags, including the bags themselves.

Completing her task, she eagerly compared the clothing listed on the receipt pulled from Bert's records. Everything was there... Except for the size twelve boots.

"Why bring the clothes back to her house?" she asked the empty room. "To make us believe she shopped and then came straight home? If that's the case, then whoever did this must not have known we'd already been here... or they were hoping no one would notice they were placed there afterwards. But why bring them back at all? Why not toss them in a dumpster or throw them in the ocean?"

After a few minutes of intense brainstorming, Lane shook her head in frustration. She hadn't been able to come up with a single answer.

CHAPTER 49

"Hey ya, Phil! How's... how's it going?" Kody quickly slid his feet off Philip's desk and nervously stood up. "I didn't know you were stopping by," he added lamely, quickly running his fingers through his curly blonde hair and straightening his tie.

He'd been enjoying a nice catnap when the slamming office door jarred him awake.

"Kody." Philip glowered at the sleepy-eyed young man. "I see you're working hard while I'm away. Another late night, last night?" He handed Kody a mini-mart bag holding two tall energy drinks. "Here, these are for you."

Kody answered with a gaping yawn and cracked open one of the cans. "You have no idea."

"Oh, I don't know about that." Philip smiled at the young man, despite the fact he'd just caught him sleeping on the job. "What's her name?"

"How'd you know I met somebody?" he asked, surprised.

"You come in every day dragging, barely able to keep your eyes open, and you're usually out of here like a shot. Wasn't hard to figure out a girl was in the picture." Philip grinned wisely.

"Phil, the things she can do with her—," Kody started dreamily.

"Gonna stop ya right there, kid," Philip interrupted with a chuckle, putting his hands up and discouraging him from continuing.

"Suit yourself." Kody gulped down the energy drink and cracked open the next can. "What you doin' here, man? Just came by to say hi?"

"Pretty much. Thought I'd check in on you and make sure you hadn't burned the place down." Philip sat behind his desk. "So, how is it going?"

"It's boring as all heck," Kody complained. "I didn't realize how slow it is up here during spring. It's a complete snooze-ville."

Philip nodded, agreeing, though he had learned to enjoy the peace and quiet of the season over the years.

"Yeah, it can be. I should've warned you, being you're typically off at college this time of year. Don't worry. It'll get busier by the end of the month."

"How are things in town? They figure out who killed Stacy yet?" Kody got up and sat on the edge of

Philip's desk, his drink already half-finished.

"Maybe." Philip leaned back and plopped his feet onto his desk, despite giving Kody a hard time for doing the same. "Can you keep a secret?"

Kody leaned in eagerly, nodding.

"Okay..." Philip made a dramatic showing of looking both ways and then leaned in, motioning for his young ranger to come closer.

"Phil..." Kody looked around the small office, confused. "There's nobody here, but us."

"Shut up, kid. I am setting the tone," Philip said defensively, and then added, in a confidential whisper, "There's gonna be an arrest any day now. Maybe even tomorrow."

"Really? Do you know who it'll be?" Kody's eyes lit up. "You do, don't you?" He scooted closer. "You can tell me."

Philip shook his head in the negative.

"I would if I could, kid. The sheriff won't tell me who it is. All I know is she's got Stacy's cell phone, and she's pulled the text messages and call log. She knows exactly who Stacy met out in the park on Monday," Philip lied. He was getting good at it.

Kody's eyes went wide.

"Oh, man," was all he managed.

"It probably won't be kept a secret for long. If I was the bad guy, I'd be making for the ferry and the mainland ASAP. Getting myself out of Dodge and in a hurry." Philip got up from his desk and Kody stood up with him.

"Getting out of where?"

"Never mind, kid. Well, I'll let you get back at it. I can tell you've got everything under control." Philip straightened a few papers on his desk and pushed his chair in.

"I gotta tell ya, Phil. I'll be glad when you're back from vacation." The young ranger flopped down into his own chair and propped his feet up onto his tiny desk.

"See ya Tuesday, kid." Philip caught himself looking at the sole of Kody's boots.

What he saw confirmed his suspicions.

CHAPTER 50

"You wanna tell me exactly who we're looking for?" Harry complained, taking another swig of his beer. They had been sitting in his truck for the last five hours staked out by the ferry dock.

The first hour and a half had been miserable, scrunched down in the cramped cab until the sun went down, hoping no one would take notice, keeping their strength up by munching on potato chips and pepperoni sticks from the store.

Now that it was good and dark outside, they could sit up and enjoy the large cooler of beer Harry had brought along.

"I told you already. I don't want to say anything until I know for sure. They could be completely innocent. I wouldn't want to drag them down into the mud if I'm wrong," Philip said honestly and fought off a yawn. It had been a long day so far, and the beer wasn't helping.

"What makes you suspect this person in the first place?" Harry dropped an empty on the truck floorboard and grabbed another beer.

"Take it easy with those," Philip warned, gripping the steering wheel, trying to stay awake. "I need you half-sober if anything goes down."

Harry just waved him off.

"And it's not me who suspects. It's Sheriff Lane. This is more to prove their innocence than it is their guilt."

"I don't get what you mean," Harry slurred a little, the beer making his thoughts fuzzy.

"Ah, forget it, Harry."

"Fine, then. When's this "person of interest" going to show up?" Harry used air quotes.

"It's a quarter to ten. We'll go home once this last ferry leaves," Philip promised.

"I gotta take a leak," Harry announced, and then opened his door, climbing out to face the back of the pickup to relieve himself. Philip rolled his eyes and started to wonder if this had been a bad idea... especially bringing the beer... and Harry.

Light suddenly reflected off the truck's rearview mirror, momentarily lighting up the cab. Philip shied his eyes and used the side mirror to see behind them, a pair of lights pulling into the Park and Ride lot.

The new vehicle parked, and the headlights went dark as a young man quickly climbed out. He grabbed a backpack from the bed of the vehicle and started for the ferry dock.

"Ah, crap. It's him!" Philip practically yelled, struggling with the truck door.

In his eagerness to get out, he'd forgotten the driver's door could jam at times, and he ended up having to body slam the door open with his shoulder.

The young man was just about to step onto the wooden dock leading up to the awaiting ferry. In a few seconds, he'd be on the boat and out of sight.

Philip yelled his name.

"Kody!"

Startled, Kody spun around and gave a searching look into the dark corners of the parking lot. He took a few steps forward, stepping out of the dock's bright lights.

"Phil, is that...?" he started to call back, when out of the darkness, Harry leapt through the air tackling the young man to the ground.

A loud and surprised "UFFH" escaped from Kody's chest as he was thrown down, the full force of Harry's clumsy tackle, practically knocking the wind out of him... and Harry.

By the time Philip reached them, Harry had pinned Kody's arms to the ground and sat straddled across his chest. Kody, for all his worth, was desperately squirming, trying to break loose.

"Got 'em, Phil!" Harry panted, obviously out of shape, using an old wrestling move from their high school days.

"What the hell!" Kody wheezed, his face red. "What are you doing, Harry? Get off me!"

"Let him sit up, Har," Philip directed his buddy to ease back.

Harry let go of Kody's wrists but kept the young man from standing.

"You wanna tell me where you're going?" Philip looked around them to make sure no one was coming to Kody's rescue.

"To see my girlfriend in Seattle!" Kody answered sourly, giving Harry a dirty look, trying to rub the feeling back into his wrists.

"At ten o'clock at night?" Philip asked skeptically. "I would have thought you'd taken an earlier ferry. Like the six o'clock, right after work?"

"She doesn't get off shift until ten! She's supposed to pick me up at the ferry terminal. If you don't believe me, check my phone!" Kody nodded his head towards the ground a few feet away, where the phone had been flung from his hand during the tackle.

Philip walked over and picked the cell phone up, wincing at the large crack running across the screen. If he was wrong, he was gonna owe the kid a new cell phone.

"I've been going over each night to see her. I tried to tell you about her today at the office," Kody called after him.

Philip swiped his finger across the screen and read the last text message received from a girl named Amy. The things she suggested they do... Philip was glad it was dark, feeling a heated blush rising over his face. No wonder the boy headed over the ferry each night to see her.

"Let him up, Harry. He's telling the truth." Philip returned and watched his buddy, with some difficulty, untangle himself from Kody. Once fully upright, Harry stooped and reached for his lower back.

The young ranger began to brush the dirt from his clothes.

"If you were worried, I was going to be late to work tomorrow, I was just gonna hit it and quit it. Come back on the 5 a.m. ferry," Kody complained and then swore when he saw his phone's broken screen.

He roughly stuffed the cell into his front pocket and snatched up his backpack. "Even ripped my shirt," he muttered, giving Harry a dirty look.

Ashamed and embarrassed by his friend's exuberant tackle, Philip wasn't exactly sure what to do next.

"Sorry about your cracked screen. I'll buy you a—."

"Yeah, you will!" Kody snapped. The shock of the attack had faded, anger replacing the fear. "What the hell is going on?" he repeated his previous question and gestured towards Harry, his face furious. "Why's this guy tackling me?"

"Phil thought you killed Stacy," Harry said bluntly, now earnestly rubbing his lower back.

"I never said that, Harry!" Philip pointed at him and then turned to Kody. "I never said that, Kody. I swear."

"Ohhh, I get it now. That's why you came to the office today and checked up on me. And what? Hoped to lure me out here?" Kody shook his head, disbelieving. "You thought it was me! That I killed Stacy."

"Kody, I can explain. I actually thought you DIDN'T do it. This was just my stupid idea of trying to prove it." Philip frowned. "But when you showed up here so late...," he trailed off. There was no good way the conversation would end now.

"You thought I was making a run for it," Kody finished for him.

He slung his backpack onto his shoulder and started to stomp up the dock, then suddenly stopped.

"How many years have you known me, Phil?" he suddenly asked.

"Kody, listen. I'm sorry..."

"How many?"

Philip shrugged. "I've known you since you were nine, kid."

Kody nodded, agreeing.

"Long enough to know I'd never... never hurt

anybody." He made a fist with his hand and then suddenly pointed at Philip. "When you get back from vacation, I quit!" He turned and ran up the plank to the ferry deck as the large ship signaled it was leaving the shore.

Left standing on the dock, Philip and Harry watched as the ferry pulled away, making its way across the choppy water. After a minute of silence, Harry sighed heavily and then slapped his buddy on the shoulder.

"Well, this was fun!"

CHAPTER 51

"You did what?" Lane about toppled the TV tray, slamming her coffee mug down.

"I know, I know. It was extremely stupid." Philip admitted, reaching over and stabilizing the small stand.

He'd showed up at her apartment bright and early with coffee to confess. At her reaction, he wondered if he should have brought donuts as well... maybe with sprinkles.

Lane stared, dumbfounded.

"What... were you thinking?"

"You haven't heard the worse part." Philip scrunched up his face in an apologetic grimace.

She sighed heavily, "Tell me."

"I knew it wasn't Kody because his boot size was too small."

"So, why the stakeout then?"

"Because... well. You made a good point about Kody and I wanted to prove you... I mean, I wanted to prove the theory wrong."

"No, you said it right the first time, Phil." Lane got up and tossed the rest of her coffee into the kitchen sink, slamming the mug on the counter. "You wanted to prove ME wrong."

"That didn't come out right. It's not what I meant."

Lane leaned up against the kitchen counter, her arms folded and faced him. "Tell me, Ranger. What if you had been wrong and I had been right? What if Kody had been our killer and he'd pulled a gun or a knife? What if he had gotten away?"

Philip shrugged his shoulders.

"I didn't consider it because I didn't really think it was him."

"I don't believe you," she said crisply.

"Okay. I was worried it might be him, but I didn't really think it was. Is that better?"

"It's more honest."

Philip couldn't meet her eyes.

"And what's worse, is now, ten to one, nobody will talk to YOU or me because they'll probably be worried the finger will be pointed at them next."

"I've already straightened it out with Kody this morning, and I've apologized. I met him at the early ferry and begged his forgiveness. Luckily for me, he'd calmed down. He won't say anything and has agreed not to quit. Harry already knows to keep his mouth shut."

"That's another thing! Dragging Harry into this. You two are not Cagney and Lacey." Lane pushed off from the kitchen counter and sat down next to Philip on the bed. "I think you need to realize when or if we catch Stacy's killer, it's going to be someone you know. I need to know you can handle that."

Philip nodded his head and then met her frosty blue eyes. At the moment, they didn't look any friendlier than they had the first day they met.

"I can handle it," Philip promised.

"Good. Because today might be hard for you," Lane said gravely, and stood up, patting the bed-spread flat.

"You plan on interviewing Shelby today, don't you?"

"I'd like to. But I can't without Roberta being present since I might be accusing the girl of a crime. The girl is a minor." Lane started to fold up the TV tray. "My plan is to ask her about Bridget taking the knife from the antique shop and depending on how that line of questioning goes, and if she can produce the knife, it'll end there."

"Can I be there when you do?" Philip asked, already knowing the answer.

"I don't think it would be wise," Lane said, with frank honesty.

Philip sat silent for a moment, disappointed, and then slapped his hands on his knees, standing up.

"Well, let me know how it goes and if I can do anything else to help."

Lane looked over at him, her blue eyes still cool.

"I will, Phil."

CHAPTER 52

With the rain clouds parting and the sun beaming down upon the Esten's cabin, Lane pulled into the graveled driveway and parked, blocking both vehicles.

About to step out of the rig, she decided to peel off her yellow parka, pulling her trusty notepad from the pocket, and smacked her lips together, discovering they felt slightly chapped. She opened the glove box, and rummaged through, looking for her lip balm, and used the rearview mirror as a guide to apply the ChapStick.

Upon closer examination of her reflection, it revealed, a small blemish starting to form on her chin. Tempted to do something about it, it suddenly occurred to Lane, she was stalling. She really didn't want to do this...

The front door of the cabin suddenly swung open, and Shelby's head popped out, having heard someone pull into the driveway. The teenager gave the sheriff a warm smile and a friendly wave.

Lane took a deep breath and climbed out of the truck.

"Hi, Shelby! How's your day going?" Lane made her way up the paved walkway to the front door where Shelby was waiting.

"It's going." Shelby's answer was accompanied by a shoulder shrug.

"Well, good. Would it be alright if I came in and had a chat with your mom? She's home, isn't she?" Lane's voice was light and upbeat, her stomach twisting in knots.

Shelby shrugged but left the door open. Lane interpreted this as an invitation and followed the girl inside, the teen announcing loudly they had a visitor.

As they progressed from the short hallway into a large living room, Lane noticed all the lights on in the house, including the TV in the living room, a smaller TV in the kitchen, and some hip-hop music blaring from one of the back bedrooms. She could even hear the dryer going in the small utility room.

"I hope your mom is feeling better? I'd heard she had a migraine yesterday," Lane ventured, the young girl bellowing a repeat of her previous declaration.

"Yeah, much better. Her headaches are funny.

They come and go, just like that!" She snapped her fingers and then plopped down onto the sofa. "You can sit down," she offered.

"That's all right. I'll stand for now. Thank you, though."

Bert emerged from a hallway on the right and took in the sight of Sheriff Lane standing in her living room, her reaction a mixture of surprise and irritation.

"Oh, well... Sheriff! I didn't realize it was you. What can I do for you?" Bert motioned for Lane to have a seat. "Is Phil with you?"

"Thanks, and no, it's just me." Lane took the offered seat, Bert sitting next to her daughter on the couch. "I'm glad I caught both of you at home. I need to ask Shelby a few questions about her friend Bridget and a minor theft down at the antique shop. However, I need your permission since Shelby is still a minor." Lane had addressed Bert directly but heard a groan escape from Shelby.

The moan caught Bert's ear as well, and she looked at her daughter, asking sternly, "Shelby? Do you know what this is about?"

"Roberta, do I have your permission?" Lane insisted. "I need for you to say yes or no before this conversation continues."

Bert ignored the question and stared at her daughter.

Shelby, for her part, seemed to be intently looking at her nails and then at her shoes. Looking everywhere, but her mother's eyes.

"Yes, Sheriff. You have my permission. I'm curious as well to hear what she has to say about this." Bert pulled her eyes away from Shelby and faced Lane. "But I'll call an end to it if I think we need to get a lawyer involved. We use Mr. Allister. In fact, maybe I should give him—"

"Oh, no need to give him a call. It's nothing serious," Lane said soothingly. "It's just a minor shoplifting accusation."

At the mention of shoplifting, Bert's eyebrows raised, and Shelby's head popped up, her eyes wide.

"Me?" she squeaked.

"Yes. I wanted to—," Lane started.

"Shelby, I want you to tell the truth to Sheriff Lane. No fibbing." She gave her daughter a warning look and then turned back to Lane. "Sorry. Go ahead."

Lane flipped open her notepad and smiled at Shelby, who nervously peered back, biting her nails.

"I wanted to let you know Bridget has confessed to stealing something from the antique shop for a friend. Do you know who the friend was, Shelby?"

"Um... Yeah." She licked her lips and looked at her mother, who nodded for her to continue. "It was me."

"I see. Thank you for your honesty." Lane gave her a reassuring smile. "That's helpful. Now, why—"

"Wait a minute. You had a friend STEAL some-thing for you?" Bert interrupted. "What was it? Clothes, a new purse, jewelry?"

"No!" Shelby crossed her arms, clearly not want-ing to say more.

"Then what, Shelby?" her mother demanded.

The teen huffed and scooted to the edge of her seat. "Mom, don't freak out, okay?" She waited for her mother to give any kind of indication she would not freak out, and not seeing it, the girl begrudgingly answered, "A hunting knife."

"A hunting knife! What in the world do you need a hunting knife for?" Bert stood up, raising her voice. "Shelby Ann Esten, you better start explaining yourself."

"I wanted it for protection," Shelby's voice was barely above a whisper. "You're always saying how much safer you felt when dad was here and how good it is to have a man around again." Her voice grew stronger, almost accusatory. "You're always telling me to double check the locks whenever I come in the house, even making sure my windows are locked before going to bed... Like someone is go-ing to sneak in or something." Shelby grabbed one of the decorative pillows from the couch and start-ed tossing it in the air. "I just wanted it because dad wasn't around anymore, and it made me feel safer. That's all."

Bert snatched the pillow out of Shelby's hands and tossed it back on the couch. "Stop that! You are in a lot of trouble, young lady."

"It's no big deal," Shelby responded, a little too much sass in her tone.

"You watch it, Shelby Ann," her mother warned.

"If I may interrupt..." Lane cleared her throat. "Shelby, I think we can clear this up easily enough. I need you to give me back the knife."

The teenage girl suddenly looked extremely alarmed. "What if I don't have it anymore?" she asked, timidly.

"What?" Both women blurted in unison.

"I was keeping it under my pillow at night, in case someone broke in, and... well, it's not there anymore."

"Young lady, we are going to clean that room from top to bottom till you find it and return it!" Bert scolded and then turned to Lane. "I am so embarrassed. Can you give us a day to get her things organized, and we'll return the knife to Sue or pay for it? If you saw her room, you'd know what I'm talking about," Bert pleaded and then addressed her daughter, "If you thought a week of being grounded was bad, you just wait."

Lane was sick to her stomach, her mind racing. Would they really find the knife or did somebody steal it from under Shelby's pillow? Or worse, did she already have it in an evidence bag?

"Shelby, did you tell any of your friends about the knife? This is important," Lane suddenly asked, a new idea flashing into her hectic thoughts.

"Sheriff, I'm sure it's somewhere in her room," Bert reassured her. "Really. It's like Armageddon in there."

"Anybody, Shelby. Did you tell anybody else about it, besides Bridget?" Lane insisted and tapped Shelby's knee, drawing the girl's attention from her mother.

"Um..." She picked up the little pillow again and hugged it against her chest in deep consideration. "Just Stacy. We kind of told her everything when she was around."

"Just Stacy, huh?" Lane closed up her leather notepad and then said under her breath, "Great. That's just great."

CHAPTER 53

"How'd it go?" Philip asked, pacing back and forth on the small landing outside of Lane's apartment.

He'd spent most of the afternoon sitting at the picnic table inside Hattie's, watching the road impatiently for Lane's return. His fellow occupants at the picnic table, Glen and Dub, had tried to encourage Philip to join their debate. Mulch vs. compost... but Philip wasn't interested. Instead, he'd kept his eyes glued to the window and drank his coffee in silence, an hour passing before he spotted Lane parking across the street, and immediately making his way straight to her apartment.

"We've got a slight problem." Lane walked past him and shouldered the door open.

"She couldn't produce the knife?" Philip guessed, feeling a minor wave of nausea come over him.

"No, she couldn't. Roberta thinks it's in her room and that they'll find it once they clean it out. I've given them until tomorrow morning to retrieve it and hand it over. The problem is, the last time Shelby said she had seen it, the knife was under her pillow. When she went to go look at it again, the damn knife was gone."

"She could be lying?" Philip could hardly believe he'd said it. He was starting to sound like Lane.

"That's the problem. I'm not convinced she is lying." Lane opened her small closet and hung up her light coat and rain parka. "And there's something else."

"What?" Philip continued to stand in the middle of the apartment waiting for his guts to settle.

"I asked her if there was anyone besides Bridget who knew about the knife."

"And there was?"

"Yes! She told Stacy." Lane sat down on the bed and kicked off her boots. "Which means Stacy could have told someone else."

"And that someone else could have decided to use the knife to kill her with no suspicions coming back on them," Philip said slowly, stunned at the revelation.

"Or... here's an even more wild theory. Stacy could've taken it herself." Lane flopped backwards on the bed.

"We're never gonna solve this thing," Philip sighed, defeated.

"Who would she have told?" Lane ignored him,

placing her hands behind her head.

"Let's see..." Philip unfolded the TV tray, thinking out loud, "A number of people." He sat down and put his elbow on the stand, resting his chin in his palm. "She could have told her boyfriend Rick. Pastor Jonas? Maybe, Harry?" Philip shot a quick glance at Lane, but she didn't rise to the bait. "Lacey?" he continued.

"Or our mystery person," Lane finished for him. "I keep thinking about something Jerry had said." Lane used her elbows to prop herself up. "Why did Sue Carter have a new knife in her antique shop?"

"I think we should find out." Philip got up, intending to make his way to the antique shop right then.

"Sit down. I'm still thinking..." Lane flopped back on the bed and stared at the ceiling. "You know, there's someone we forgot she might have told."

"And that would be who? The butcher, the baker, the candlestick maker? Who's the next lucky suspect?"

"Tim Esten." Lane sat back up, ignoring his jab. "Do you know if Roberta changed the locks after he left?"

Philip shrugged. "I'd assume not... but it's never crossed my mind to ask her."

"Follow my train of thought here, Phil." She swung her feet back onto the floor. "Tim reconnects with Stacy, and they arrange a rendezvous. But not before she tells him his daughter is so afraid to be without him, she sleeps with a big bowie knife underneath her pillow. Tim comes over early. He knows Roberta is working at the shop and Shelby is probably still at school. He lets himself in with his old house key, takes the knife, and then meets Stacy at the arranged location either in town or at the park. Maybe lures her into the woods with the promise of sex or to show her something? That's when he kills her and leaves the knife behind, not dreaming it would be tied back to his daughter."

"Or knowing it would be, and he's using her as a scapegoat," Philip practically growled.

"I'm heading over to the mainland tonight to meet with my buddy from OPD. He promised to track Tim down for me and see if he could find out if the guy has an alibi or not. I'll make sure to stop at the station too while I'm over there. I'll have them pull Tim's DMV photo and see if they can spot him on the ferry video we pulled for Monday." Lane stretched. "If he's on there, we've got him. We'll have motive, opportunity, and a tie-in to the weapon. Shouldn't be hard to get a warrant for his arrest." Lane couldn't help but feel like a thousand pounds of stress had been lifted from her shoulders.

"What if he's got an alibi?" Philip played devil's advocate.

"Then we'll see if it can be broken!" Lane said stubbornly. "Besides, if he's on the ferry video, he's as good as caught. I feel good about this, Phil. I really do. We may have our man."

"Do you think Bert and Shelby are in any danger?" Philip felt as if a thousand pounds were suddenly added to his already stressed shoulders.

"That depends. If he feels like they're a threat... possibly. If not, he'll probably let them be. In my opinion, the only reason why he's resurfaced at all is because I think Stacy found out where he was and tried the pregnancy scam on him. He's got a new life in Olympia, living with a new love, and here she comes from his past about to destroy it all."

"So, he destroys her first." Philip clenched his jaw as another thought crossed his mind. "Do you think we should still look into why Sue had a new bowie knife in her display case?"

Noticing the time, Lane stepped into her boots and peered up at Philip as she tied the shoestrings. "Be my guest. If for nothing else but to satisfy our curiosity."

CHAPTER 54

Lane walked to the front desk of the mainland sheriff's office and waited patiently for the receptionist to hang up the phone. The young woman, who Lane didn't recognize, seemed to be having a hard time transferring her caller to the correct department. After two unsuccessful tries, she accidentally dropped the line.

"Shoot." The young girl looked up to find Lane staring and gave an apologetic smile. "Sorry to keep you waiting..." She squinted at Lane's name tag, wrinkling up her face as she did so. "Sheriff... Lane."

"Hello, ...Monica," Lane read her name tag in return. "You new?"

"Second day." She blushed and quickly picked up a clipboard sitting by the phone. "What can I do for you, Sheriff Lane?"

"I wanted to see Eddie," Lane said, shrugging a backpack off while putting two large evidence bags and the rice container on the counter. "I plan on dropping these off with forensics."

"Eddie? Um... hold on... I don't..." The girl ruffled through papers attached to a clipboard. "I don't see we have an Officer...err Deputy Eddie." Monica squinted at the clipboard, vainly searching her list of personnel.

"Correct. Eddie is the IT guy."

"Oohhh... you're wanting to go back to the dungeon." Monica smiled, happy to be in the know. "Please sign in here, and... Oh, I suppose you know the drill."

"I do," Lane acknowledged, moving the rice container out of her way and signing the visitor's log.

The Tupperware caught Monica's eye, and she squinted at the container, spotting something pink among the white blur. Curious, she tapped it, seeing if anything would move inside. Hiding an amused smile, Lane suspected Monica either needed glasses or had forgotten to put in her contacts.

"Thank you for your help, Monica." Lane put the pen down and gathered up her belongings. "You're doing a great job." She smiled goodbye and made her way through the beehive of activity.

Having walked the full length of the station, Lane stopped in front of the dungeon door and read the scotched taped sign.

Before you knock, ask yourself...
Have I tried turning it off and on first?

Lane snorted and gave the door a firm knock.

"Enter at your own risk!" Was bellowed from the other side and then followed up with, "Come on in!"

The dungeon, also known as the IT department, was run by Eddie Jones. The department earned the name not just because it was small, dark, smelly, and stuck way in the back of the station... but because Eddie was a nerd and proud of it. Dungeons and Dragons, Star Trek, Star Wars, Game of Thrones, comic books and comic heroes, Japanese animation, Lego competitions, gaming systems, and gaming universes... It didn't matter the genre, he loved it all, and wanted everyone to love it with him.

"Hey, D.M." Lane swung the door open, greeting the Dungeon Master, a nickname he'd chosen himself.

She left the evidence bags outside the door and walking through the threshold, instantly struck by the office's anomaly of culture, chaos, and entertainment all rolled into one.

On the IT side of things, Eddie had three large computer screens mushed together, two laptops, (one broken), and several software disks scattered across his workspace. Behind the desk stood modems and servers stacked high upon each other, beeping and bopping along to the harmonic hum of their powerful fans. Ethernet cords hung like jungle vines along the walls with computer drives, keyboards, mouses, and various components frankenstein'd from other computers filling the remaining free space.

On the entertainment side, every crook and cranny was filled with popular pop culture references or items. Small character figurines lined the desk and shelves, precariously balanced on top of various boxes and semi-flat surfaces. Behind the hanging wires and cables, peeked posters and comic book art. Lego sets of various movies were displayed on the window sill proudly, everything from Harry Potter to Minecraft. Even the window had Spiderman curtains. It was a sight to behold.

"Halt!" Eddie spun his chair and faced his visitor. "My fair lady knows the toll upon which is required to seek knowledge from the Dungeon Master, does she not?"

Lane rolled her eyes, a smile cracking her face. She placed the rice container on the floor since there was no room on the desk and opened her backpack, dumping several candy bars in his lap.

"Toll paid."

"Wow, Lane... you didn't scrimp. Hershey bars WITH almonds. Nice," he said with a pleased smile and gestured towards a bar stool crammed in the corner. She had to remove several files before she could sit down.

"Need your help, D.M." She handed him the container full of rice. "I've had this cell phone in there for a couple of days. I'm hoping it's dried out enough so you can power it up? I don't have a cord for it."

Eddie popped open the air-tight seal and dug the pink phone out, dry rice spilling everywhere.

"Well, the phone looks like it's got one of those super hard cases on it. If you look here, you can pull this flap down before you can even stick in the charger. May not have even gotten wet... I mean, the inside." He rolled his chair over and opened the bottom drawer of his desk. The action sent his toy figurines wobbling as the drawer shuddered open. He dug around, yanking out a white cord. "You're in luck. I've got a charger for it."

Lane scooted the stool a half-inch closer, careful to not bump the Millennium Falcon dangling from the ceiling, and watched as Eddie pried off the heavy-duty case. He then checked the charging prongs, blowing on them lightly, and attached the charger, sticking the other half in the wall socket. Lane held her breath and said a small prayer. The pink phone suddenly gave out a loud beep, a lit battery symbol appearing on the screen.

"It's taking a charge," Eddie said, slamming the bottom drawer shut, the figurines precariously wobbling once again. "We'll have to give it a minute or two before I power it on. Was this at a bottom of a lake or something?"

Lane shook her head no. "Small puddle... but for several days."

"This for a case you working on?" He unwrapped one of the candy bars and took a bite, offering the rest to Lane.

She politely declined.

"Better not be your boyfriend's phone." He eyed her warily, straightening a tumbled stack of Pokémon cards.

"It's evidence in a murder case," she said, keeping her voice low.

"And why pray tell, is it not in the forensic tech's office? Why seek the counsel of the Dungeon Master?" Eddie grinned slyly, already knowing the answer. "Cell phone records taking forever?"

"That they are," Lane admitted. "And I need action on this case. I'm at a dead end. I just want a quick peek."

"You know, Lane, they say curiosity killed the cat," Eddie warned and took another bite. "But... what else are you gonna do with nine lives? Let's see what's on this thing." He pressed down on the power button and the phone lit up, making another loud beep, the welcome screen appearing.

"If it's got a security code on it, you might still

take this to a forensic tech," Eddie cautioned, hitting the home button. He looked up with a bright smile. "No security code. That's lucky."

"Can you see the text messages? Who was her last phone call from? Does her calendar show anything for last Monday?" Lane stood up from the stool, trying to see the screen.

Eddie continued to press buttons, a frown forming and deepening with each push and swipe of his finger.

"What's the matter?" Lane asked, her hopes failing. "Why are you looking like that?"

"The phone has been dumped," Eddie said flatly, still pushing buttons.

"Dumped?" Lane asked, confused.

"Yeah, everything is erased. Pictures, messages, voicemail, notes... It's all gone. It's almost as if you bought it off the shelf."

"Well, can you get any of it back?" Lane returned to the stool, flustered.

"I could try... but I wouldn't be any faster than a forensic tech. At this point, it's probably best for you to go through the right channels. Sorry, Lane. You just ran out of lives." He handed her the pink phone with an apologetic smile.

"Is it blank because of the water?" Lane looked at what was now considered a pink paperweight.

"No. Somebody manually erased everything. If they'd put it back to factory settings a different way, then some of the applications would be gone. But there were a few there which didn't come with the phone right out of the box. Sorry, Lane. Looks like somebody was covering their tracks."

CHAPTER 55

Philip frowned at the "CLOSED" sign hanging in the antique shop's window, and peered down at his watch, confirming it was thirty minutes before the place was supposed to be closed.

The storefront dark, he stubbornly tried the door, then knocked loudly, peeking through the windows and rattling the door knob. No one came to the answer. The only thing he could figure was that Abby and Bridget, knowing the bosses were away for the weekend, had taken it upon themselves to cut out early.

He turned to leave, hearing a familiar voice call his name.

"Hey, Phil! Hold up! Jerry Holmes was walking down the sidewalk towards him, two dogs leading the way.

"Hi, Jer. How's it going?" Philip greeted, shaking

Jerry's hand once he came to a full stop. "Enjoying an evening stroll?"

Out of breath, Jerry nodded his head yes before responding, "Yup." The chocolate Labrador retriever and Jack Russell terrier at the end of the leash seemed to be taking Jerry for a walk more than him taking them. "Gotta let my patients stretch their legs a bit. Hate keeping them cooped up in crates all day. Besides...," Jerry lowered his voice and patted his tummy. "Helps keep my beer belly from growing."

Philip subconsciously sucked in his own small beer gut and gave a light chuckle. "Well, have a good walk. I'll see ya later." He turned to leave.

"Phil... um... just a second," Jerry lightly grabbed his arm. "Are you going to be seeing Sheriff Lane anytime soon?"

Philip gave his friend a big grin and nodded. "Probably tomorrow. She's gone to the mainland this evening."

"Oh, okay. Would you mind asking her to call me?" Jerry wrestled with the leashes, the Lab eager to be on the way.

"Sure! You gonna ask her out on a date?" Philip nudged his buddy's arm, giving him an encouraging grin. Jerry twirled his mustache, a nervous gesture, and smiled shyly.

"I might. But uh, I also wanted to tell her something my Amy said."

"Amy! How is your daughter doing?" Philip asked politely.

"Better. She's back at her mom's, which I feel good about. I don't like her bouncing around. But, um... she came over last night. She was supposed to come over on Friday but she ended up missing the ferry and standing me up for dinner."

Philip let the dogs smell his hand, introducing himself, before petting their heads.

"We were talking about Stacy's death, and I was telling her about how we had found her and about the black bear... And... that's when she remembered." Jerry suddenly stopped talking, looking almost apologetic. "You know, it's not important. Have the sheriff give me a call when she can." He smiled, making as to leave.

"Oh, come on, Jerry. Spit it out. What did Amy remember?" Philip encouraged, somewhat impatient.

It was hard pretending to be on the outskirts of the investigation. Being the sheriff's sidekick wasn't the same as being the sheriff. And if Philip was being honest, he was annoyed Lane had once again gone to the mainland station without him. Not only that, but she'd asked for the rice container with the cell phone. He had really wanted to be there when they turned the damn thing on. Instead, he was peeking through darkened store windows.

Jerry twirled his mustache again and said, "For

the record, Amy could be wrong, and this could have absolutely no bearing on the case. And maybe the sheriff already knows about it, but I figured if she doesn't, it might be worth mentioning... but then again, I don't want to kick the hornet's nest either. It's just, I got to think—"

"Jerry! Get to the point," Philip said sternly, but not unkindly.

"Sorry. Amy had come over to the island last Monday night to visit Kody. They've apparently been seeing each other."

"I didn't know that," Philip said, embarrassed, suddenly knowing way too much about Jerry's daughter via the text messages on Kody's phone. "That's to say, I knew he was sweet on a girl, but I didn't know it was YOUR Amy. He's a good kid, Jerry. She could do worse."

"Yeah, sort of what I thought as well. Anyway, she'd come over to see him, and one of her friends drove her out to the park for a short visit. While she was out there, she noticed a red Jeep with its lights on and hood up sitting on the side of the road."

"If she thought it was Stacy's, she was right. We found it parked in the towing yard at Edgar Rowles's place," Philip said, kneeling down and giving the Lab a good scratch. "Kody had called him, not realizing anything had happened to her."

"Well, there was also another vehicle parked next

to it. That's... that's what I wanted to talk to Sheriff Lane about," Jerry said, hesitantly.

"Really?" Philip stood up, his full attention on Jerry. "Did Amy know whose rig it was?"

"No... but when she described it to me, it sounded a lot like Harry's brown beast." Jerry's lips twisted into an apologetic wince.

"Did she actually see him, though?" Philip asked, trying to not sound defensive.

"No, Amy didn't see anybody in either vehicle and she didn't think anything was strange. It wasn't until I mentioned Stacy had been murdered in the park that she remembered seeing her Jeep that night." Jerry patted the smaller dog and told him sternly to sit before looking back up at his friend. "I know it's kind of dumb to even mention it because you and I both know Harry is a big teddy bear. But I didn't know if he might know something or if he even realized the Jeep was Stacy's. Which would really surprise me since he was her boss... but... I don't know... I just thought I should mention it." Jerry looked at Philip's scowl and thought he'd said enough.

Philip was about to ask Jerry another question when his cell phone rang.

"Well, I better let you go. Have a good night, Phil."

"Thanks, Jerry... And... I'll tell Sheriff Lane to give you a call." Philip gave a quick smile, trying to not look unnerved, and answered his cell phone.

"Hi, Bert," he said distracted, scenarios running through his head.

"Phil! Shelby has run away!" Bert's panicked voice came over the phone in a rush.

"She's what?"

"We got into a fight, and she left to go to the store, and that's been two hours ago. I think she's run away," Bert's voice broke into a sob.

"Hold tight. I'm on my way."

CHAPTER 56

Oh, I'm so glad you could make it!" Mindy gave her sister-in-law a big hug and then stepped back, running her fingers through her mop of a hairdo. "Sorry! Did I get anything on you?" Mindy's apron was covered with two different colored sauces and a powdery substance.

Kent's high school sweetheart and soon after wife had been a part of their lives for the last twenty years. Quickly becoming the female patriarch of the family, Mindy opened her home to all and encouraged visits whenever possible. She was the sister Lane never had growing up.

"A little, but it's all right. Here." Lane smiled, handing her a six-pack of beer, which Mindy frowned at. "Oh, and this." In her other hand, she produced a bottle of red wine. This garnered a delighted smile.

"I knew there was a reason why you were my favorite sister-in-law!" Mindy took the wine and ushered Lane into the house. "You'll have to forgive me but I need to get myself back to the kitchen. I've got something boiling."

"Want any help?" Lane offered, taking her coat off and tossing it over the nearest chair.

"Oh, thank you, but no. I've got it all under control. Fix yourself a drink and go keep Jimmy company. I've relegated the kids to their bedrooms till their dad gets home, so you guys will have some peace and quiet before dinner. Then after that, you're on your own." She gave Lane a playful wink.

"Forewarned is forearmed," Lane acknowledged.

"Kent should be home shortly. I made him stop by the store for some more ginger!" Mindy yelled over her shoulder, already halfway through the kitchen archway.

"Sounds good!" Lane lightly tossed back and walked into the dining room, a large table already set, and a drink tray waiting. She happily made herself a double whiskey on the rocks and ventured into the small sitting room.

"Well, aren't you a sight for sore eyes!" Jimmy said, getting up from a large overstuffed chair facing the TV, the Mariner baseball game on the wide screen.

"Hey there, Jimmy!" Lane gave the big man a squeeze and felt her feet lift from the ground.

"Can I just say..." Jimmy grinned at her, setting her back down. "You look awfully smart in your uniform." He let her go and went to sit back down in his overstuffed chair. Lane could tell Jimmy was a little red in the cheeks, which probably meant he'd had a couple double whiskeys waiting on her.

"Sorry. I just came from the station and didn't have time to change." Lane looked down at herself, suddenly feeling a little embarrassed. Even though she'd been in the sheriff's department for six years, none of her family had seen her dressed in uniform before. At least, not in person.

"Here, take a load off." Jimmy pointed to a second chair as he put his feet up on the ottoman. "So, kiddo! Kent tells me you're working on a murder case?"

Lane twitched at the word "kiddo." The ever-favorite term of endearment used by her brothers. Even Alex, the youngest, had started using the nickname. They all knew it drove her nuts.

"Yeah, I'm not even day one into my office, and I'm already neck-deep in one." Lane took a sip of her drink, feeling the ice cubes clink against her teeth.

"Any strong leads?"

Talking shop was one of the things their family did really well together. It had been routine, growing up, that whenever their dad came home from working a twelve-hour shift at the police station, he'd sit down at the dinner table and run scenarios past his kids. As a family, they problem solved cases, debunked possible alibis, and imagined motives. You could say from a very young age their father had started to train them for police work.

"Not any that I like," Lane said, honestly.

"Run me through it," Jimmy offered and listened quietly as Lane described the circumstances in which the body had been found, the coroner's report, along with his black bear alibi theory, and the early suspicions of Harry, the dead girl's employer. She continued with the discovery of Stacy having an affair with a married man, which then led to the revelation of her money scheming efforts, and added the laundry list of people they had suspected but seemingly cleared: Rick, Harry, Kody, Edgar, Pastor Jonas... each a serious conclusion at one time.

Then she ran down the current list of possible suspects from Tim Esten to his daughter Shelby, even the mystery person she thought they might not have discovered yet. She ended with the dilemma they were having with the missing bowie knife. Did the girl really lose it, was she hiding it, or had someone taken it?

Jimmy, nursing his whiskey while his attention was consumed, listened with eyes closed. At times he had nodded in agreement with her conclusions, and at other times, he'd simply shaken his head severely. Periodically he'd ask a question, but mostly he just listened. When she had finished, he leaned forward, placing his empty glass on the ottoman.

"What about this park ranger that's helping you out? You've checked him out thoroughly? He'd be the perfect guy to dump the body and then find it. Might be worth a second look?"

Lane gave her big brother a smile and shook her head. "He's a good man, Jim," she said, with all seriousness.

Jimmy, knowing his sister and what kind of person you needed to be to elicit any kind of respect, left it alone.

"All right, back to person X. What would be their motive?" Jimmy got up to refill his drink.

Lane's brow knitted as she mulled the question over, taking another sip from her whiskey.

"Well, it could be a stranger kill, as in, she was in the wrong place at the wrong time, and she just happens to not be a real nice person in real life... but none of it's connected to her death."

"However," Jimmy prompted.

"However, the scalping of the victim is odd for a stranger kill. Unless someone was trying to make a souvenir out of it."

"And why would they do that?"

"Well, it could have been their first kill or if they're a serial killer, part of their MO... or a sign of some kind? Like a disfiguring of the body. To make her ugly?"

"I agree. That seems more personal."

"Very personal."

"Why would someone who knew her, want to disfigure her corpse?"

"Jealousy? Rejection? Revenge? Obsession?" Lane ticked each word with a finger. "It could be dozens of things."

"What does your gut say?"

Lane pondered and then answered, "Revenge."

"You three!" Mindy's voice broke in, giggles rising from behind Jimmy's chair. "What are you kids doing out of your rooms?" She addressed the adults second. "All right! Enough shop talk. These three trouble makers have been eavesdropping for the last five minutes," she scolded, pointing to her kids.

"WHAT! The tickle monster doesn't like eavesdroppers!" Jimmy's voice boomed as he stood up and loomed over the accused listeners.

"Tickle fight!" The boys championed before tackling their Uncle Jimmy in force.

Immune to tickles, he made short work of them and wrestled the two boys to the floor, while his niece scooted to the sidelines. She made sure to stay out of arm's length of the tickle monster and worked her way over to Lane.

"Hi, Auntie! Want to see my room?" The girl gave her a side hug, wrapping her short arms around her waist. Lane squeezed back and patted her head.

"Sure, sweetheart. But first, I gotta teach these boys how to take down your uncle."

CHAPTER 57

"Tell me what happened." Philip had flagged down a ride to Bert's cabin and was now sitting in her small kitchen watching her pace the room. Bert, clutching her cell phone, shook her head seemingly unable to come up with the words to explain.

He watched her continue to pace.

"Take a deep breath," Philip suggested. "Come on, Bert." She stopped pacing, and with eyes closed, inhaled deeply. "That's better. Now, what happened?"

Her voice shook, "Sheriff Lane came over to the house because Bridget... She's one of Shelby's friends, shoplifted from the antique shop, and gave the item to Shelby." Bert neglected to mention what the item was. "You can imagine, I was pretty mad, to say the least. I grounded her for two months and threatened to take away cheerleading."

Philip let out a low whistle.

"Oh, boy."

"Yeah. She argued with me, but I'd put my foot down." Bert shook her head, her voice cracking. "We, uh... we started cleaning her room because that's the last place she had this... this thing and, uh... I was starting to get a headache, and I'd run out of aspirin. I got worried it might turn into a full-blown migraine, so I sent her to the store to buy some more while I kept looking."

"Here. Sit down before you fall down," Philip said sternly and pulled a chair out, ordering her to sit. "What happened next?"

"Well, I finally found what we were looking for and reali—"

"You found the knife?" Philip about jumped out of his chair.

"Oh. Sheriff Lane told you then," Bert said deflated, giving Philip a disappointed look.

"I just happened to be there when she discovered Bridget took it," Philip said innocently, a big smile on his face. "Where was it?"

"Is that really important right now, Phil?" Bert scolded.

"No... no, you're right. Go on," Philip agreed sheepishly, still wanting to know.

"I'd just found the... the hunting knife, and that's when I realized an hour had gone by. Shelby hadn't come home. I waited another hour, thinking maybe there was a line at the store or she was just mad and driving around downtown. You know, cruising... Phil, she's not even answering her phone! I think threatening to take away cheer was a mistake." Bert laid her head in her hands and unblushingly cried, large streaks of tears rolling down her flushed cheeks. He'd never seen her this upset before.

In an effort to offer comfort, Philip rubbed her back and told her softy it was going to be all okay. He would get a search party together, and most likely, she was right. The girl was probably driving around blowing off steam. He'd barely gotten the words out when Bert's cell phone rang and she snatched it up, standing up from her chair.

"SHELBY! Where are you?" Relief flooded through Bert's voice and body.

Philip could only hear Bert's side of the conversation. He tried to follow along as best as he could from her facial reactions and tone of voice.

"You had me sick to my stomach, Shelby. Just sick!" Bert's relief briefly turned into motherly rage. She listened for a few seconds before saying, "I want you to know I found it. So, you can tell her everything is going to be okay." ...a few more seconds went by... "I don't think, Shelby..." a few more... "All right. But after tonight, you are grounded for three months. Yes... I said THREE." "Well, you should have called me sooner. Now you better call me first thing in the morning and let me know when you are on your way home." Bert nodded her head as Philip heard wisps of Shelby's voice come through the phone speaker. Bert's tone softened, "I love you, honey. Please be safe." She hung up the phone.

"She's okay, then?" Philip asked, watching Bert's shoulders relax, and her hands unclench.

"Yes, thank God." Bert gave Philip a relieved smile and a quick hug, hampering him from standing up. She lightly pushed him back into the chair with a smile. "She ran into Bridget at the store, and they got to talking. She said she just lost track of time. She's going to spend the night over at her house."

"Think Bridget is such a good influence?" Philip didn't like the idea of Shelby hanging out with the klepto redhead.

"I don't care for the girl either, but it'll be the last friend she's gonna see for a while. Three months of being grounded is really gonna kill her social life." Bert flopped into her own chair, running her hands through her long hair in relief.

"Well, I'm just glad she's okay." Philip stood up to leave, grabbing his coat from the table.

"Where are you going?" Bert asked surprised, reaching across the table to touch his arm.

"I've got to talk to Harry about something, and then I've got to track down Sheriff Lane," he explained in a rush. Philip started to put his coat on. "I hate to go."

He had both arms in his jacket's sleeves, trying to shrug the coat over his shoulders when he started to say he'd call her the next day. However, Bert had stood up and walked herself over, slipping her arms around his waist. She leaned into Philip, pressing herself up against him, determined to change his mind.

"Do you really have to go?" she asked huskily and nuzzled his chin with her lips. "I mean... We've got the whole house to ourselves. Shelby is out for the night. No pesky sheriff dragging you all over downtown... seems to be a waste of a perfectly good opportunity." Bert's hands wandered up and down his chest as her lips moved to the base of his neck.

Philip's brain formed the words telling her why he really needed to go. It was his lips that couldn't push the words out. They were preoccupied at the moment returning Bert's wanting kisses.

Mentally he reasoned, Lane wasn't going to be back from the mainland for at least a few more hours, and Harry... Well, Harry would be there in the morning as always. Neither one of them was in front of him right now, and a beautiful woman who wanted him was.

CHAPTER 58

With dinner consumed and enjoyed, everyone dispersed to different parts of the house. Mindy had begun clearing away the messy dining table before tackling the kitchen. While Jimmy, who volunteered to read the kids a bedtime story, was down the hall in the boy's room. This left the two middle siblings free to hide out in Kent's den.

"The kids love it when you here." He shut the den door behind them and nodded for his baby sister to take a seat. "We need to do this more often."

"I'll come visit more," Lane promised, taking a quick sip from her whiskey on ice. It was her third one of the evening, and if she was going to be able to drive in an hour, it would need to be the last.

"How's the new assignment on the island?"

"I like the place and the people... however, it's

been hard to warm up to anybody. Especially when looking for potential suspects," Lane confessed.

"What's the population out there anyway?"

"Oh, I'd guess there's roughly about a thousand people or so, counting kids. Nice small community. It takes a special kind of person to live off the mainland. Help isn't right around the corner."

"Yeah, I don't know how you'll do it, kiddo. I know you. You like hopping in your car, going for long drives, taking in a movie on a rainy day. Not to mention, it's going to be hell on your dating life."

"HA! What dating life?" She shook her head as a sudden image of Philip and Jerry standing by their trucks popped into her head. "Besides, I can still go on long drives. It'll just be in circles." She cracked a smile.

"Still. You're not worried about going stir crazy out there?"

"Nah. Once they get the office finished, I'll have loads of paperwork to catch up on, and it's not like there's not anything to do. I mean, the island is basically a grownup's playground. I can canoe, hike, go off-road Jeeping, wildlife watching, possibly take up photography?" Lane listed all the things she could do with her spare time... but probably wouldn't.

"Do they even have a doctor's office there?" Kent had tossed her a coaster for her drink and put his glass down on one as well.

"Of course. Though he's on vacation right now.

We've also got a small volunteer fire department and a three-person manned post office. Oh, and a one-screen movie theater. See, we're not completely backwoods."

"We? Already counting yourself among the locals, huh?"

"Guess so." Lane realized with surprise. She liked the fact she did. "Enough about me. How are things on your end with work?"

A slow smile spread over Kent's face. "Got our gang yesterday. Five million dollar bust! Booyah!"

"Kent, that's great!" Lane leaned over and gave her big brother a loving punch in the arm.

"Well, I had to bring in the DEA to stitch it up, but we got' em. They were running drugs out of Mexico and then dispersing the load from here to all over the country and Canada."

"DEA, huh?" Lane's face showed marked amazement. "That had to have impressed them."

"It did." Kent's smile widened further. "Meeting with them for a possible transfer on Monday."

Lane held up her drink in a mock cheer.

"Congrats, bro. They'd be nuts not to take you."

"It's not much more money to start, but it's where all the action is. Oh, and speaking of action." He got up and pulled a well-worn leather notepad from his pocket, sitting back down, the leather notepads being a Christmas gift from their father. Lane pulled hers out as well, her pen at the ready.

"I didn't forget about the little errand you sent me on. Or..." Kent gave her a stern look. "Should I say wild goose chase?"

"No luck finding his parents or him?" she asked, disappointment underlined in her voice.

"Oh, I found the parents alright. Though they were shocked to hear their son was living in Olympia with a new girlfriend. The last time they'd talk to him was around..." He referred to the notepad. "The beginning of November, last year. Been in limited communication with his wife, um... Roberta... but I guess, she goes by Bert?" He looked up at his sister to confirm. Lane nodded her head it was so.

Kent went on, "They've talked to her a couple of times. The last being right around New Years. This Bert lady has been saying their son is working deep in the jungle on a once-in-a-lifetime photography expedition. The Congo or some crazy place like that. No internet, no cell phone reception, and no snail mail." He shut his notepad with a light smack. "During my visit, they asked if they should open a missing persons report."

CHAPTER 59

"I'll just ignore it." Philip offered between hurried kisses, his cell phone obnoxiously vibrating against Bert's nightstand, his attention momentarily distracted.

The cell phone went quiet, then promptly started a new, scuttling across the surface. It repeated the action, and on the third missed call, Bert reluctantly pushed Philip away, demanding he either answered the damn thing or turned it off.

Not to be deterred, Philip reached behind and blindly searched the table while his lips busied themselves elsewhere. His hand, by chance, landed on the phone as it started buzzing once more, and he snatched it up, fumbling as he tried to press the power button on the side. Not coordinated enough to kiss and work electronics simultaneously, he was forced to break away from Bert's luscious lips, and crossly looked down at the caller ID.

"Ah, crud," he moaned. "I... I better take this. Sorry."

"Fine, but no peeking till you're off the phone," Bert gave him a sultry smile as she brought the bed-sheet up and tucked it under her chin.

Philip groaned in protest and answered the call, the phone still buzzing in his hand.

"Yeah!" he barked; his frustration apparent.

"Took you long enough!" Lane barked back.

"In the middle of something, that's why. What do ya need?"

Philip friskily tugged at the bedsheet with his free hand as Bert giggled, and gripped the cloth tighter, shaking her head, and laughing, "No, stop it! No peeking!"

Lane's voice echoed over the line.

"Phil, listen to me very carefully. Bert LIED about Tim living in Olympia. I'm on my way to you now." Her voice was terse, the sound of a fog horn and the cry of seagulls heard in the background. "I think we've been looking at this all wrong."

The smile on Philip's face fell, and he let go of the bedsheet. He held up his index finger and whis-pered, "Give me one second, Bert."

He climbed out of bed, grabbing the crumpled jeans from the floor and his t-shirt from the bed-post on his way to the bathroom, looking for privacy. He turned to shut the door and gave Bert a long-ing look, the bedsheet still tucked under her chin, a playful pout upon her lips.

With a wink and devious smile, she dropped the sheet, the fabric falling to her waist, her beauty exposed.

Philip shook his head, taking her in, and reluctantly closed the bathroom door."HELLO! Are you there? Phil! Did you hear what I said?" Lane's voice ratcheted up a notch.

"What the hell are you talking about?" he practically hissed into the phone.

"OPD looked up Tim's parents because they couldn't find any record of a Tim Esten living in Olympia. No power bill, no water bill, no address. His parents have not talked to him since early November of last year. They told OPD Roberta has been telling them he's on a photo expedition in some jungle." Lane's mind was working furiously. "I'm starting to think Tim is actually missing, and maybe he didn't leave on his own accord."

"Whoa, whoa. Slow down." Philip sat on the toilet, one leg in his jeans already. "What are you, nuts? That's a HUGE leap to make, Lane."

"Phil, do you think it's possible Bert knew about the affair with Stacy? I know you asked her, but do you think she could have been lying?" Lane raised the question, bracing herself for his reaction.

"No." Philip shook his head and then shook his leg out of the jeans pant leg. "I'm not doing this with you, Lane. You've accused everyone I'm close to. Harry, Kody, Shelby, and now Bert? And every time you do this, I get sucked into thinking you're right. I'm not doing it again! You're on your own!" he finished angrily and ended the call with a hard press. "Insane!" he said out loud to himself and roughly tossed the cell phone onto the bathroom counter. "Absolutely insane!"

He braced himself over the sink and gazed into the oval mirror, fuming at the accusation Lane had thrown at Bert. It was ridiculous and outlandish... and foolish. He debated on calling her back and telling her exactly how insane she was being, but heard movement outside the door and remembered Bert was still waiting.

He flipped the faucet on, hastily splashing cold water onto his face, and ran his fingers through his bed-tussled hair.

"Forget her," he muttered and took a deep breath, catching his reflection in the mirror. With a crooked smile, he playfully posed with his chest puffed out, and his gut sucked in, analyzing his new form.

"I gotta lay off the beer," he chastised himself and reached for the bathroom door, swiftly kicking his jeans out of the way. He swung the door open and sucked in his gut. "Sorry about that, Bert. Now, where were we?"

CHAPTER 60

"Phil, ...I know it may seem like it, but... just listen to me," Lane had started to say when the line went dead. She immediately hit re-dial, the call going straight to voice mail. "Dammit!"

She couldn't blame him. Throughout the whole investigation, she HAD been pointing fingers at practically everyone they came into contact with. Suspicious of every little comment, every little facial tick, every little movement. Maybe he was right? Maybe she was going down another rabbit hole?

After all, Bert had tried to be helpful throughout the investigation. She'd volunteered freely that she had seen Stacy on the day of the murder and provided videotape. She'd even given a reasonable explanation for the in-store credit. Not to mention, letting her question Shelby about the bowie knife. If she really had something to hide, wouldn't she have refused?

Bert seemed to strike Lane as a loving and doting mother. The idea of her using her daughter as a shield with the murder weapon seemed almost laughable. Lane took a deep breath through her nose and closed her eyes, exhaling out her mouth.

The slight swaying of the ferry was making her sleepy, and it had been one heck of a long day. The guys at the station had ribbed her about taking so long to come up with an optimal, single suspect, teasing her, hinting maybe this case was too hard for her. Basically, insinuating she never should have been given the post on Rockfish Island. The jealous bastards.

And, maybe, she shouldn't have been? Perhaps, she was reaching for straws? And, possibly, all Bert had been doing was saving his parents some heartbreak? But why lie to Philip about him living in Olympia with a young girl? Unless she figured he'd drop the subject, and they'd leave her and Shelby alone. Could be why Bert had asked him specifically NOT to tell her?

Then again, why say it at all? Why not just stick with the story that he's gone and she's never heard from him again? Was she trying to throw him off Tim's trail? Maybe she does know where Tim is? Maybe, she knows Tim did it and she's protecting him? Her daughter's father. Maybe...

Lane looked at her cell phone, sitting in her lap,

and hit redial again.

"Straight to voicemail," she sighed, and put the truck into drive, awaiting her turn to disembark. She would just have to talk to him in the morning, that is, if he was willing.

CHAPTER 61

Harry was locking up the store when his cell phone started ringing. Digging it out of his pocket, he thought he heard his name being called and shielded his eyes from the downpour coming off the broken gutter overhead. He saw in the distance, a small, yellow-encased figure crossing the street towards him.

"Sheriff, is that you?"

Lane, decked in her oversized rain parka, was indeed, making her way toward him.

"Hi, Harry. Glad I caught you."

"What are you doing out in this?" he asked, taking the store keys from the lock, shoving them into his shirt pocket, and fumbling for his umbrella.

"Oh, I finished parking the patrol truck and was walking back to the apartment. Saw you and thought I'd say... Hi!" She gave him a friendly smile, suddenly looking shy.

"Well... Hi, back." He smiled in return, at a loss, if he should add more to the greeting.

They stood in awkward silence.

"Hattie home already?" Lane asked, suddenly looking around them, spotting his brown truck empty.

"Yeah, I had today off. I just ran down here because Missy misplaced her keys and was needing me to lock up the place." He tipped his umbrella, so it covered Lane a tad more than it did him.

Lane nodded awkwardly, giving him a grateful smile, then suddenly asked, "Hey, Harry?"

"Yeah?"

"I... ah... I wanted to apologize to you for thinking you might have had something to do with Stacy's murder. I was wrong, and you're a... you're a good guy," she finished slowly, lightly patting him on the arm.

"Thanks." Harry didn't quite know how to respond to the suddenly friendly and tongue-tied attractive sheriff, so he fell back to his good ol' reliable standard. "You wanna go get a beer?"

"Oh, no." Lane shook her head, her smile dampening, and her eyes growing wide. "No. No, I don't. But... thank you for asking. I'm going to head home now. I only wanted to say I was sorry and hope there are no hard feelings between us."

"Yeah, okay. Um, no hard feelings at all!" Harry smiled, a little stung by the rejection, but never one to give up added, "And if you change your mind on the beer, just let me know!"

"I'll do that. Thanks, Harry. You have a good night." Lane patted him on the arm again and then turned into the alley between Hattie's General and the bank building next door.

CHAPTER 62

Lane numbly climbed the apartment steps, not minding the rain as it slowly slid off her parka. Her mind was flat-out exhausted, and her heart was heavy. She was happy to have made peace with Harry, though Philip was still heavily on her mind, and she idly wondered if she was coming down with a cold as she normally wasn't this sappy.

Making it halfway up the stairs, she'd started to take off her duty belt, pulling her shirt from her slacks through the rain parka. She was ready to get inside and map out her ideas, her thoughts on Bert and Tim still bouncing against her skull.

Lane's foot grazed the second to the top stair, and she lightly stumbled the rest of the way, her boot clumping down on the warped wooden deck.

She was obviously distracted.

An idea had popped into her head when she'd driven back onto the island from the ferry, and the more she thought about this epiphany, the more and more she was sure she was right. If she could just talk it out with Phil...

She shook her head at the thought, knowing it wasn't a possibility. Her notepad would have to do for tonight.

She put the key in the lock, the deadbolt flipping over, and gave a hard push. The door stubbornly stuck, the rain swelling the wood. With a sigh, she tiredly heaved against it, throwing herself at the fixed barrier, and slipped, the slick deck causing her feet to slide out from beneath her and fall flat on her knees.

It actually saved her life.

A loud bang echoed down the alleyway, sharp and cracking. It took Lane less than a second to recognize the sound and her situation, and she quickly slammed herself to the deck, lying flat on her belly. She inched forward and pressed her palm against the bottom of the door, and pushed with all of her might. It refused to budge, leaving her without cover, stuck on the landing, visible under the porch light.

Crawling into a crouch and staying low, she stretched for her duty belt, her slick fingers trembling as they fought with the snap, her eyes frantically scanning the alley below. She managed to pull her weapon free from the holster, another bullet flying loose, this one hitting the deck railing.

Out of pure reflex, she jerked back from the splintered wood and lost her balance. Falling backwards, she tumbled down the steep apartment stairs and landed in a heap at the bottom, dazed and cold, her brain screaming at her to move.

Agreeing it was not a good idea to lay in a puddle of rainwater for much longer, Lane scrambled to her feet and reached for her service weapon, the gun having toppled over the stairs with her and landing near her head. Her palm grasped the grip, and she hunched down low, trying to get her bearings, her eyes squinting through the rain and darkness.

Another shot echoed off the walls, and Lane quickly realized there was no standing her ground. She needed to run and find cover. She took off down the darkened backstreet and darted behind the store, using the wall as a shield, straining to hear footsteps, knowing her assailant must have seen her run behind the building. How could they miss her in this bright yellow parka?

Taking in her new surroundings, she was disappointed to discover she was now trapped. Sandwiched between the back of Hattie's General and the butcher shop, a large air conditioning unit blocking her only other exit out of the alley.

Lane, realizing she had nowhere to go, took a deep breath and dared a peek around the corner.

Another shot rang out and the bullet chipped the brick by her face.

She jerked back, pressing herself hard against the wall, her hand flying to her eyes and cheeks, scraping away the bits of masonry peppering her skin. She shook her head, scolding herself for being reckless, having almost taken a bullet to the head, and squinted at the surface of the building, searching for a fire escape or utility ladder, finding bare brick.

Blinking the rain out of her eyes, Lane pulled her cell phone from her parka and dialed nine-one-one, the cracked screen lighting the dark alley, her bars of service, zero.

"Dammit!" She shoved the phone back into her parka, her breaths heaving as she brainstormed. "Think... Think."

Her options were limited and time was fleeting. The idea of running down the alleyway, out the back side, occurred to her. But she didn't feel like taking a bullet in the back and quickly reversing and trying to shoot her way out, only really happened in the movies. Out of options, Lane committed to the only choice.

It took a few tries, and she hurt her knee in the process, but she managed to kick in the back door of Hattie's General and quickly slipped inside.

"Please have a silent alarm, please have a silent alarm," she muttered to herself and tried to find something to barricade the door. She didn't have much time as whoever was taking potshots, would most likely figure out where she escaped to.

Manically searching the nearest grocery aisle next to the busted door, the only thing she could find was a mop. She snapped the handle in half over her knee, stifling a painful whimper, and then jammed it underneath the door handle, unconvinced it would hold but hoped it'd at least give her enough time to get to a good place of defense and a landline phone.

Hattie's General had been left partially lit, the main front lights hanging over the picnic table and coffee station still on, the back of the store completely dark. Lane slowly worked her way across the aisles, avoiding the lighted area of the store. It would be too easy for someone to double back and try to take a shot through the front window.

With her gun in hand, she found the swinging doors leading to Harry's office, where she knew there was a landline sitting on his desk. Stepping past and through them, she put one hand behind her, steadying the doors to a full stop.

The place was as it always was. Empty cardboard boxes stacked haphazardly, two lit freezers, and one unlit. A large pallet of kitty litter and a half-opened pallet of dog food sat a little ways in front of the doors.

Suddenly, all three freezers went dark, and the backroom, pitch black. Lane blinked, and quickly realized the power had been cut.

Was it done from the outside or had they flipped the store's fuse from the inside?

As in answer, a loud clang echoed from the opposite side of the doors, the mop handle rattling to the ground, followed by the distinctive sound of footsteps, rubber soles squeaking across the waxed, linoleum floor.

As quickly and as quietly as she could, she ran behind the large pallet of kitty litter, the footsteps stopping just in front of the swing doors. The store itself became deathly quiet and Lane stepped into a shooter's stance, leaning against the pallet for support, shuffling a little to the right, the slight movement gratingly loud against her ears as her plastic parka rustled with every move she made.

Outside the doors, it sounded as if the footsteps were fading, leading away. Then, with a loud squeak of rubber, her purser turned on their heels and headed for the backroom.

Lane held her breath, waiting, the swing door on the left slowly opening, dim light from the front of the store shining through. She squeezed the trigger, the shot ringing out, the bullet missing its target and clipping the right door, it swooshing back and forth in the darkness, the left side suddenly flying open, and a dark figure running in, engulfed in the blackness.

Lane was no longer alone in the backroom.

"Don't you find this a bit silly? All this cat and mouse hiding?"

Lane's heart stopped, immediately recognizing the voice.

A flashlight swept past her face, and she squeezed her eyes shut against the light, moving behind the pallet and hunkering down, trying not to move a muscle.

"I mean, it's rather pathetic hiding back here. Behind some empty BOXES!"

The cardboard boxes, haphazardly stacked, tumbled down onto the concrete floor scattering in a loud commotion. "Or behind the freezers." Gunfire briefly lit up the room as shots were put into each cooling unit, shattering the glass doors from the back side.

There was a sudden hysterical laugh, and Lane's heart sped up with the crunch of glass underfoot, falling footsteps coming closer. She moved as silently as possible towards the office, praying the door wasn't locked.

"But you're not hiding behind those things, are you? Why don't you come out from behind the kitty litter, and let's talk?"

Lane reached the back office with relief and turned the doorknob, only to find it securely locked. There was now no other way out of the backroom but out through the swing doors. She turned around and headed for the extensive metal shelving, choosing to hide behind it, using the grocery items as cover, and pointed her gun in the general direction of the flashlight beam.

"Okay, Bert... Let's talk."

CHAPTER 63

Philip opened his eyes and tried to focus. Everything was fuzzy and his eyelids felt heavy. So heavy, he couldn't keep them open. There was also a massive weight on his chest, like an elephant, crushing down on his ribs, and he half-wondered if he was having a heart attack.

He decided not to worry about it.

A sharp bloom of pain lit across his face and he opened his eyes, blinking away tears. There was another smack against his opposite cheek, even harder than the last. He tried to turn his head away from the blows, but they were repeated in quick succession.

"Come on, Phil! Snap out of it. Open your eyes, buddy!" a voice said, and he tried to determine where it was coming from. He willed his eyes open and looked aimlessly around, his head flopping to the right.

With blurred edges, he could see that his arm was being held high in the air. Jerry holding onto it at the wrist and looking down at his own watch. Philip tried to say hello, but his tongue felt swollen, stuck to the roof of his mouth. Instead, he closed his eyes and decided to sleep some more.

There was another smack to his face, and the heavy weight on his chest shifted.

"Phil, ya gotta keep your eyes open. Focus on me. Come on, buddy."

Philip moaned to let the voice know he could hear them.

There was another voice, younger and female, off to his left asking if he was going to be all right. Philip thought that odd.

Why wouldn't he be all right?

Maybe he WAS having heart attack?

"Get a big glass of cold water, Shelby," the third voice said to his right. Philip thought hazily it was probably Jerry.

The heaviness on his chest abruptly lifted and he felt someone grab him under the arms and prop him into a sitting position.

"Jerry, I think he's starting to wake up," Harry said, substantial relief in his voice.

Philip mumbled something, sort of sounding like, "HiiiiHarree."

"Keep him talking, Har." Jerry let go of Philip's

wrist and placed it back on the bed. "His heart rate is fine and his motor skills seem to be coming back. I think he was just given a heavy dose of sleeping pills... but, not enough to kill him... I think."

"Thank God," Harry said earnestly and turned towards the door, Shelby running in with a large glass of water.

"Here you go." Grim concern was etched on her young face. "How's he doing? Has he said where my mom is?"

"Not yet, honey, but we'll find out." He took the water from her hand and tilted the glass against Philip's lips.

"No, Harry. It's not to drink." Jerry snatched the glass from his grip and threw the contents in Philip's face, who sputtered, fully opening his eyes for the first time. "Shelby, get me two more glasses, please."

Philip heard hurried footsteps retreat from the room.

"Wha... go'n on?" he managed to get out.

"Phil, do you know where Bert is?" Harry held his head in both hands so it wouldn't flop forward onto his own chest.

"Strip teaseeeee," Philip slurred, and Harry slapped him hard across the face, Shelby returning and handing Jerry two glasses. Once again, water was thrown in Philip's face, Jerry letting him drink from the other, Philip gulping half the glass down before he pulled it away.

"Shelby, would you mind making a big pot of coffee now? We're gonna see if it will help Phil, and then maybe he can tell us where your mom is, okay?" Jerry handed the water glass to Harry to hold and lightly guided the girl out of Bert's bedroom, shutting the door behind her.

Philip yawned and moved into a more comfortable position against the headboard, accepting the half-filled glass of water from Harry. He was becoming clear-headed, and his face hurt.

"Thanks, man," Philip mumbled and finished off the glass, then blinked a couple more times. When he was sure he could keep his eyes open, he looked at his best friend, who was sitting on the edge of the bed next to him.

"You scared the crap out of me, Phil," Harry admitted, and then pulled up the bedsheets to cover Philip, dressed only in boxer shorts.

"What are you guys doing here?" Philip motioned between the two men as Jerry walked to the nightstand, picking up and sniffing empty beer bottles.

"Shelby called us. She'd come home from visiting a friend, who I guess she got into a fight with. Not knowing you were sleeping over; she came into the bedroom wanting to talk to her mom. Instead, she found you and no sign of Bert. When she couldn't get you to wake up, she called Jerry..."

"Dr. Hadley is on vacation, so I'm the next best thing, apparently," Jerry interrupted, picking up another bottle off the nightstand.

"And then Jerry called me and we busted our butts to get here as soon as we could. Found you unconscious."

Jerry sniffed at a beer bottle that had fallen on the floor next to the bed and suddenly jerked the bottle away from his nose.

"Phil, what's the last thing you remember from tonight?"

"Um, I was in the bathroom..." Philip ran his fingers through his hair and frowned. "Talking on the phone with Lane, I think."

"Sheriff Lane?" Both men asked at the same time.

"Yeah... still sort of fuzzy. I... I had hung up on her. I was mad about something... I, uh, I opened the door from the bathroom... and Bert was out of bed. She said she had a surprise for me... then told me to have a beer, and she'd be right back." Philip licked his dry lips and tried to remember. "I waited a while, and when she came back, she was all dressed... even had a coat and hat on." He shook his head side to side. "Last thing I remember was wondering if she was gonna do a striptease... and then I guess, I fell asleep?"

"More like passed out. You were drugged, Phil." Jerry handed Harry the empty beer bottle. "Here, take a sniff."

Harry did and then jerked the bottle away.

"Smells funny."

"Yeah, probably didn't smell so strong when there was actual beer in the bottle." He turned to Philip. "Did any of your beers taste funny to you?"

"The last one was a little bitter. It was a micro-brew. I normally don't drink those, so I didn't think anything of it." Philip frowned, trying to concentrate. "Wait, are you saying BERT drugged me?" He blinked a few times, not comprehending. "Why would she drug me? ...Oh, Shit! Where are my pants?"

CHAPTER 64

Bert lowered the flashlight and, surprisingly her gun, leaning casually against the pallet of kitty litter.

"There you are."

"Here I am," Lane acknowledged, pointing her gun directly at Bert's chest. "Now, put your weapon down on the ground and put your hands up in the air."

"I don't want to," Bert said, leaving her handgun resting against her leg.

She was dressed in all black, wearing a black baseball hat with her hair up in a ponytail sticking out the back. Lane noticed she had dangly earrings in her ears as well. If someone wasn't looking closely, they would most likely think they were looking at Shelby.

"I mean it," Lane ordered through gritted teeth.

"I'm sure you do." Bert shrugged her shoulders, not seeming alarmed in the least.

"Bert... I don't want to have to shoot you."

"Oh, but I bet you do," she said sarcastically.

"Bert... I need you to—"

"You never did like me, did you?" Bert snapped, suddenly pointing her flashlight directly into Lane's eyes.

Blinded, Lane turned her head to the side, trying to minimize the glare. She kept her gun tracked on Bert the best she could.

"If I'm being honest. NO," Lane confessed, debating if she should squeeze off a shot. She hesitated, knowing if she missed, Bert had a perfect yellow bullseye to take aim at.

"Shame," Bert said, lowering the flashlight out of her eyes. "Phil did. Which I bet he'll regret in the morning..."

Lane's heart skipped a beat and her knees weakened. "What have you done to Phil?" she asked panicked, her voice tinged with fear and anger... more anger than fear.

"I knew it. I just knew it!" Bert lifted herself up from the pallet and trained the light back into Lane's eyes.

Lane kept her gun tracked on the flashlight and took a step back, trying to distance herself from the glare.

"I knew you had a thing for him." Bert suddenly snapped the flashlight off, and the room went dark.

Lane blinked a few times, trying to dispel the purple dots from her vision. "I want you to know I heard him arguing with you on the phone. It was sweet how he stood up for me, don't you think?" Bert gave out a loud sigh, "I'm sure you realize, I can't let you keep filling Phil's head with all of your little bright ideas. You've forced my hand."

"So, you plan on killing me?"

"Obviously," Bert retorted with annoyance.

"Killing me isn't going to stop the investigation, Bert."

"Of course, it won't," she spat. "But it will slow it down."

"Bert, put the gun down. We can still work this out," Lane tried again.

"I'm curious. Why zero in on me?" She ignored the offer.

"The lie about Tim living on the mainland. It didn't make sense."

"Ahhhh... it was a stupid lie," Bert admitted, shaking her head regretfully.

"It made me realize we'd been looking at everyone around you and not at YOU." Lane quickly crouched down and steadily inched her way past the shelved aisles, stopping behind the laundry detergent. "You killed Stacy. It wasn't your daughter or Tim."

"You know. I'd asked Phil not to tell you... I knew it was a mistake when I said it. He'd caught me off

431

guard, and I panicked. Silly of me to think he'd keep his word," Bert's voice floated to Lane's left. "So, you think you've got this all figured out then?" Bert was moving in the dark, still in close proximity to the freezers as the broken glass crunched under her feet.

"Think so. My guess is Stacy had an affair with Tim, and you were seeking revenge, by killing her." Lane checked the clip in her gun.

"Revenge? I suppose it might look that way," Bert said, nodding her head in the dark, contemplating the idea.

Lane turned down another aisle, her shuffling feet accidentally kicking an empty cardboard box, sending it skidding across the concrete floor.

"Careful, Sheriff! There's another box, right in front of you," Bert warned playfully. Lane tensed, realizing there was. The other woman had the upper hand, and she was enjoying herself.

"Tim didn't really leave the island, did he?" Lane stepped over the box and kept her voice steady. "He's been dead this whole time."

"Yes, he has."

The voice was now coming from her right.

"Did you shoot him?" Lane asked, wincing as she hit her knee on the metal shelving's sharp corner. Her poor knee was taking a serious beating.

"No," Bert's voice grew closer and impatient, "Why don't we dispense with the twenty questions?"

"Fine by me. Tell me all about it. Unburden yourself, Bert." Lane sensed the other woman truly wanted to tell all.

"Unburden myself? Where would you like me to start?" Bert stopped and leaned against the shelving, unconcerned.

"Ohhh, at the beginning is always a good place," Lane suggested, trying to rip her snagged parka free from a bolt sticking out of the metal shelf.

"You're absolutely right." Bert thought for a moment and then took a deep breath. "Tim and I... Well, our marriage hadn't been good for a while. We'd married young, and just when we both figured out, we'd made a huge mistake, Shelby came along. I wanted to try to make things work, but his unhappiness became more apparent as Shelby got older and especially after we'd taken over my dad's shop. I knew he didn't like it here on the island, but I never dreamed he'd actually leave it, me... or Shelby." Bert paused. "Especially for a practical child, twenty years younger than himself. The idea of being with a girl just a few years older than Shelby! Sick bastard..." Bert tightened her grip on the gun.

"It wasn't like I had planned to kill him. The truth of it is he really just had lousy timing that night. Sorry, if that bursts your bubble, Sheriff. There was never any elaborate scheme to do my husband in." Bert paused again, tilting her head to see if she could still pinpoint Lane.

Distinctly hearing the rustle of the rain parka at a safe distance, Bert continued, "It was a normal weekday night. I'd come home, checked the mail, and made dinner like a devoted wife should. Shelby was at a friend's house, and Tim wasn't home yet. So, I threw his dinner in the oven to keep it warm and sat myself down at the kitchen table opening the mail. A knife company had sent me a package with their product, hoping I'd consider selling them in the store. I had just tossed the contents of the box onto the table when he came through the door."

If Lane had been able to see Bert's face, she would have realized the other woman was completely caught up in her memory. A look of dazed recollection in her eyes.

"We immediately started to argue. I was angry he was late for dinner, and he wasn't in the mood to hear me bitch and moan, so I started to clean up. It was between bites that he told me Stacy was pregnant and the baby was his. That he was going to do the right thing by her and start a new life. How he wanted to set up visitation arrangements for Shelby and how he hoped our daughter would one day look upon Stacy as another mother," Bert's voice cracked with angered emotion.

"No apology. No begging for forgiveness. No shame... Just smugness. As if throwing away the life we built together didn't bother him... and was of no importance to ME. No concern his actions might hurt ME. No realization he was tearing MY world in two! Ohhhh, I was seething!" Bert's voice rolled across the backroom, echoing the sheer anger she'd felt.

"With tears streaming down my face, I begged him not to leave. Begged him! All the while, him shoveling bite after bite into his big smug mouth." Bert took a shuddering breath. "Next thing I knew, I'd picked up a sample knife from the kitchen table and stabbed him in the back of the neck." Bert snapped out of her memory with a slight jerk. "He always was a sucker for blondes," she added, as an afterthought.

Lane, who had been busy moving as stealthily as she could while Bert was talking, stopped mid-motion.

"How did you dispose of his body?" She was trying to double back and get behind Bert, back to the swing doors.

"That was really quite more gruesome," Bert confessed, and then lightly continued, "He had left a large suitcase by our front door, I assume, to pack his crap in. So, I dragged him to the tub, chopped him up into manageable pieces, and packed him in the very same suitcase he was going to leave me with. The next day, I took a leisurely drive through the park and spread the ashes, so to speak. Then a day or so later, I started to tell people he had left, taking all our money with him."

"Did you smother his body parts in honey, like you did with Stacy?" Lane was back to the kitty litter pallet and only a few feet away from the swing doors.

"You might not believe me, Sheriff. But I had no plans to hurt Stacy. It wasn't her fault my husband was a backstabbing, worthless, unfaithful creep. The problem was she started to feel guilty about the affair. Or... so she had said when she showed up at my store one day in tears." Bert straightened the baseball cap and continued, "When she saw I wasn't going to be as sympathetic as she hoped, she started to wave around a positive pregnancy test. Demanding money or she'd tell Shelby she was going to be a big sister. I had no choice but to give her what she wanted. I pretended to befriend her. Told her we'd both been screwed over by Tim and I was so sorry she was going through this alone... and if there was anything, I could do to help..." Bert suddenly turned on the flashlight, quickly scanning the room, then turned it off.

"Don't go too much farther, Sheriff. I'm just getting to the good part," she warned.

"Go on." Lane shifted her weight and pointed her gun in the direction of the light flash.

"I gave Stacy money, her demands being small to start. Of course, I knew they would eventually grow and never really stop. She was quickly becoming a financial thorn in my side... and her belly wasn't growing. I finally realized she'd been lying the whole time. Still scared she'd tell Shelby about the affair, I pretended not to notice. That's when I came up with the idea of telling Stacy I wanted her to be the model for the store catalog," Bert's voice seemed to smile at the recollection.

"She thought herself a budding supermodel already. So, when I told her to keep it in the strictest of confidences, to not even tell Shelby, she obeyed. Selfishly worried once word got out, everybody in town would want to be in it. She was only too happy to keep her mouth shut and all eyes on her," Bert's voice sneered with contempt. "It was with the guise of the catalog shoot that I instructed her to come down to the store and pick out some items. A few things the same, but in different colors. A wide variety for people to choose from, I told her."

"You purposely wanted us to see her on your security tape," Lane said astonished, realizing they'd been played from the beginning.

"You bet I did! It gave me a perfect alibi! You got to see Stacy and I interact with each other on friendly terms, and her leave the store safely, going who knows where next. Then a few minutes later, I seem to start suffering from a migraine and go home to sleep it off. Where my daughter is at home and can be my alibi."

"What was the deal with the boots?" Lane suddenly asked, painfully curious.

"Yes... the boots. I told her I wanted to advertise footwear as well. However, we didn't have her boot size. I managed to convince her the size of the boots didn't matter because she'd be wearing them in the shots from a distance. She grabbed the first pair she saw." Bert sat down heavily on something, the plastic wrap crinkling under her weight.

"After she left the store, I grabbed a matching pair in type and size, then feigned my migraine, and went home. Slipped a minor sleeping pill into Shelby's soda pop, and after she crashed out, I took the bowie knife she'd been hiding under her pillow."

"The one you used to slice Stacy's throat," Lane sneered, overly disgusted Bert was framing Shelby.

"No, that knife was the knife I used to kill Tim. The knife Shelby had was the second sample knife. You can't possibly think I'd ever frame my daughter for murder," Bert's voice was harsh, protective. "If you hadn't told Phil you found out I lied about Tim, you would have been surprised to have been given back the knife Bridget stole from the antique shop. Shelby would have been cleared and you would've stayed completely confused."

"That's why you left the murder weapon behind...," Lane's voice was hued with awe. She was now struggling to pull the rain parka off, trying to remove it as quietly as she could, the parka protesting loudly with each snap of a button and squelch of wet rubber.

"Ideally, if the animals had done their work and Phil hadn't stumbled across the body, then one day a hiker would have randomly found a bowie knife left in the woods. Leaving the knife behind was my contingency plan."

"That was smart," Lane admitted, lightly tossing the yellow rain parka behind her.

"Oh, it gets better," Bert bragged. "Once I knew Shelby was sound asleep, I hopped into her car so that if anybody saw me, they'd just think it was my kid cruising around town as she loves to do." Bert stopped and listened. "I hope you're not trying to sneak up on me," she cautioned, her voice full of malice.

"Wouldn't dream of it," Lane lied, almost to the swing doors.

"Good," Bert's voice sounded pleased. "I told Stacy where to meet me in the park. Even bought a throwaway phone and texted her, pretending to be the photographer waiting for her at the photo shoot site. She was so gullible." Bert suddenly chuckled. "The stupid girl didn't even realize there wasn't another car around. In fact, she didn't even find it funny when I asked her to wear the oversized boots while we hiked in. She just pulled them out of the box and popped her shoes in. We grabbed the bags of clothing and made our way to the spot." Bert suddenly sighed heavily. "She did start to wise up when we got to the clearing and there was no photographer or equipment. By then though, she had her back to me. It was easy. I simply walked up behind her, grabbed her chin in one hand, and sliced with the other."

Lane, having been at the clearing, could picture the scene in all of its bloody detail.

"And then you put her white shoes back on to disguise the boot prints you both made when you walked in."

"That I thought was a stroke of genius!" Bert said, proudly.

"Squirted honey on the body to draw in the bears, probably threw the empty containers in the shopping bags, and just walked yourself out. Then you put the note on Stacy's Jeep and drove back home in Shelby's car," Lane finished, her hand on the swing doors. She was going to have to make a run for it. "You got away with murder... twice."

"And now, I have to do it again."

CHAPTER 65

Harry's hands were shaking so bad he could barely get the store key into the lock.

After Philip had gotten dressed and Jerry had agreed to stay behind with Shelby, they'd grabbed the shotgun from Jerry's rig and hauled ass downtown, Philip, during the five-minute drive, giving the digest version of his conversation with Lane. Harry, to his credit, hadn't asked questions and kept the gas floored.

When they'd arrived at Hattie's, squealing into the handicap parking spot, the first thing they noticed was the lights, the storefront dark. This did not bode well. Harry had, and always did, leave the lights on by the main window.

Jumping from the truck, the two split up, Philip making a mad dash down the alley to the upstairs apartment, Harry to his shop.

Peeking through the windows, Harry cupped the side of his face, squinting, his nose pressed against the glass, unable to make anything out. He took a step back and started towards the alley, intending to check the back door when Philip rounded the corner and informed him the above apartment was empty, with a bullet hole in the door and no sign of their sheriff.

"Did you check the back of the alley?" Harry asked incredulously. "She could be hurt!"

Philip, out of breath, nodded in the affirmative.

"Another thing... Your back door... It's busted in. I can't get it to open. It's jammed."

"You think she's in the store?" Harry almost sounded relieved.

"Maybe. But if she is, I don't think she's alone."

"Not good, not good," Harry muttered nervously, turning the key in the lock.

"Harry, breathe. You're shaking like a leaf." Philip reached out and laid his hand on his friend's outstretched arm. Harry, in turn, nodded and then pushed the door open.

The golden bell jingled above happily, announcing their arrival to the store. Philip quickly stretched up and grabbed it, silencing the little bell with a grimace. If they were hoping to sneak in, their cover was just blown.

Philip brought Jerry's shotgun to bear on his shoulder and slowly entered in the lead. For his part, as soon as they stepped into the store, Harry flipped the four light switches by the door. Everything stayed dark.

"Powers out," he whispered and then, as if to assure himself, Harry looked over his shoulder across the street at the lit-up single gas pump, which normally fueled the whole island.

"I see that." Philip waved Harry ahead of him. "Hurry up and get it."

Bent over at the waist to stay out of Philip's line of sight, Harry crossed in front and scurried to the cashier counter. He quickly punched in his code for the small gun safe sitting under the register and pulled out a snub-nosed revolver, the little bit of insurance he kept in case the store ever got robbed.

With shaky fingers, Harry pushed the cylinder release and made sure it was loaded, then flicked it closed with a loud metal clank. He then ran back, Philip peering down each aisle in slow progress, returning to the cashier counter.

"I think I can hear someone talking in the backroom," Philip reported, his head towards the back of the shop.

"I'll get the lights back on and then meet you at the swing doors," Harry said, more confident than he felt.

"Okay." Philip moved forward and then suddenly stopped, Harry a few paces behind him. "Hey, Harry? Don't accidentally shoot me, okay?"

Harry gave Philip a firm nod, and a crooked smile. "I'll do my best, buddy."

CHAPTER 66

Bert switched on the flashlight and caught Lane, her hand on the swing door, both hearing the golden bell chime in the stillness.

"Back away from the door... NOW!" Bert hissed, training her gun on Lane, forcing her to squint through the flashlight's bright beam once again and slowly back away. The light followed her, and even though Lane had her gun in her hand, it was basically useless if she couldn't see her target.

Bert quickly moved to the swing doors having to push up on her tiptoes to look through the small windows. She couldn't see anything but knew someone... or somebodies was out there. The question was, did they know they were in the backroom?

She brought her full attention back to the irritating sheriff, making sure she kept her blinded with the bright flashlight. Bert had to get rid of her, and the rest could still be salvaged. She'd drugged Philip but not enough to do him any harm. He'd just wake up with a terrible headache and find her sleeping peacefully next to him in bed, none the wiser.

If she played this right, Sheriff Lane's murder would be blamed on Stacy's unknown killer. With everyone's assumption being Tim, who they'd never find. It would probably be a cold case for the books.

As she saw it, she had two choices in front of her. See if whoever was in the store would eventually leave without them being discovered or take a huge risk and get her hands dirty... and then sneak back home. Bert tucked her gun into the waistband of her jeans.

She'd decided on option two.

CHAPTER 67

Lane's mind raced as Bert's flashlight went dark... and the world filled with blobs of purple and green imagery. She instinctively took a step back and found herself against the pallet of kitty litter, quickened steps coming towards her, scuttling across the concrete floor.

Suddenly a hand groped for her neck in the dark, and another hand grabbed for her gun. Lane pulled the trigger, a small blast of light emitting from the barrel, giving a brief Polaroid image of the backroom. Bert had managed to get one hand around her throat and was trying to grab her weapon with the other.

As the two women wrestled, the gun went off again, this time straight up in the air. Bert punched Lane as hard as she could in the stomach, and Lane let out a loud "Oufff," dropping her weapon. Stunned by the blow, she went to take a breath, but Bert had both hands around her neck, gripping tightly.

Scratching desperately at the hands throttling her throat, Lane struggled for air, her eyes watering as she blinked in the darkness. She couldn't see anything, but she could hear the backroom doors swooshing open and closed, open and closed... Her lungs beginning to burn as if on fire.

CHAPTER 68

Harry met Philip outside the swing doors and reported that the fuse had been flipped and that the front lights were on, the back of the store remaining plunged in darkness.

Philip pressed his index finger to his lips and gave Harry a severe, "Shhhhhh!"

Harry, in return, pursed his lips together and nodded an apology.

"I thought I heard somebody moving back there, but it's gone quiet," Philip relayed, putting the shotgun butt down on the ground. "I'm gonna go in there, and I want you to...," he started to say when both heard a shot fired. Philip brought the shotgun to his shoulder and looked at Harry, his eyes wide. "Stay low and to my right."

Another shot boomed, and Philip busted through

the swing doors. Harry followed suit, staying low, to Philip's right as directed, and made straight for the light switch.

"I'm there!" he yelled into the darkness, hearing gasps of air and scuffling sounds.

"Now!" Philip yelled.

Harry flipped the switch, and the room flooded with light, a peculiar site coming to his eyes.

The sheriff was bent over a large pallet with Bert's hands wrapped around her throat, a gun protruding from Bert's waistband, and another lying on the floor, Philip's shotgun pushed up against Bert's back, the latter standing stock still.

"Let her go, Bert," Philip said, anger and sadness mixed in his growl.

"Phil?" Bert asked, stupefied, her head slightly turned in recognition.

"Put your hands up where I can see them, Bert."

"Nooooooo... no, no, no... no...," Bert's voice shook with bewildering denial, but she didn't move.

"Now, Bert! Where I can see them."

Slowly, she lifted her hands, and Philip grabbed the gun from her jeans, tossing it to the side, then kicked away the gun next to the pallet on the floor, keeping his shotgun against her back.

Lane inhaled a deep breath of air free from Bert's grip, bending herself upwards, back into a standing position.

"Get her... away... from me," Lane wheezed, rubbing her sore neck, still pinned by the other woman's body against the pallet of litter.

"Come on. Towards me," Philip commanded, taking a step back to give Bert room to move. She slowly turned around, her hands still up in the air, her eyes glued to the shotgun barrel pointed at her chest.

"Phil, ...tell Shelby I love her," Bert choked with emotion, never meeting Philip's eye. "Tell her I'm sorry... about her dad."

"You can tell her yourself," Philip snapped through clenched teeth, leaning to the side, wanting to look at Lane.

"Please. Phil?"

He ignored her and called over his shoulder, "Harry, grab that pistol." He nodded to the gun on the floor, but nothing happened. Philip turned his head, wondering where Harry had gone, and yelled towards the office, "Harry? ...Harry! You calling the mainland?"

What happened next, happened fast.

Bert suddenly gripped the shotgun barrel, yanking it from Philip's grasp, and stepped towards him, pushing the muzzle hard against his chest.

Still weakened by the lack of oxygen, Lane slumped to the ground, scrabbling for her gun. It just out of reach.

Philip took a step back and managed to get the

451

words, "Bert, wait!" out before falling backwards, tripping over his own feet. There was a loud BANG, and Bert crumpled to the ground, the shotgun hitting the floor and sliding several feet.

"Jesus," Philip said, shaken. It wasn't a curse as much as a plea.

Harry suddenly appeared, rushing from his back office, his revolver out in front of him. He stopped dead and pointed the gun to the ground, taking his finger off the trigger. There was no point.

Bert laid on his backroom floor, bits of gore speckled across the concrete, blood spreading out about her like a blanket.

CHAPTER 69

The next couple of days were a blur for Philip as he was accosted by law enforcement detectives, reporters, and neighbors... all wanting to know what happened. It still wasn't public knowledge that Bert had killed her husband and the cheer coach, but it soon would be. As much as he wanted it all covered up for Shelby's sake, it was just too big of a crime and too small of an island. Not to mention, he was still nursing a broken heart... salted by betrayal and the fact he'd never know for sure if Bert had attempted to kill him or simply tried to keep him out of her way.

Every night he woke up from a dead sleep, covered in sweat, his heart beating through his chest from the living nightmare of watching her put the shotgun to her face and pulling the trigger. He'd hoped, in time, the image would simply drop from his unconscious mind, and he'd be able to move on. Though he figured the nightmares would be a hell of a lot worse if he'd been the one to have to pull the trigger. He shuddered at the thought.

Everything was hindsight... Lane had just gotten her gun in hand from the backroom floor when Harry returned from his office with his revolver... Bert didn't really have a way out if he tried to look at it from her point of view. She was going to go to jail. Well, maybe she did find a way out. His brooding thoughts just went in circles, so he tried not to think about it.

For now, he was happy to be back in the woods, surrounded by peace and quiet, with the occasional interruption from Kody. The kid had forgiven him, but Philip didn't think he was quite done being mad at him. The young ranger had been spending most of his time cruising the park instead of hanging out in the office as per usual. Partially because there was a forensics team with cadaver dogs searching the island for Tim's remains and partially because the kid just didn't know what to say... it was obvious Philip was grieving.

And it was true. Philip was still having a hard time reconciling the woman he loved was a murderer twice over and that he didn't... or to be more truthful, hadn't wanted to see it at the time. Though that's the thing about psychopaths. They seem like your everyday kind of people. Family members, co-workers, close friends... lovers. He simply had been fooled and because his judgment was clouded, it almost got Lane killed. Not forgetting he might very well have been another victim himself. What was even more distressing was he missed Bert. He felt guilty about that too.

After Lane had recited her conversation in the backroom, Philip still had questions. He still wondered why Bert had scalped the young woman after slicing her throat. Lane said Bert had muttered something about Tim being a sucker for blondes and how she surmised, it was Bert's way of defacing the young beauty. It wasn't enough to take her life, she had to make her ugly too.

The thought upset Philip... He understood the concept of someone being pushed to their mental limits, to the point where their ties to morality just snapped. But at some point, when the reality of black and white comes crashing back in... You have a choice to make. And Bert decided to stay in the world of gray morality, where he never would have been able to follow.

There was still the question of how the bowie knife showed up at the antique shop. After Lane revealed there were two knives from the very beginning and how Bert had manipulated Shelby into being scared of being home alone... they both came to the conclusion Bert had probably tossed the knife into one of the many boxes of junk left by the Antique shop's back door. Bert knew Bridget had sticky fingers, and behind the scenes, she pushed the girls into taking the knife for protection. If they hadn't, Lane was pretty sure, Bert had a backup plan to somehow get the weapon into Shelby's hands.

And lastly, he wondered, if she'd never killed Stacy, would she have killed again, eventually?

He tried to tell Harry how he was feeling, but Harry didn't understand and frankly had more pressing things on his plate. His business had turned into a crime scene, and he was still struggling to find a night cashier. The last time they had talked, he was buying paint to cover the bloodstains on the back-room's concrete floor.

Philip hadn't wanted to, but he managed to ask Harry why he was parked next to Stacy's Jeep the night she was murdered out at the park. Harry swore it wasn't his truck, and he was home with Hattie, as he had previously stated. Philip figured it might have been a tourist looking to help a stranded driver and pushed it away with the rest of the unpleasant thoughts.

Thinking of Hattie reminded Philip of their conversation and her words of wisdom.

"Love triangles are dangerous."

Philip half-wondered if it had been a warning.

Hattie was a pretty smart lady.

"Knock, knock," Lane said, rapping lightly on the door before popping her head into the park ranger's office. "Mind if I come in?"

Her voice was still raspy, and Philip could just make out the small finger-sized bruises on her neck, especially with her hair up in its usual styled bun. She was dressed in her sheriff uniform, her shoulders wet from the rain drizzling outside. She'd most likely never wear a rain parka again.

The two of them hadn't talked much after the incident. When help from the mainland arrived, they'd whisked her off for medical attention and quarantined him and Harry for questioning. Philip knew when she was well enough, she had been cross-examined herself and then scrutinized for her actions. However, they must not have judged her too harshly. They kept her assigned to the island and also recruited a deputy to work with her when the office opened up in a week. Philip's assistance most likely would not be needed in the future... which made him sad as well.

"Yeah. Come on in." Philip gave her a small smile and stood up, indicating for her to take Kody's chair. Lane grabbed it and brought it around to the front of Philip's desk. She was still limping a great deal as well.

"I wanted to stop by and check on you. See how

you are holding up." She sat down, flopping back into the chair, finally at ease in his presence.

"As best as I can be, I expect." Philip did the same, equally comfortable.

"I, uh... I also wanted to say, thank you." She looked him in the eye. "For saving my life."

He met her stare and saw tears, warmth, and friendship as well. Philip swallowed the lump in his throat.

"You are welcome, ma'am," he said sincerely, and suddenly busied himself with moving a few things around on his desk. "You know," he cleared his throat, "there's been something I've been dying to ask you." Philip sat forward and rested his elbows on his desk, leveling Lane with a look.

"Really?" she asked surprised, blinking her eyes dry.

"Yup! Ever since the day we met and had our first discussion at the picnic table over at Hattie's." Philip smiled, remembering how they bumped heads... and probably still would occasionally.

"What's the question?" she asked, with a nervous chuckle.

"What's your first name?"

Lane tilted her head and looked at him in playful annoyance. "I thought we agreed you'd just call me Lane?"

"Yeah, but I think after all we've been through...

not to mention you shot up my best friend's business, cost me my girlfriend, and almost my deputy... we're now close enough to be on a first-name basis." He counted the actions on each of his fingers.

Lane sighed heavily, looking up at the ceiling in dread. "Promise, you won't laugh."

"No can do." Philip shrugged his shoulders. "Sorry, you're just gonna have to risk it."

Lane took a deep breath and said, barely above a whisper, "Lois."

"Lois... Your name is Lois Lane? As in like, Lois Lane from the comics?" Philip snickered, a big smile cracking across his face.

"My dad is a big Superman fan."

"What's your brother's names?" Philip asked, wildly curious.

"Clark, Kent, Jimmy, and Alex. But dad calls him Lex for short.

"Don't tell me your dad kept having kids till he got a girl!" Philip was thoroughly enjoying the notion.

"Okay, I won't," Lois Lane quipped, and then stood up. "My office should be ready in a week. Think you'll come by and visit?" She walked to the door and opened it, making her way to leave.

"Most definitely."

"Good. Be there early and bring coffee."

The story isn't over!

Don't miss the next exciting and intriguing adventure with Lane and Philip in **BOOK II:** *The Push*.

THE PUSH

CHAPTER ONE

Birds exploded from the trees below, their wings furiously flapping against the damp air. Her feet stuttered to a stop, and she watched as they scattered, startled by the loud noise as much as she. Was someone behind her? Another hiker, perhaps? She heard, more than saw, the swaying of motion further down trail. A heavy movement against the bushes.

There again. Closer. Another crack, a snapping of branches underfoot. She sharply turned her body towards the sound.

"Hello?" she called out, a friendly lilt to her voice.

Adjusting the strap around her neck, she waited for a reply. There was nothing... only the sound of pattering raindrops bouncing off the plastic protecting her camera. She adjusted the strap again and took a halting step forward, straining to see through the shroud of morning mist. Was something there? It was hard to tell.

Fidgeting with her ponytail, she unconsciously leaned forward, her eyes raking across the scenery below. The trees and bushes, as if sensing her full attention upon them, sat motionless in the settled silence. An eerie silence she suddenly thought and then scolded herself for being so dramatic. She was alone.

Relaxing her stance, she took a deep breath, slowly exhaling. It must have been nothing. The wind tossing and creaking the branches of a tree. A chipmunk or squirrel jumping from one limb to another. Nature simply being nature.

Even so, her sense of unease still lingered. Keeping her eyes down trail, she anxiously fumbled her cargo shorts. Feeling a familiar lump, she pulled a can of bear spray from her pocket and curled her thumb over the safety clip.

Rumor was, there had been a bear attack earlier in the year, around springtime. She hadn't seen any bear tracks in the mud. However, this didn't mean they weren't around. Not to mention, there were cougars to be concerned about as well. Yet, here she was, up there all alone with just a can of bear spray. Or was she?

Curtly dismissing the thought, she suddenly felt

silly. She was being paranoid and wasting time. Standing there, peering at nothing, while clutching a can of bear spray, wasn't going to get her to where she needed to go.

Shoving the can roughly into her pocket, she gave the slate gray sky an appraising look before tugging her windbreaker hood further over her forehead and trudging ahead. There was still half a mountain to climb and not a lot of time to do it in.

So far, the morning mist layering the rugged terrain had made it hard to see her footing, and the steady drizzle of rain was making it hard to keep it. Both did little to hamper the young woman's mood. The fact that this was her third morning climbing up The Mole Hill, a local nickname for the 5,372-foot mountain, with no sign of a mountain goat to be had... However, did dampen her mood quite a bit. Especially, since this was to be her last day before heading back home to the grind of the Emerald City.

Instructed to visit Rockfish Island by a local Seattle activist magazine, she had gone in hopes of attaining a few picturesque photos of the goats atop their craggy rock perches. The idea had seemed simple enough. Scramble up the rocky terrain. Find a few large, white-haired, black horned herbivores. Snap a few pictures and then down the mountain, she'd go. But the large goats weren't as plentiful or as easy to spot as she had imagined they'd be. This was in part, she was finding out the hard way because the goats hadn't taken to the island. At least, not as well as they had in more conducive areas.

According to her research, the mountain goat population had been introduced to the Rockfish National Park back in the 1920s. Around the same time as their introduction to the massive Olympic National Park where they flourished. So much so, several decades later, the Olympic National Park was wanting to re-home the goats to their natural habitat in the Cascade Mountains.

The magazine, which had contracted her agent for the photographs, wanted to stop the relocation. With their strongest weapon of opposition being the public, the magazine strategized the need to pull on people's heartstrings. A good picture could do just that.

Janie, as most people called her now, intended to go to the Olympic National Park at first. However, her new agent and the pushy magazine editor suggested Rockfish National Park instead. Stating it was a far better example of how a small community could live in harmony with its wildlife neighbors. They also knew her aunt lived on the island and figured it would save the nonprofit magazine a hotel bill. Begrudgingly agreeing to their plan, Janie now found herself hiking up The Mole Hill once again.

Having kept a steady pace for the last twenty minutes, she broke through the thick tree line and found herself staring up at open skies. At her feet, the ground blanketed under muddy layers of pine needles and crushed pine cones had unexpectedly turned bare and rocky. Boulder-like rocks, iced with lime-green moss, speckled the new landscape. Ahead, freed from the masses, sparse and looming trees boasted their towering height with their tip tops swaying lazily in the breeze. At their stumpy bottoms, feathered ferns sprouted flamboyantly, taking root where they could in the rocky terrain.

Janie walked a few paces to the largest tree and gratefully plunked her knapsack down against its trunk. She needed a breather and leaned up against it, looking up at The Mole Hill's peak with an exhausted sigh.

"I swear this mountain gets taller every day," she declared, flipping the spout on her water bottle. "But the rain has lightened up. So, I've got that going for me."

She started to bring the bottle to her mouth, then suddenly stopped, placing it carefully on the uneven ground. With eager tension, she grabbed the camera dangling from the strap around her neck and brought it up to her right eye. Squinting the other eye closed, she fiddled with the focus rings till she was able to bring a large nanny goat into view.

"I should've brought the other lens," she scolded herself.

Even with the zoom feature at full tilt, she knew

it was not the crisp, clean, up close, and personal perspective the magazine was asking for. She was still too far away.

"At least I finally found them," she said, giving herself a mental pat on the back and lowering the camera to her chest.

Suddenly from behind, an earsplitting snap broke the stillness, echoing up from below and jerking her to attention. It sounded as if several branches were breaking at once. Her first thought was a tree had fallen, but as she twisted to peer into the dense tree line she'd come from, she could almost see it. Something was coming, something big.

In one quick motion, the camera was back to her eye, and she peered through the viewfinder, zeroing in on the thick berry-lined brambles. There was a patch of black. It appeared through the swaying bush and then disappeared. Janie held her position, and when she saw it again, her index finger automatically pressed down. The camera made a long shuttering noise capturing repetitive shots in succession. She lifted her finger and fretted her bottom lip. Was that a black bear?

Unsure of what she saw, Janie tried to think of options as she pulled the bear spray from her shorts pocket once more and scanned her immediate area. There was the looming tree behind her. Maybe she could climb that? No good. Bears could climb trees extremely better than she. Quickly she gauged the distance to the large uphill boulders. She might be able to hide behind one of those? She immediately nixed the idea. Bears were scary fast, it would be a short chase. Fighting down her panic Janie shot a fleeting look at the can of bear spray in her hand and made up her mind.

Gripping the camera and spray awkwardly, she peered through the viewfinder catching another brief glimpse of black. Letting the camera heavily drop to her chest she braced herself before squeezing her eyes shut and letting out a large throat-wrenching yell. It wasn't a panicked scream, but a throat burning bellow.

"GO AWAY!"

Janie waved her hands in the air and began to jump up and down, whooping and hollering as loudly as she could.

"GOOOOO AAAAWWWWAAAAY!"

She knew she was bringing attention to herself, but that was the whole point. She wanted the bear to know she was there, and hopefully, all the noise and racket she was making would force it to head in a different direction.

Down trail, the swaying of the bushes abruptly stopped. Janie dropped her arms and brought the camera up. She was breathing heavily now, adrenaline vigorously coursing through her veins, the camera trembling in her hands.

"Go away... go away.... go away... please go away," she chanted to herself.

Another flash of black appeared. Keeping her eye to the viewfinder, she watched intently as the brush suddenly parted. She let out a surprised, "OH!" as she found herself looking at a man. He was wearing a black jacket and baseball cap with a black knapsack on his back. He was also looking up at her with great concern. The new arrival, having seen her yelling and waving at them like a crazy person, called up to her.

"You okay? Do you need help?"

Janie dropped the camera with relief and let out a nervous laugh. She began to shake her head no, then realized the hiker might not be able to make the motion out very well.

"I'm okay! Thought you were a bear!" she hollered down in an apology.

The fellow hiker waved as if he couldn't hear Janie and started to make his way towards her.

Feeling greatly relieved and more than a little foolish, Janie quickly gathered up her water bottle, stuffing it into her knapsack. She hoisted the bag onto her back and took a quick glance downhill. The hiker was making excellent progress. By the time she had gotten herself situated she could make him out clearly.

"Uh, Hey!" Janie said, her heart skipping at the moment of recognition. "I didn't realize it was you." She dropped her head back in relief, letting her hand drop from her heart. "Hi!"

"You okay?" he asked, a warm smile on his face.

"Yeah," she laughed. "I'm fine. Thought you might be a bear. I was trying to scare it off."

"Well, you sure succeeded in scaring ME!"

"I suppose I probably did!" Janie laughed again, more relaxed. "Sorry about that, Brent. How... how have you been?"

"I've been good. Heard you were in town visiting your aunt. Whatcha doing all the way up here?" Brent removed his knapsack, unclasping the dangling water bottle from the side. "Just out taking pictures?" He nodded towards her camera before taking a drink.

"Sort of. I've got a piece to do on the mountain goats," Janie explained, shaking her head no as he offered her his water.

"Any luck?"

"Spotted them for the first time today. They're elusive little buggers. All my yelling probably scared them off. I had just spotted a nanny when I heard you."

"Have you been coming up this trail the whole time?"

"Well, yeah. It's the easiest way up."

"That's your problem. You need to cut over more east. It's way rockier, and the climb is harder. But you'll find more goats."

"Yeah. I'd rather—"

"I can show you. I know another trail. We'll have to watch our step, especially with this drizzle. But you're a good climber, right? You can handle it." Brent gave her a confident smile, lightly patting her on the shoulder. Janie paused at the offer and looked at Brent warily. He was a very good mountain climber. She was so-so.

"Uh, okay. Sure."

"Great! This will be nice. Gives us a chance to catch up while we walk." Brent clipped the water bottle back onto his pack. "By the way, you can put away the bear spray. Pretty sure you've scared every bear off the mountain."

Janie looked down at the can of spray still clutched in her hand and blushed prettily.

"Yea, guess so." She stuffed it back in her pocket and stepped aside to let him lead the way.

Thank You!

Thank you for reading the first book of the Rockfish Island Mysteries series, Black Bear Alibi, A Rockfish Island Mystery:I. The Push, A Rockfish Island Mystery:II and False Findings:III are now out and available on Amazon.

If you enjoyed Black Bear Alibi, would you be so kind as to put a review on Amazon, Goodreads, and Bookbub? Thank you for your support!

ALSO BY J.C. FULLER

A ROCKFISH ISLAND MYSTERY SERIES

Black Bear Alibi

The Push

False Findings